THE GIRL HE KNOWS

A FRIENDS TO LOVERS ROMANTIC COMEDY

KRISTI ROSE

Vintage Housewife Books

Cover Design © 2022 Qamber Designs and Media

The Girl He Needs/ Kristi Rose. -- _2nd edition_

ISBN: 978-1-944513-39-9

Previously published by Kensington Lyrical with the same title.

Print ISBN-978-1-944513-39-9

*For DHM. I'm the luckiest girl in the world
And*

*For Anya, Eryn, Gary, and John. Without you, this book
wouldn't exist. I turned my can't into cans.*

INTRODUCTION

She wants one night, he wants forever.

Three reasons I slept with my best friend's brother by Paisley McAllister:

1. We laughed all night, the drinks were strong, and I needed to sleep somewhere.
2. I have a weakness for military men.
3. I know he won't kiss and tell.

... but lord when he kisses, he makes me forget I've completely broken the best friend code.

So when he makes me a no strings attached offer, I figure we've already done it once. But Hank has never been the type for casual. He's husband material, and I should've seen the problems with this plan from the beginning.

As good as he makes me feel, the ink's just dried on my divorce papers. I'm no longer **the girl he knows.**

1

"HANK, HONEY. TIME TO GET UP." Hank's mom, calling through the door, wakes me from my sleep.

Disorientated, I sit up with a jerk. The blanket falls, exposing my bare breasts. Gasping, I pull the sheet up to my chin, squint, and do a long blink. My contacts are dry, which makes them feel stiff and scratchy and my vision blurry. Each blink offers a short snapshot of my surroundings.

I know where I am. Mortified, I drop my head and cover my eyes with the sheet. Why had I agreed to come here? What would make me throw caution to the wind and risk ruining a friendship?

Lust. That's what.

"Hank, Dad says you have a tee time in one hour. Time to get up, sleepyhead," his mom calls.

"Sweet Jesus," I whisper. Panic seizes me as I glance to my left. Lying next to me is my best friend's older brother,

Hank. I've known Gigi and Hank my entire life. This is her childhood bedroom, now a converted guest room, and the voice on the other side of the thin door is their mother, Ms. Becky. I'd rather face all of hell's demons than have her find me here, in her guest bed, naked, with Hank.

"Hmmphh? To slee…." Hank mumbles and his warm body rolls away, exposing his firm, well-defined backside. I close my eyes and count to ten. Now is not the time to get distracted by his assets or lost in the memory of how wonderful last night was. Now is the time to get the hell out of Dodge. I clutch the sheet to me as I shake his shoulder.

"Wake up," I whisper. When he doesn't move, I lean close to his ear. "Wake. Up. Your mom is at the door."

He opens his eyes, or at least the one eye I see as he's lying on his stomach.

The doorknob rattles, and I fling myself back, pull the covers up over my head, and try to burrow underneath him.

"I'm up, Mom," Hank says, not even moving an inch.

"Well hurry. Dad's anxious to get to the course." Her voice fades, indicating she's moving down the hallway.

"You can come out of hiding," he says.

I flip the covers off my face, then clench them to my chest, "Hush. I don't want them to know I'm here."

"I figured. I don't think they'll care if they find you here." His voice is a low baritone and I worry it will carry.

"Whisper," I say. "I don't care what you think. I don't want them to know. I don't want Gigi to know. I don't want anyone to know." Just saying it makes my stomach clench with apprehension.

"I don't see the big deal."

I sit up, rest on my elbow, and face him. "Of course you don't. Let me tell you how it will go down if anyone finds out about last night."

"This should be good," he mumbles.

I continue, "I've been divorced a year now. Everyone wants to set me up because they think I need to be getting serious again. If our family gets wind of this...they'll go nuts." I shake my head. My mother would put an announcement in the social page of the paper, the engagement section, not five minutes after gaining this knowledge.

"I'm not so sure they'll react like you think." He's a guy so he doesn't understand the way a mother's mind works, or his sister's for that matter.

"You tell no one." I point to emphasize my words.

"How do you figure you're getting out of here if not through the front door? Dad and I are headed to the golf course. My mom is staying home." I give the room a quick scan. I want to leave unseen.

"There's my exit." I point to the window. I roll away and sit up again, tucking part of the sheet under my arms and wrapping the rest around my backside. I search for my clothes.

"The window? Really?"

"Sure. Trust me, it's easy. I've done this before. Lots." I wave my hand to emphasize that it's no big deal.

Hank raises a brow. "You've done...what before?"

"Oh my God, not that. I mean, I haven't done this"—I point to him—"but I've snuck out the window. With Gigi."

His lips twitch. I'm prepared to slap my hand over his mouth should he start laughing.

"What if someone goes outside and sees you? It's"—he turns to look at a clock—"eight-thirty."

"They won't know I've come out the window. They'll think I'm coming from the back." Gigi's bedroom is on the side of the house. Gigi and I have run every possible scenario. This is something I've done often enough I could label it a skill. "And you'll be in the kitchen distracting your parents. Close your eyes."

"Huh?" He rests his arms behind his head and yawns. It must be nice to be so relaxed.

"Close your eyes. I want to get out of bed and get dressed." I'm not ready to be naked in front of Hank in broad daylight. I'm pretty confident my backside isn't as well defined as his.

"Do you not remember last night?"

"Just shut up and do it." When he closes his eyes, I toss my pillow over the top of his head. I swing my feet out of bed and lower them to the ground. The crinkle of a wrapper halts my flight.

I peer over the edge of the bed where condom wrappers lay scattered.

"Holy shit," I whisper and look over at Hank to find him smiling.

The light of day casts a whole new perspective on last night's choices, and even though I thought I was making a sound decision, it's obvious now I was conned by lust...and alcohol. Enough to impair my common sense and my moral compass, but not so much I can't remember.

"Hurry, I want to get up, too." He grunts when I punch him in the gut.

I slide out of bed, pulling the sheet with me. Hank pulls back when I'm three feet away, my bra and panties are just out of reach. I give a firm tug and meet resistance. Hank still has the pillow over his eyes, but is it enough? Will he look? I snap the sheet in a hard tug and let go when he resists. The fabric floats back, covers his head, and I dash to scoop up my panties and bra. I have one leg in my jeans when another knock at the door startles me, and I fall back onto the bed. When the doorknob rattles, I roll onto the floor and try to crawl under the bed, but bump my head on the frame. I don't fit.

"Hank, here's coffee," his mom calls.

Hank jumps off the bed and snatches up condom wrappers. He puts his pants on with amazing speed, tucking the wrappers into his front pocket. I jump up and hop toward the closet as I pull on my pants, stopping only to gather my shirt, purse, and boots. I ease the folding door closed. The closet is empty save for a few Rubbermaid bins. I dress with deliberate movements, careful not to bump a wall, pausing, one arm in my shirt, the other midair, when the low creak of the bedroom door opening paralyzes me.

"Oh, you're getting dressed. Good. I thought you might be having a hard time waking up. You got in pretty late. Did you have a good time last night?"

I cover my mouth with my hand to keep from snorting. He'd better say he had a fabulous time. I press my head into my palms. What is wrong with me? I'm talking about Hank. Yes, last night I experienced alter-my-psyche, toe-curling sex with him, my best friend's brother. It's the last part that makes me want to hurl. If our acquaintance was recent, not a familiar one with the baggage of a past, if I wouldn't have to hear about it for years to come from my family or his sister, if I knew he could walk away after a few more encounters wanting nothing more, I wouldn't hesitate to repeat last night. Often.

This is wrong on so many levels I can't even wrap my mind around it.

The last thing I should care about is whether or not he enjoyed last night. I should care about leaving without doing any more damage. Still, I wonder—what did he think of last night?

"Yeah, it was fun. Tell Dad I'll be ready in a minute."

Fun? He closes the door and I resume dressing. My bra is on inside out, but I don't care, I want to leave. I put my purse on messenger-style and reach to pull on my knee-high socks.

Hank opens the closet door. "You can come out. She's gone." He has a mug of coffee in his hands and a grin on his face.

"Remind me why we came here?" I look up from the closet floor. Neither of us lives here, in Lakeland. We spent last night at a concert in Orlando and could have gone north to my house instead of coming south.

"I'm helping Dad balance his business accounts this weekend. You said you thought it'd be fun to come with me."

"Yep, fun." I say. There's that word again. Fun. Clearly, it's synonymous with stupid.

"I've had fun. You haven't?" He offers me his hand.

"You would describe last night as fun?" I pull on my boots, forego his hand, and scoot past him until I can stand.

"Yeah, fun. What did you have?"

"I don't know." Maybe I had my mind blown, a fantastic night, or experienced a whole different level of pleasure. Whatever I had, Hank had fun.

"Never mind. Help me with this." I walk to the window and ease up the blinds.

Hank doesn't move, just stands by the closet with his coffee. His dark hair is so short it hardly looks mussed and last night's smooth face and jawline are now covered with the shadow of a beard. When we first kissed, yesterday, I held his face between my hands. Today, I want to stretch across the space, hold his face again, and compare the touch, to commit both to memory. My palms itch with need.

"You're really doing this? You think this is a better option than going through the front door and saying you crashed here because you drank too much?" he asks.

"Yes, I do." I ease up the well-oiled window and pop out the screen like a pro. Ten years later and I still have skills. Gigi and I used to sneak out of her room without even waking the dog. I lean over to lower the screen to the ground and check to make sure no one is outside. The desk chair is the perfect height to get me up onto the windowsill, and Hank steps aside to let me drag it over.

I whisper, "I'll hand you the screen, you can put it back, and then you'll need to go distract your parents." I climb up and lower one leg over the sill.

He sips his coffee, makes a face, and puts it on the desk.

"Did you hear me?" I ask in a loud whisper. If I wasn't sitting on a windowsill, half in, half out, this moment would be like all the others I've shared with Hank: comfortable, easy, laughable at one point or another.

"Yeah, yeah. I heard you." He shakes his head with what I'm sure is disbelief.

After all, I'm a twenty-five-year-old sneaking out a bedroom window like a fourteen-year-old.

"Just do it," I tell him then jump off the sill onto the ground. I hold the screen and wait for his head to appear. When it does, I hand it to him.

"Don't forget to distract your parents."

"How could I?" he mumbles and fixes the screen.

When he turns away, I pull out my car keys. My SUV sits on the road between Hank's parents' house and the neighbor's. It'll be a run since Hank parked it on the far side of the house. At least I have an escape method and won't have to walk a street over to where my sister lives. She would never buy any story that brought me to her doorstep, without my car, looking like I do.

I stay crouched below the window, fidgeting with my keys until the bedroom door gives its telltale moan. I count to ten then I take off like a shot straight across the yard toward my Pathfinder. Like the dummy I am— sleeping with Hank proves that point—I press the unlock button on my keyless entry. When the horn gives two loud beeps to indicate the lock releasing, I stumble, almost wet my pants, and hit the ground.

I roll over, look at the houses, and wait a breath.

Nobody comes out, including Hank or his parents. Relieved, I pick myself up and sprint to my car. I fling the door open, jump in the driver's seat, throw the key in the ignition, and take off, letting acceleration close the door as I floor the gas.

I do quick calculations. Should I make an unscheduled family visit or haul ass home, leaving no one the wiser I was in town? With a groan, I remember this is the weekend my sister is hosting a family dinner. Having begged off with a poor excuse, I'll have to recant if I stay.

A look in the mirror shows circles of mascara under my eyes and a rooster tail on the back of my head. Clearly, it's not wise to see my family in this condition. Mothers are perceptive, at least mine is, and she would know in an instant how I spent my night.

I pull into the lot of the local quickie mart, and make a mental list of necessities as I walk in. My bladder gets top priority. I wash my hands, splash lukewarm water on my face, and pat it dry with a scratchy brown paper towel. It's a start, and it helps clear my head.

I make my way to the toiletries. After grabbing a bottle of saline solution off the shelf, I rip off the security tab and do a continuous squeeze of solution into my eyes.

"Ahh. Boy, that feels great," I tell the clerk.

Blinking rapidly, I enjoy the saline as it sluices down my face in cascades of pure relief. The clerk, who'd been staring at me as if I were a three-headed freak, begins running a total of my damage in the cash register. I snag a package of tissue off the shelf to wipe my face and head toward the fridge, where I grab a Yoo-hoo. On my way to the counter, I pick up a box of Krispy Kreme Doughnuts and eat one while I pay.

"Paisley?" someone behind me says.

I close my eyes in dread. Maybe, if I stand here long enough, they'll go away.

"I didn't think you were coming to town this weekend. Thought you were running a 5 K or something...."

I turn and look up at my sister's husband, Dan.

I'm cold busted. Of all the rotten, stinking luck.

"Hi, what are you doing here?" There's a box of Krispy Kreme Doughnuts in his hands.

Damn those irresistible doughnuts.

"I think the question is what are you doing here?" he says.

He pays and follows me outside. He's parked next to me. I guess he came in while I was in the restroom.

"I was in Orlando and figured I'd come on in." My voice quivers.

"Mmm-hmm. Reckon we'll be seeing you for dinner," he says.

"Uh, yeah. I'll let Sarah Grace know." He nods and moves toward his truck.

"Hey, Dan," I call. "I would appreciate you not telling anyone what you saw."

"See you later." He waves, gets in his truck, and drives away without a backward glance.

I sit in my SUV. My only real option is to go to Gigi's. I need a shower and a change of clothes. I'm not up for any more run-ins with people I know, so that rules out Target and a glance at the clock tells me the mall is closed. I'm pulling into traffic when my phone rings. More focused on avoiding a collision than checking my caller ID, I bring it to my ear.

"Hello?"

"You're in the clear," Hank says. His voice catches me off guard and I fumble my phone and drop it between my legs.

The irony.

With trembling hands, I switch the call to Bluetooth.

"Paisley?" he says.

"Sorry, I dropped the phone. Does anyone know I was there?" Honestly, this is the first time he's had me twisted up in knots.

"Nope. Not a clue. I still think you should have stayed for breakfast." He yawns. The simple sound brings forth the sensation of our naked bodies nestled together, the comfort of our sleep entwining us, and I suppress the urge to fan my face.

"Are you crazy? Was I supposed to walk out in your shirt and join your parents? Morning, Poppy. Morning, Ms. Becky. Your son and I had sex all night long and I'm famished," I mimic and Hank laughs.

"Well it wasn't *all* night. We did sleep the last few hours." His voice is like chocolate, rich and creamy, and I kick myself for not staying around for a second helping.

"Hank Lancaster." I pull into a strip mall parking lot, unable to concentrate on driving while talking to him.

"Where are you right now?"

"About to get on I-4," I lie. I don't want him to know I'm staying in town. If we get together again, I'll probably want a repeat performance, and then I won't be able to call our night of sex a mistake. He'll accuse me of wanting more.

He'd be right, but there is no need to have *that* conversation.

"You know not to head home without me, right?"

Bam! It's like being slapped upside the head. The aftermath of this impulse doesn't ever seem to end.

"What? Why?"

"Because my truck is still in Orlando and you are my ride to get it."

Stupid me. Telling him last night I wanted to go to Lakeland, too. If we'd gone to my apartment in Daytona Beach, I would not be in this predicament.

"It was stupid to come here."

"It was stupid to climb out the window," he retorts.

"It was stupid to hook up."

"Face it. What happened between us last night was bound to happen at some point. Heck, look what happened last week when we met in Cocoa Beach for the surfing competition. We've been gearing up for this since high school."

"We have not."

Liar. Liar. I know he speaks the truth. If I admit it, I'm breaking some unspoken friendship rule between Gigi and me, even if this is her fault for canceling on us and not attending the surf competition. She's directly responsible, leaving us unchaperoned.

When I accepted the invitation, I was excited to hang with an old friend. I never imagined we'd spend the evening on the beach, under blankets, learning each other's body.

I drop my head onto my steering wheel. Something about being with Hank makes me not think things through.

"In my opinion, hot weather and too much booze are the root cause of these slip ups." I toss out the lie and hope it sticks.

"OK, you keep telling yourself that." He chuckles. "I'll see you bright and early tomorrow? The folks leave for church at eight."

"All right. Listen, are you planning on seeing your sister today?"

"No, should I?"

"No, I'm heading to her house. I need a change of clothes before I visit my family. You cannot tell your sister what we did." I hope he gets the severity of my words through my tone. I rub the space between my eyes.

"Roger that," he says, his smile coming through the phone.

"Promise?"

"Yeah, sure."

"Say it."

"I promise, Paisley McAllister, to never tell my sister we made hot-monkey love in her childhood bed."

I groan. I can tell this is going nowhere fast. "I gotta go."

"I'll see you in the morning."

"Gee, I can't wait." I end the call.

I pull out of my parking spot, travel around the backside of the strip mall, and decide to take back roads to Gigi's house since I'm having attention issues.

I need a cover story, and a good one at that; otherwise

she'll see right through me. I dread facing her. I know I have to at some point. Why not today?

The consequences of my actions plague me. It's quite possible I may have set in motion the end of my friendships with Gigi and Hank. It's ironic, this is exactly what I promised myself I would do once my divorce was final. Not sleep with Hank, but start getting a life. Married the summer before my last year of college, I veered off onto a path quite opposite my friends. While they were enjoying life after college with extra cash in their wallets, I was supporting a medical student. Now it's my turn. Of course, I'm doing a bang-up job so far.

What if he wants something more? I'm not interested in going there. My journey is just getting started. What if our families find out? They are entwined enough for me to know it would be damn near impossible for my mother not to exaggerate our one night and push for a permanent union. Because I'm the only divorced person in my immediate family, pairing me off with someone as fantastically magnificent as Hank Lancaster—my mother's words, not mine—would go a long way toward putting the blight behind us.

Maybe one day my mother and I will want the same thing: me, happily married.

Right now we don't.

I pull up to Gigi's house and park. If best friends could be soul mates, Gigi would be mine. I don't think there's a thing she doesn't know about me, until now. Which makes this all the more difficult because she's who I go to for confession and guidance.

While I was in the midst of my divorce and on the

edge of a nervous breakdown, it was Gigi who came to me with the soundest advice. "You get a second chance," she told me. "A second chance to do it right. Pick wisely and do it for those who are stuck." I have every intention of getting it right this time, no matter what.

2
___

I LIKE to think there are golden rules for every aspect of life. The one between best friends goes like this: Thou shall not covet a friend's old boyfriend or brother, and thou shall not fornicate with either of them.

If Gigi finds out I used her brother for sex, that I consider last night a jumping off point for starting my single life, I don't know if she'll forgive me.

I want to idle in front of her house, but her husband, John, is leaning against his truck, smoking. With no, "Hello, how are you" or even a comment about my appearance, he points me in the direction of his wife. I walk through the fence gate to the backyard where she's cleaning their pool. She does everything: cleans the house, mows the yard, runs their kid to and fro and even works the grill.

Personally, I think yards and grills are for men. It irks me she does so much. When they first started dating, Gigi was on the back end of a bad breakup. John seemed nice enough but secretly I've always thought of him as her rebound guy and I'm pretty sure research exists showing relationships with rebound guys don't last. They married six months after graduation. I'm not convinced John makes Gigi blissfully happy, no matter how much she swears he does, certainly not lately.

"Hey." I toss the box of Krispy Kreme doughnuts on the outdoor table.

Sometimes a good doughnut can fix anything.

"Hey yourself." She runs the net through the water and does a double take when she looks at me. "I didn't know you were coming to town."

"Surprise," I mumble. I pick up a water noodle and start twirling it.

"What the hell happened to you? You're a wreck." She's staring at my hair.

I swat at her with the pool noodle. "I need to borrow some clothes."

She hangs the long-handled net up and sits down to a pitcher of tea, pouring a glass for both of us, and helps herself to a doughnut. "Clearly. You getting laid?" I cough and look away. Gigi points at me and laughs.

"Good for you. Anyone I know?" She wiggles her brows at me, reaches into the wet bar they keep on the porch, and pulls out a bottle of Jack Daniels.

"No," I squeak. She pours a good splash of booze in her tea. I dare not make eye contact. She hovers the bottle of Jack over my cup and I shake my head. My stomach is churning. Though I'm not exactly sure if it's from the dare-I-say excitement or my now raging headache.

"Tell me about this." She waves her hand toward me.

I suck in a breath and in a rush of words spit out the story I'd rehearsed.

"It's nothing. I went partying with my Daytona friends last night. Met up with this guy I know and did something stupid. I believe it's the alcohol's fault, thank you very much."

It comes out fast and jumbled. I hold my breath and hope sticking to some semblance of the truth will work to my benefit.

She chuckles. "I guess you're ringing in your freedom like you planned. You gonna keep a journal? Notch your belt?"

I feign indignation. "I don't have a quota I'm trying to reach or anything like that. I only want to get some more experience. Figure out what it is I want from life. My previous life's plans were based on Trevor's and what I thought they *should* be. Now, in my new single life I'm trying to make some new ones."

The moment passes between us, and I'm reminded why Gigi has been and always will be my best friend. When her eyes catch mine there isn't an ounce of pity in them.

"Why'd you drive here looking like a college coed sneaking out of a frat house?" In a snap, we shift gears.

"Because I have a dinner tonight at Sarah Grace's and...you know." I want to leave it at that but her expression is open, waiting for me to continue with my story. "I mean this guy, he like lives in Orlando and I um...didn't have the time to drive home. Now I'm up shit creek. I guess I didn't think it through."

If that isn't the understatement of the year I don't

know what is. I catch my lower lip in my teeth but quickly release it. What if that's my "tell" and she knows I'm fabricating the truth?

"You wanna shower here, too?"

Slowly, I let out my breath and nod as I reach for a doughnut. Maybe it will be OK after all.

"OK, I'll lend you clothes and you can shower in the guest bathroom, but I want details. Every juicy one. I want to know everything about this guy."

I may throw up. I put the doughnut back and wipe my fingers on my jeans.

"Can it wait until after the shower? I feel pretty skanky."

She laughs and gets up. I follow her into the house and down the hall to the bedrooms, stepping over a boy's oversize dump truck. Gigi and John have a four-year-old who defines the word rambunctious. She pauses at a closet, opens the door, pulls out a fluffy blue towel and washcloth, and hands them to me.

"Aside from this event, how's the single life?" This is her favorite question and

I'm afraid she'll compare my answer to her life, weighing what she has and what she's given up. I follow her into her room and watch her pull clothes out of her closet.

"It's all right. It's an adjustment." Mostly good, I want to add, but why rub salt in a wound? All my money is mine, I can shop when I please, keep dirty dishes in the sink without a care, and don't have to worry about someone else making poor decisions and messing up my life. I'll leave that part to me.

She hands me some clothes.

"I need underwear." We both grimace, she pauses before snapping her fingers.

"You left a swimsuit here that you can use. It's not like I don't want to give you some underwear, it's just... You get it." She runs down the hall. The French door opens, slams shut a moment later and she comes back carrying my old bikini. She tosses it to me.

The elastic and fabric are separating, "I don't know if I can wear this all day." I pull the elastic, puckering the fabric, and let it go in a snap.

"Only until the mall opens and you can go buy your own skivvies."

She breaks into a smile and when I look at her dimples, so similar to Hank's, my knees quiver. I look at my bikini bottom and figure it's better than nothing.

Gigi is an amazing hostess who keeps her bathrooms stocked with spare everything: toothbrushes, shampoo, soap, and lotion. Her mother does the same. I take the best, albeit shortest, shower of my entire life and don a short, navy-blue T-shirt dress and flip-flops. Thankfully, we're close in size. Gigi's clothes are perfect for the warm Florida spring day.

Outside, I find Gigi sipping iced tea by the pool. The bottle of Jack is sitting out, the box of doughnuts half-empty. I plop into a chair next to her and reach for a doughnut.

My headache is finally fading.

It dawns on me something isn't right.

"Why is your house so quiet?" Come to think of it, I haven't seen her son. "Where's Pete?"

"He's at John's mother's house. We're supposed to be having a romantic weekend. But, he got called in to work, of course." She leans in, her eyes suddenly bright. "Hey, stay over and we'll get our party on."

If memory serves, I believe I got my party on last night.

"I can't. Sarah Grace's dinner remember?" I do an eye roll.

My sister, Sarah Grace, is perfect. She married her high school sweetheart, is blissfully happy, has a twin boy and girl, a beautiful home, and makes me feel inadequate simply thinking about her. Sarah Grace would never get divorced, my mother once told me.

"Sounds nice." She wears her oh-poor-me face.

"Seriously? You don't want to come with me do you?"

"What are my options? John will be at work tonight, I'm kid-free, and you won't ditch your family for me." She looks at me. "I could go to my parents' I guess." Holy shit.

My headache flares up. "That would suck, huh?" I whip out my phone and send a text to my sister.

"It's OK, I'll figure something out." She sighs, takes another drink, and watches me text.

I give her my knock-off-the-pity-party look. I'm like a juggler. Only my balls are on fire. Chances are I'll get her to my sister's house and she'll still want to pop over to her parents', say hi, and find Hank there.

Without a car.

She'll put two and two together and kick my ass right there in front of my nana.

Gigi once said no girl would be good enough for her brother. She's certainly not going to approve of me and my actions. I may be her best friend, but I'm her divorced, train-wreck best friend.

"You're coming. Y'know my sister is an amazing cook, so the meal will be good. You'll have a decent time, if a bit tame." I finish my text and put my phone on the table to wait for a reply. It comes in an instant.

"Sarah Grace says to bring wine. You're locked in. It'll be mandatory fun. No good time for you, my friend," I tease. "And certainly no S.E.X.," I say, reminding her of her lost romantic weekend.

"You suck." She laughs and throws her teaspoon at me. "Hey speaking of things that suck, did Hank get a hold of you the other day? He misplaced your number."

I nod. Thinking of Hank makes me blush. I try to hide it by guzzling my tea. She quirks a brow, and I look at my watch. Well, what do you know? The mall is open.

I pop up out of my chair.

"You in a hurry?" She pours more Jack Daniels in her tea.

"Yeah, the reason I left this swimsuit here is it's a bit small. It's chafing me in a few uncomfortable areas. Let's hit the mall. You're coming, right?"

"Yeah, I guess so."

"Jeez, don't look so excited. What else you got going on?"

I guess I strike a chord, because when she looks up at me she looks sorta sad and I hate that for her. Is her life what she wants it to be? Are her dreams coming true? Did she think these things about me when I was married to Trevor? Seems like neither one of us are doing too well in the whole make-your-dreams-come-true department.

"You're right. I have absolutely nothing going on. What I do have is chocolate-covered strawberries and champagne in my fridge going to waste. I guess a bit of retail therapy will boost my spirits."

"Plan a trip to Daytona and boost your spirits. We'll meet with my Daytona gang and have a great time." I reach over and give her a hug. My Daytona gang consists of four other women who get together on a monthly basis for girl's night out.

"When?"

"Next weekend, any weekend. Just come." I pull her up out of the chair and push her toward the house.

"Now go turn your frown upside down and let's go get our shop on." I fidget with the suit as it decides to ride into my crack.

The way I see it, this is a win-win situation. I'm cheering up my best friend by keeping her busy. If she's busy she won't wander over to her folks, see Hank, visualize how we spent the night, and take me out. No doubt I'll score some crazy-good retail deals because Gigi is the bargain huntress of the world.

Totally win-win.

3

WHEN GIGI and I roll to a stop at my sister's house, the tension returns, my blood pressure rises, and nausea joins the party. I want to turn around and go speeding back to Daytona. I don't have the energy for my family.

With flowers and wine in hand, we head inside. I give the customary polite two knocks, open the door, and stick my head inside. You never know with Sarah Grace. She's blindsided me before by bringing home one of Dan's employees to dinner as a setup. It's happened twice, once when I was dating Trevor and once right after our divorce.

Nana, my father's mother, comes around the corner and smiles. My mother is right behind her.

"Hi, Nana." I give her a kiss. Two years after my father died, my mom spiraled into a dark depression. It was clear she couldn't keep it together any longer. Without any living relatives from my mother's side, Sarah Grace and I were at a loss as how to help her. Thankfully, Nana stepped up. She came for a visit and never left. They've been thick as thieves since.

Nana waits for Gigi to give her a kiss before she pats us on our cheeks and walks away, cocktail in hand. That's my Nana, quiet. Though when she has something to say, it's wise to listen up. I hug my mother, who is scanning me up and down.

"Are you staying long enough to see the hairdresser?" My mother, a Georgian Southern belle, never goes out of the house unless fully coiffed. My appearance this morning at the Circle K would have given her a coronary.

She met my father at the University of Georgia. Dad was a foreign-exchange grad student in the engineering department, and Momma was getting her MRS. Degree. According to them, it was a whirlwind courtship. They moved to Florida when my sister was a baby.

I reach up and try to pat down my wayward curls. It's not my fault I inherited my father's light complexion with the uncontrollable reddish-orange hair, nor can I help my mother wants me to dye it some color close to a Crayola crayon. Magenta, I think it's called.

"Leave her alone, Helen, I like her hair. Don't ye worry, me dear, it'll brown out as ye age," Nana, who has ears like a bat, says from the other room. I've been waiting for it to "brown out" most of my life. She's right about it getting darker, though it seems to be taking forever. Sometimes I wonder if the darker color she refers to is gray.

Thankfully, Gigi distracts my mom with her clever conversational skills. We follow her into the great room and kitchen combination. Oversize French doors separate the inside from a large outdoor deck and even larger pool. Sarah Grace's kids are outside running around the yard. They catch sight of me and come rushing in.

"Aunt Paisley," they cry and lunge at me when they get close. I hug the best niece and nephew in the entire world with all my strength.

"Did you bring us anything?" Jill, the youngest by three minutes, asks.

"No," my sister answers for me. She's standing in the kitchen, tossing a salad.

"Yes, it's in my car. Front seat."

They run out before I can say any more, Jackson in the lead, and I follow behind. Jackson pulls a bag out of my car and holds it up for affirmation. When I give him the nod, he pulls out two books.

"Yippee. Thanks, Aunt Paisley." They give me hugs and kisses before running off to fight over their new books.

"At least it's books," my sister says. She thinks I spoil them. "Hello, Gigi, it's great seeing you. How's little Pete?"

They exchange hugs and cute stories about their kids and I try not to let it bother me. This is one area I have nothing in common with Sarah Grace or Gigi. We are at such different places in our lives.

"You look pretty, Paisley." Sarah Grace hugs me close. "I'm glad you changed your mind and decided to come."

"You look pretty, too. The house looks great." It doesn't hurt that Sarah Grace is an interior designer.

In high school, she was the *it* girl and it's still obvious as to why. Tall, with long, blond hair, and big green eyes, she looks as much like our mother as I look like our father. She is perfection, gives perfection, and expects nothing less from others.

Sometimes it's hard to be her sister. Sometimes it isn't. Like when I was going through my divorce and she called me every day to check up on me. She's sweet.

I glance outside. Dan's in the yard staring at some folding tables he's been tasked to assemble. He gives me thumbs-up with a smirk.

"Why's Dan outside?" I snag a chip and dip it in salsa.

"We are dining alfresco tonight."

My vision blurs, and I choke on the chip. We cannot eat outside. Sure, it's a wonderful idea and even though Sarah Grace's seven-foot privacy fence blocks any view to Gigi's folks' house, Gigi will still think about them. Knowing they are right behind the fence, she'll feel obligated to go say hi, see Hank, do the math, come back, punch me in the face, and end our friendship. My family will figure it out. My mother and Nana will gush with joy and start scouting for wedding locations, and Sarah Grace will shake her head with disappointment. I don't want anyone to know what Hank and I did.

"What about the mosquitos?" Any state in the South will claim mosquitos as their state bird. Florida included. I start chewing my fingernails.

"I bought some of those large citronella candles. According to the package, we shouldn't be bothered."

Desperate times call for desperate measures and, even though I know it's a cheap shot, I don't hesitate.

"Oh, OK. So you aren't worried about the study that came out?" There is no study.

Sarah Grace stops cutting vegetables. "What study?"

I pick up a second chip and dip it. "The one linking childhood learning disabilities to West Nile Virus. It stated citronella and pesticides are ineffective." It's low, I know. I also know the safety of my niece and nephew is high priority for Sarah Grace and about her natural proclivity to go to the extreme.

I use it to my advantage.

Sarah Grace pauses for a beat and marches outside. I watch her discuss something with Dan, turn, and march back inside. Dan shoots me a lethal look. I give him the thumbs-up. I bet he's happy I came.

He takes down the table he struggled to get open and carries it to the screened portion of the deck, closer to the house. It's still outside, but if I can get Gigi to sit facing toward the inside of Sarah Grace's house, maybe I'll be OK.

"You don't have to change eating outside, Sarah Grace. It's one study. I'm sure one night of citronella smoke and the odd mosquito bite won't hurt them. Much." What's the point of putting a blade in if you don't twist it?

"Better to be safe than sorry." She finishes loading the appetizer tray and hands it to me. I scurry off to my mom and Gigi like the rat fink I am.

Not fifteen minutes at my sister's house, and I've chewed my nails down to nothing, made small talk with everyone, eaten all the carrots, half the salsa, and drank one and a half oversize piña coladas. I slow down on the booze, considering being drunk will probably not work in my favor, and I reassess the situation. No one is the wiser about last night. I'm in control.

Tonight might turn out all right.

Maybe.

And then my very own mother throws me under the bus.

"Mercy, Sarah Grace. You certainly can host a dinner. You've enough food to feed the neighbors," she says, taking in the smorgasbord Sarah Grace has prepared.

Sarah Grace shrugs and smiles, her head snaps up, her smile widens, and she looks right at Gigi. My stomach plummets.

"Gigi," she cries. "Why don't you invite your parents over? It's been forever since we've seen each other."

4

I PICK up the remainder of my piña colada and toss it back. Gigi calls her parents. I pour another one and start chugging. Screw being in control. All hell has broken lose. It was stupid to think I could avoid Gigi's family. Stupid.

"My brother is visiting?" Gigi poses the question to my sister. My mom and Nana ooh in unison.

"That's even better. We haven't seen Hank since the homecoming party. When was that, two? No, nearly four months ago. Dan, get the other table out of the garage."

Sarah Grace takes off for her linen closet and starts gathering table-setting items.

My mother turns to me and attempts to fancy me up. She pinches my cheeks, straightens my dress, and squashes down my hair before she steps back to assess the results.

"Go put on some lipstick, sweetheart. It wouldn't hurt you to try to impress Hank. He's a nice boy. Imagine how lovely it would've been if you had married Hank rather than Trevor." She shakes her head in what I can only assume is disappointment.

My mother never wastes a moment to point out my failed marriage. She didn't seem to object six years ago when I was engaged to Trevor, pleased at his quiet, gentle nature. Now, a year after the divorce was finalized, all she can talk about is how she knew he was wrong for me, how he probably never loved me, and how he was probably always cheating on me. Though her remarks are heavy with truth, they are better left unsaid.

I bite back a snarky reply. "Marrying Hank would have been unlikely since we were never like that."

I get myself another drink and catch my reflection in the mirror above the wet bar. My eyes are large, and my skin is pale. I look guilty.

"So you slept with him. Big deal. There's no need to panic. It's about time you slept with someone," I whisper to my reflection. "Maybe next time pick someone more removed from the family." With a firm nod of my head, I pour another drink and make my way back to the group.

People bustle around, setting up a second table on the deck, getting dishes, and moving chairs around, excited to see Poppy and Becky Lancaster. It's clear how my one night can backfire in ways I never imagined. What I do out of town, where my family cannot bear witness, makes it seem as if it never really happens. But this, this was right under everyone's noses.

"Paisley, don't just stand there," Sarah Grace calls to me as she carries chair cushions outside. "Grab the pruning shears and cut some hydrangeas. The vase is on the counter." She stops and gives me a look. "What's wrong with you?"

I tip my drink back and return her stare. I don't see her. I only see a catastrophe in the making.

"Paisley," she shouts.

I jump, put my drink down, and move toward the kitchen.

Gigi rushes by, shoots me a broad smile, and squeals, "This is going to be so much fun."

Yeah, until she puts it together and the world implodes.

I try to return her grin, but I can't force my lips to make a real smile. Instead I stretch them back. They curl upwards and I show teeth, hoping it's enough. I move in what I'm sure is the opposite of warp speed, like an out-of-body experience. I head toward the kitchen and everyone's running past me, chatting excitedly, yet it's all white noise. It takes all of my brainpower to put one step in front of the other. Maybe I'm drunk? Maybe this is the afterlife. Gigi has worked out what's happened and separated my earthly body from my spirit. Maybe it's hell.

I snort. It's definitely hell.

I don't know how I do it, but I make it to the garden, snip some hydrangea blooms, walk them back inside, and put them in a vase. I'm heading back out to the table when I realize Gigi's family has arrived.

Everyone's talking, hugging, and acting as if they live hundreds of miles from each other instead of around the block. I'm afraid to make eye contact. Gigi's father, we all call him Poppy, pulls me into a bear hug.

"Paisley, we don't see enough of you. You need to come over more often," he says.

They could have seen a whole lot of me this morning.

"I'll try, Poppy," I say. Looking at him, I see what Hank will look like when he's his father's age. He passes me over to their mom, and my eyes meet Hank's, who is hugging my mom. He winks and I glare. His mom gives me a warm embrace, and I feel dirty. If she knew, would she be disappointed?

"You look lovely. You doing OK out there in Daytona by yourself?" Ms. Becky asks.

"Yes, ma'am. I'm doing all right. It's good to see you."

When she lets go, I head inside to the bar and refill my wineglass. Goose bumps cover my arms, and I sense rather than see Hank come up behind me. I'm caught off guard at how close he's standing. He takes my glass and finishes it off.

"What are you doing later?" He wiggles his brows. My knees threaten to buckle.

"Ahh. I...I...Uh." I'm tongue-tied. I step back as Gigi approaches. She pours a glass of wine and gives me a curious look before turning to Hank.

"I didn't know you were coming to town," she says.

Using telepathic means, and what I hope are pleading eyes, I try to convey to him not to say anything, but he refuses to look at me. It's odd having this secret and pretending otherwise. It makes me nervous and sweaty. I struggle against the maddening urge to chew my already ravaged fingernails. Instead, I clutch my hands in front of me.

"I don't run everything by you," he teases.

There's a pause lasting longer than it should.

"Hey," she says, wagging her finger between us, "did you two hook up?"

Hank is still holding my glass or it would have crashed onto Sarah Grace's perfectly polished hardwood floors. Panic has shut down my bodily functions, and I'm going to wet myself any minute now.

"Huh?" It's all I can come up with.

Hank, the big oaf, takes another drink.

Gigi looks at me, puzzled. "You know. Last week at the surf competition in Cocoa. When I canceled. I'm sorry I bailed last minute. Did you two get together?"

Hank drops an arm around my shoulder. "Sure did. We made out, didn't we, Paisley? Competition was fun to watch, saw some sharks, scored some free surf stuff including a Ron Jon's Surf Shop T-shirt." He squeezes my shoulder, pulling me toward him.

"Yep. It was fun." I nod uncontrollably. I try to pull myself together, stamp back the panic, and force a smile. I focus on a spot over her head and try to think of something other than the make-out session Hank and I had on the beach that night, because tingly heat is climbing up my neck and I'm trying to beat it back.

Gigi leans toward me. "What's wrong with you? You're acting weird." She sniffs my breath. "I think she's drunk. Cut her off, Hank," she teases as she walks away.

"Relax," he whispers. He drops his arm off my shoulder, pinches my ass, and leaves with my drink.

I berate myself for drinking too much, for not being quick on my feet with a response, for going to the stupid beach to begin with because, let's face it, all roads lead to here. At this very moment, I'm experiencing the infinity wheel of karma hell.

Sarah Grace comes over and asks me to help her set out the food. It's a distraction I welcome. Dan's put two tables in a figure-eight layout so no one will sit with their back to another. It's like watching a bad comedy as people jockey for various seats and my mother's obvious attempt to make sure Hank and I are seated together. Try as I might to avoid it, I end up sitting next to Hank anyway.

Before we pass the food, Nana raises her glass for a toast. It's a family tradition done at every meal. Everyone picks up their glasses.

"*Slainte*," my nana toasts.

"*Slainte*," we repeat and clink glasses, but I need something more than a toast for good health. How about some good luck?

I pick at my food and notice Hank is picking at his, too. Will this new awkward always be a part of us? I reach over, take my wineglass from him, and toss back a gulp.

"You should slow down on the hooch," he whispers.

"You should shut it," I whisper back and take a second gulp.

"You keep it up, you might find yourself waking up in the same bed tomorrow you did today." He squeezes my knee.

I choke on my wine. The ugly kind, where you can't talk because you are too busy gasping for air, the kind of choke where people stop eating and look at you, waiting to see if you'll need the Heimlich or not. Hank continues eating with one hand and stroking my knee with the other.

"Paisley dear, ya OK, darlin'?" Nana asks, while whacking me on the back.

I nod, wheezing as I suck in air and grab Hank's hand on my knee, twist it, and try to push it off. He chuckles and removes it.

"How are you liking Jacksonville, Hank?" my sister asks.

"It's nice to be close to home. That's for sure." He leans back and puts an arm across the back of my chair. "It's the little things you miss. You get a good idea of how you define home when you're homesick. Puts it in perspective."

Everyone nods and looks thoughtful, as if he's shared the path to enlightenment. I do an eye roll.

"You dating anyone special yet?" Of course, my mother is the one to ask this nosy question.

"Momma, he's only been home four months." I give her the stink eye, but she doesn't care.

"Hush, Paisley. For all I know he met a nice Asian girl and brought her back."

She dismisses me with a wave. The women in my family turn toward Hank to wait for an answer.

"Yeah, he's left her in the car outside," I mumble to Gigi across the table and she sniggers.

"I didn't bring anyone from Japan home." He laughs. "It takes a special person to be with a service member. The hours are crazy and the deployments can be long. I was deployed a fair amount in Japan, so it wasn't easy to meet people. Besides, I find most girls want to stay close to home. Moving halfway across the world takes an adventurous spirit."

My mother and Nana exchange looks. The scheming has begun.

"I'm the perfect example. I won't even move the fifty minutes to Tampa for John's work," says Gigi.

"Paisley couldn't wait to get out of Lakeland." Momma pitches to Hank.

"That's not true. I love Lakeland. It's just easier to stay in Daytona." Plus my job and network of friends are there, but never mind that.

"Pish." She doesn't even look at me, her focus solely on Hank. "You *do* know Paisley's free now, and she's always had such an adventurous spirit. You may not want to date a divorcée, not many people do, but she's a good worker, and if she would do something with her hair, she'd be rather pretty."

"Momma," Sarah Grace exclaims on my behalf.

Momma smiles at the group and winks at me. "Hush. Y'all know I'm not being ugly. I have good intentions."

"She always does," I whisper to Hank, who cuts his eyes to me before looking at his plate.

I can sense everyone's eyes on me. The room is quiet except for the scraping of Momma's fork on her plate. No one knows what to say.

"And her teeth are real, too," I say, showing off my pearly whites before I reach over and toss back the rest of my wine.

It's gonna be a long night.

5

———

AN ANNOYING BUZZ rouses me from my slumber. I bury my face in the pillow and hope it goes away.

It doesn't.

I crack an eye and sigh with relief when I recognize Gigi's guest room, in her *current* house, not her childhood bedroom.

The buzzing starts up again, and I swat at the bedside table, desperate to smash whatever is causing my disturbance. My hand grazes my phone; its vibration tickles my fingers. Squinting at the screen, I take a second before recognizing Hank's number.

"What?" I croak. Cotton mouth, a sure sign I drank too much.

"You might want to drag your sweet ass out of bed. You've got a thirty-minute window to pick me up before the folks get home from church, or your secret will be out." He's matter-of-fact.

"I'll be there in ten." I hang up and fling my phone on the bed.

Fueled by adrenaline, head pounding be damned, I pop out of bed, pull on new undergarments, my jeans, and a clean T-shirt. I stuff my possessions into one of my large shopping bags, straighten the bed covers, and bolt for the door.

Gigi's husband, John, stands in the kitchen drinking coffee. He takes one look at me, pulls out a travel mug, fills it with coffee, and passes it to me while I'm putting on my shoes. The civility of it startles me, but I'll take it because I'm desperate.

"Thanks. Tell Gigi I have to get home and I'm sorry I didn't help clean up." I look at the remains of the strawberries and champagne we finished off, after my sister's dinner, with regret. Had I refrained, my head might be more amiable to movement.

He reaches in the cabinet, pulls out a Tylenol bottle, and passes me two capsules.

"Thanks again," I say and dash out the door.

It's breakneck speed to get to Hank's parents' house before they come home. Naturally, I catch every red light. I chew five sticks of mint gum and my thumbnail.

I dread this drive home. A speeding ticket may be worth getting, to shorten the time we're in the car together. I pull onto his parents' driveway within ten minutes of hanging up and am not the least bit surprised to see Hank waiting outside. I'm tempted to blow the horn nice, long, and loud, three times, right in his face, but the early hour and the pounding in my head make me suppress the urge. He bends over, picks up a small brown-paper bag, comes to the driver side door, and pulls it open.

"Is there monkey bread in that bag?" My stomach growls as I take in a deep breath of the delicious caramel smell. Ms. Becky makes the best monkey bread in the entire world.

"Yes. Is that coffee?" He nods at my travel mug.

"Yes, it's mine though." I hug it to my chest. "Go get your own. Now give me the bag."

Hank shakes his head and tucks the bag under his arm. "My parents drink awful chicory coffee. Can't stand it. Move over." He unbuckles my seat belt.

"What? Are you kidding me? You're not driving. I am." I grab at the belt, but he leans, blocking me with his body, and waves the bag of yummy goodness in my face, taunting me. The aroma of melted sugar and cinnamon wafts around the car, filling the space. I make a grab for it. When I come up empty, I cross my arms, shrug, and purse my lips. Hank tosses it onto the passenger seat.

He smirks at my annoyed look. "You can't drive and eat monkey bread."

"Yes, I can." I hold firm.

"No. *You* can't. Other people can. Time is ticking." He taps his watch and pushes me again. I snatch up the bag, hold tight to my coffee, and scoot across the center console onto the passenger seat.

"You're a jackass," I mumble and reach in the bag to pull out the small bundle of decadence wrapped in wax paper.

"Maybe, but this jackass is the reason you have monkey bread."

Mmm, good point. I'm about to pop a chewy morsel of bread, cinnamon, and sugar in my mouth, when it dawns on me his parents have to wonder how he's getting home, or how he even got here for that matter.

Hank backs out the drive and gives me a grin.

"Uh, what did you tell your folks about how you're getting home?"

"They didn't ask." He chuckles and pushes my hand holding the monkey bread toward my face. "Stop worrying, Paisley."

We don't get ten minutes away when he pulls over into a shopping plaza and parks in front of a small café, Bert's, known for its fine breakfast.

"What are you doing? You can't stop here. What if someone sees us?" I scan the parking lot, wondering if anyone we know will be inside.

"Sees us doing what? Eating? I'm not making the trip home without coffee."

I grab his arm before he gets out of the SUV. "Seriously, Hank. They'll know we…uh…you know." I want to get as far away from Lakeland as possible so I can put this weekend behind me.

"How? No one knows we had sex. Stop acting squirrelly, or they'll figure it out. We've been to breakfast together a thousand times."

He gets out of the car and heads toward my door, but I jump out. He's right. No one has to know I'm giving him a ride back to his truck because we rode into town together as a prelude to our hook up. Besides, I'm hungry and the monkey bread only whet my appetite. I gesture for him to lead the way and he holds the café door open for me. He's that kind of guy. He's also the kind of guy who stands when I enter the room, which I like. He looks at me when I pass, gives me his fabulous crooked smile, and I can't help but smile back. Maybe he's right. We've eaten out in public before. There's nothing odd about that.

"Hi, Bert," he calls to the man standing at the register and pulls me toward two seats at the counter and helps me onto one. The restaurant is packed.

"Hey, Hank. Welcome home." Bert waves and narrows his eyes at me. "You mind your manners here, Paisley McAllister." Bert wags a finger at me, his grin large, taking up half his face.

"Jeez, Bert, I was thirteen years old when I rolled your house. My daddy gave me a whipping I'll never forget. I've apologized until I was blue in the face. Can't we get past this? I don't even have toilet paper in my car." I feign being mortified.

It isn't a stretch considering how an act I committed twelve years ago still haunts me. It was bad enough my father drove by and caught me midtoss as my friends, Gigi, and I wove toilet paper in and out of Bert's large box elders.

Hank laughs while I busy myself with a menu, wondering what will complement the monkey bread. When I look up, the reason why I rolled Bert's box elders is standing in front of me. My appetite disappears.

Melinda Bane, Bert's youngest daughter and part owner of the café, stands on the other side of our counter, looming like the black widow she is, having spotted her next victim.

"Hello, Hank," she coos.

Melinda graduated the year between Hank and I. In high school, she was the one girl who was very comfortable with her sexuality, something I've never experienced but plan on fixing. She used to joke she needed suspenders to keep her pants up. Apparently, this skill came in handy after graduation and now, two husbands later, I hear tell she's looking for Mr. Third.

"Hey, Melinda, how ya been?" Hank, not one to be rude, leans over the counter and hugs her. It surprises me when he leans back and puts his arm across my chair.

"Oh, hello, Paisley. I didn't see you there. Though I'm not surprised to see you. You always did follow Hank around in school. Some things never change." Flipping her pale blond hair over her shoulder, she smiles at Hank, her focus never wavering away from him.

What a bitch.

I only followed him around at the end of the day because he was my ride home and I knew he'd leave me if I wasn't ready when he was. I don't bother with a response since she isn't interested in one.

Melinda is Hollywood beautiful. Next to her, I'm like worn flannel socks or a well-washed quilt. Where she is tan, blonde, and made up to perfection, I'm pale, ginger, with a slash of freckles across the middle of my face, and that's on a good day. It doesn't help I'm still hungover, haven't brushed my teeth and hair, or even washed my face.

"I heard you'd moved back. Is it true?" She bats her eyelids, and the monkey bread churns in my stomach.

"I moved back to the States a few months back," he tells her.

"It sure is good seeing you." She leans forward, smiles, and gives us a cleavage shot. I lean my elbow on the counter, my face resting against my palm. Perhaps I'll get some sleep while we wait for this to play out. I certainly don't want to watch any longer.

I close my eyes.

"Thanks. It's good to be home. Do we order with you, or is there someone else?" Hank asks.

"You can order with me. What can I get you?" she purrs.

I gag.

"I'd love a large black coffee and an everything bagel with ham, egg, and cheese, and the home fries. Paisley, you?"

I rethink my order, a brilliant move considering she might spit in my food. She's that kind of girl. Now I'll guarantee she can't unless she spits on Hank's, too.

Without opening my eyes I mumble, "The same for me, please." I say please only because my momma raised me to have manners regardless.

"Make it to go, please," Hank says.

I open up my eyes, surprised. Weren't we eating here?

"Sure thing, hon." She strokes his cheek and sashays down the length of the counter to the kitchen. Never in a million years could I move like that. I'm known to trip over air.

Hank makes small talk with Bert, and I reach for the Sunday paper someone has left behind. I crack it open and scan the headlines, only to be cut off by my ringing phone. I pull it out of my purse and see my friend Kenley's face on the screen. Kenley is part of the group of girls I hang out with in Daytona. Before I could graduate with my occupational therapy degree, I was required to complete two internships. Kenley was my supervisor at my second one. We've been fast friends since.

"Hey, what's up?" I lean back in my seat.

"Paisley, I think Tyler's had a seizure. Heather is on the way to the hospital with him right now," she says.

I sit straight up. Heather is Kenley's sister-in-law and Tyler is Heather's four year-old son. He has special needs, though it's something Heather and Justin, her husband, aren't ready to acknowledge. Because I work in pediatrics and have more firsthand knowledge, Kenley and I have had several conversations about this. We know the importance of early intervention, the difference it could make in improving his overall development. For over a year now, we've hinted that Heather should seek help for him.

"What's happened?" I keep my voice steady.

"They were having breakfast and she said he seemed to space out. When he came to—her words—he threw up and was disoriented. She called 9-1-1 and then me. Doug and I are on the way to the hospital to meet her." Doug is Kenley's husband and Heather's brother.

"Holy cow." I knew Tyler was delayed with talking and his play skills were very immature for his age, but I never considered seizures.

"Yeah, it's hit the fan now," Kenley says. "You think you could meet us at the hospital? I could use the extra support and I know Heather could, too."

"Where's Justin?" I look at my watch and try to estimate my arrival time.

"He's golfing. I've called several times. He either has

his phone off or isn't answering." She says it as if she's swallowing a bitter pill.

If a person can be less than dependable, then that's Justin. He's a real douche.

"I'm in Lakeland but headed home right now. I'll be there in a little over two hours. I'll text you when I get to town and can meet you then."

She sighs. "OK."

"Hey, we can get her through this. In the meantime, text me if you need anything."

"See you in a bit," she says and we disconnect.

I stare down at the blank face of my phone. This could be a rough road for Heather, and I make a silent wish, hoping for it to all work out.

"Everything all right?" He reaches for me and I want to wrap myself in his embrace. Knowing our actions would set the tongues wagging makes me hesitate.

Instead, I stand, put the chair between us, and tell him what happened.

"Want me to take you straight home? I can get someone else to run me to my truck."

"No, thanks though. She's not alone. Unfortunately, this has been a long time coming. As worried as I am for her, this is going to be a good thing because now Tyler will start getting the services he needs." I stare at my phone and count the minutes it takes Melinda to return with our food and coffee. She comes out from behind the counter and gives Hank a hug.

"It was great seeing you again, Hank. Don't be a stranger, hear?" she says. She is ninja-quick and subtle and had I blinked a second sooner or glanced away I would not have seen Melinda slip a folded square of paper in his front jean pocket.

Hank catches my eye, and he knows I saw. I look away and start for the door. Hank pays and follows me out. He hands me the bag of food and opens the passenger door for me. I can't make eye contact, afraid he'll see how disgusted I am with him and Melinda. My movements are stiff, awkward and I take a deep breath, hoping to steady the whooshing sound in my head.

"You do know I'm not interested in Melinda, don't you?" He brushes his thumb along my jawline. I shrug and lean over to pull the door closed, forcing him to step out of the way.

"I thought we were eating there," I ask when he gets in. If you ignore stuff, it tends to go away. Or so I hope. I busy my jittery hands with unwrapping my bagel.

"Yeah, but we can't talk in there. We can talk in here." He backs the car out and points it toward the interstate.

"What's there to talk about?" I take a small bite but have to remind myself to chew. My mind races with the events of the last few minutes. Heather. Melinda. Hank.

"You. Me. Sex. You can start by telling me what happened between you and Trevor."

Ugh.

6

THE MOMENT MY MARRIAGE IMPLODED, I became celibate. Not on purpose, but because the drama and stress of a failed marriage and subsequent divorce took every ounce of my energy. Once I knew Trevor and I were not going to make it, specifically, when he moved out and filed for divorce, I decided to take the following year for myself and use it to heal. I took a cooking class, kickboxing, and even a financial-investing class.

I wanted to be one of those smart women who finishes rich. I realized how much I didn't do my last year of college or after. When my peers were enjoying their lives post-college, I was putting mine back together. When they were making life goals, I was watching mine disappear, unsure of how to make new ones. First, I had to know what I wanted.

Here we are. Celibacy over. Truth is, Hank came along at the right time. He's my crash course back into the single life. And that's what I want to focus on, my single life. Not my failed marriage. Thinking about retelling the story makes me weary. Heck, just thinking of Trevor makes me weary and nauseated.

"Nothing happened." I pick at my bagel, nervous about sharing my most intimate of failures with Hank. Sometimes I wish the truth was we simply didn't get along, "Why do you think something happened?"

He gives me a look as if I can't be serious and pushes me in the shoulder. "Because you're divorced. I figured there had to be a good reason."

"What did Gigi tell you?" I attempt a blasé air but it takes all my control not to wrap my arms around myself or shift away in my seat. Instead, I rip off a small bit of my bagel, put it in my mouth, and cast him a sideways glance.

"Gigi didn't say anything except you were going through a rough time." He looks straight ahead, his bagel resting on his leg, untouched, one hand gripping the steering wheel and the other massaging his neck.

I look out the window and ponder. It's funny; if he'd asked this question last month, I wouldn't feel as hesitant, or maybe would have hesitated for a different reason.

Now that we'd slept together, sharing the humiliation only makes it worse. I'd been cheated on, repeatedly. How could I not personalize it? What if the problem was me?

I glance back at him and know he's waiting for my response. His bagel is still untouched and he's sitting straight up. What does he think happened? I'm afraid to ask. What if his perception of me is different than I think? Or worse? So much has changed between us already. The only answer is to tell him the truth. Besides, it's not like my own mother won't tell him if he should ask. I'm sure his parents know. The truth has to be better than what he's imagining, I hope.

I take a big breath and spill it out in a rush of sentences. "He cheated on me. I thought it was the one time, when I walked in on him. Turns out once he got in med school it became his extracurricular activity."

"You walked in on him?" He gives me the wide-eyed, I-don't-believe-it look.

"Yeah. My whole family was in the house. We'd taken Momma and Nana to Savannah and got home sooner than he expected. Obviously. Sarah Grace was the one who walked in the bedroom with me and saw it, too." I cringe. The memory is forever burned on my brain so much that when I think of it I can almost smell the patchouli incense he was burning.

A burst of laughter escapes me. "I was too stunned. I just stood there, but not Sarah Grace. She walked right up to him, pushed him off the bed, and punched him in the nose." I watch him as I sip my coffee, waiting for his reaction.

"No way." He tosses his head back with a short laugh and smiles. I can tell he expected nothing less, because in Hank's Code of Ethics book, siblings take care of each other.

"It was pretty spectacular. She broke his nose and her middle finger." I search his face, still looking for the slightest pity, anger, or embarrassment and come up lacking.

"I bet it was. That's something I would've liked to see." He gives me a small smile and picks up his bagel. "Thanks for telling me."

We ride in silence. Eating, drinking, and, I'm sure, picturing Sarah Grace beating the tar out of people.

"Wanna get together again next weekend?" he asks.

I swivel my head to look at him. "Are you serious? No, I don't want to get together next weekend. This"—I gesture in the space between us—"cannot happen again."

"Why not?" He grins and wags his eyebrows.

"It's a disaster in the making."

"What do you mean?"

"Jeez, where do I start? This whole thing is wrong. My friendship with Gigi, our friendship. It could all go up in smoke. Is it worth it?" How does he not see this?

"I'm just talking about going out together."

"Sure, you make it sound harmless. But the last time we got together it led to sex. When I get around you, my judgment gets out of whack and I might do something stupid." OK, perhaps I should say I might continue to do something stupid. Stupid has already come and gone.

"As I see it, if you're gonna do something stupid, who better with than your old pal Hank? I can think of a thousand stupid things to do together." Does he really think it's that simple? He turns toward me, rests his hand on the top of my seat, and gives me a toothy grin.

I want to laugh or shove his shoulder because he's being flippant but he needs to know where I'm coming from, that I was once broken.

"Ugh, Hank." I groan. "Don't you get it? I've already hit my stupid quota for my lifetime with the divorce. I can't keep adding to the tally." I can't lose the friendship I have with Gigi or with him either. A possibility he doesn't seem fazed by.

"What if all those things you're worried about never happen and you actually gain something instead?" he asks.

"I don't see how that's possible." I shrug and shake my head with emphasis. "Nope."

He shifts to stare straight ahead. I can tell he's a tad bit annoyed by the set of his jaw. "Why?"

I struggle with my words, my thoughts. I'm not sure what to say. For starters, how do I explain to him I don't want to be involved with a guy who will always have women slipping their numbers, or worse, room keys, in his pocket? Sure, I trust Hank, but I've never been in a relationship with him, at least not one involving sex. Because of Trevor, I now see things differently.

Yes, Hank told me he wasn't interested in Melinda, yet her number is still in his front pocket. Then there's the issue of his chosen career. Talk about a buzz kill. Who wants to always move? Not me, I like my predictable life. Adventurous spirit my ass.

The most important reason is I'm nowhere near ready to be with someone, short or long term. This next part of my life should be all about me.

"You know what divorced means, Hank?" I'm about to tell him something I've recently admitted to myself, and it might make him understand me a little more. "Divorced means you've failed. If you stay single, you do so by choice. When you're divorced, it means the other person didn't want you."

"That's utter bullshit." He starts to say something more but instead puffs out a sigh and tosses the remains of his bagel in the bag at my feet.

"Says the guy who has never been divorced. The fact remains, I failed at my marriage and now I have to make sure not to repeat my mistakes. I have a track record, and it's not a good one. I went from high school to college to Trevor. On an experience meter, I'd be surprised if mine registers. I want to do now what I should've done in college."

I stare at his profile. He's leaning against the car door and tapping the steering wheel with his index finger in annoyance. The mood in the car is heading south fast.

Aware of the sudden thick air between us, I hope to lighten it once again with some levity. "Besides, if I see you next weekend it will be like having three dates and in my book three dates is the beginning of a relationship and that's the last thing you need. As you are well aware, I'm a relationship nightmare."

He's quiet, his lips pressed together into a thin line. My heartbeat pounds in my ears as I wait for him to decide whether or not he's going to allow the mood change.

"Who says it needs to be a relationship?" He quirks a brow at me like his sister does, and I look away.

"What do you mean?" When I think of Hank in terms of a relationship, I used to think friend, trustworthy, and dependable. But now when I think of him, I automatically relive our first kiss. How we stood ankle-deep in the sand and it felt so natural when he lowered his head to press his lips gently to mine.

"I mean it doesn't have to be serious. Just a good time. You say the last thing you need is a relationship..."

"I think I need to...want to...date...lots of guys." I chew

on my bottom lip. My brain hurts just thinking about what he's suggesting.

"Fine. You want lots of guys. I get it. My job has me coming and going and there's always the possibility of a deployment. Makes it difficult getting to know someone, much less building a relationship."

He continues, "Exactly the reason why this is so perfect. I like being with you, and I hope you like being with me. We already know each other, this is us getting together every so often to have a good time. No strings. No awkward first date. No expectations. Not even sex if we don't want to."

I stare at him, processing what he's said and I find I'm hung up on one word: deployment. To a war zone? I can't even imagine. If something happened to him... Well, I can't go there.

"Paisley?"

"Do you go to dangerous places often?" I have to know.

He looks at me, confused. "No, not often. Occasionally. About us?"

Every ounce of common sense is telling me to run, avoid this inevitable pain. My mind pulls up the memory of him, lying pale in his bed following surgery for appendicitis. It was fifteen years ago and I remember being scared to pieces then and we weren't sleeping together.

"Paisley?" he asks again.

"I'm sorry. What?"

"Just two friends getting together. Something we've done hundreds of times in the past. I like being with you and you can practice your dating moves on me. No strings," he says, again.

"There are always strings," I caution. "What if we do have sex again? I really do think it could change everything."

He shrugs. "If things start to change in a way that makes you uncomfortable, we back out and call it a day."

"It's a stupid idea."

Look what happened on one unchaperoned night together. There is no possible way we can hang out and not fool around on some level. At least *I* think we couldn't. Avoiding his repeated glances, I reach into my bag, pull out a magazine, and settle in, pretending to read the pages.

"Remember when we went tubing on the Ichetucknee?" He breaks the silence.

"Which time?"

"The time Hunter Norris swam up behind you and gave you a wedgie."

I grimace at the memory and nod my head. He not only gave me a wedgie, but subsequently flipped my tube over, allowing me to share the experience with most of Hank's senior class and a fair number of juniors and sophomores, too.

"You have the same pinched face look now that you wore then." He laughs when I narrow my eyes at him. "Relax. Pull your panties out of your crack. Have I ever led you wrong?"

"Yes." I wag my finger at him.

"When?"

My hesitation is enough of an admission.

"That's right. I've never led you wrong. I always bail you out. Have some faith." He reaches over and tweaks my nose. "All I'm asking is to hang out, get together now and then, and enjoy each other's company. I bet when you give it some thought, you'll see my idea is brilliant."

"Brilliant? Ha, not likely." I snort. "Seriously, you don't," I pause, looking for the right words and decide on being frank, "expect sex and it's not a relationship or anything? Because I plan on getting my date on. I don't plan to sit at home and wait for any guy to get back to town and call me. Besides, until this weekend, I've only been with two other guys and I plan on trying some on for size." Sounds like a good idea to me. In theory.

His knuckles whiten when he grips the steering wheel; it's gone in a blink. Did I imagine it? It's only right that he knows the score up front. If he wants no strings attached, then he can't be off getting mad if I'm on a date.

"Wait. What? You've been with how many guys?"

"You heard me. Three. Austin Calhoun." I tick off one on my finger. Hank grimaces. He never did like Austin, my first serious boyfriend. "Trevor, and now you." I hold up three fingers and wave them. "I'm a bit inexperienced, and I believe that's part of the problem."

Hank chuckles. "Your 'inexperience' is certainly not a problem and it's not *your* problem."

Steam starts to build up between my ears, "Just exactly what *is* my problem?"

"You think too much about everything and don't listen to what's going on here." He taps above my left breast where my heart is. "And here." He taps my gut. "Instead you get spun up in here." He taps his index finger against the center of my forehead.

I slap his hand away.

"I don't expect anything, Paisley, except for you to be yourself and have a good time. What happens, happens." He shrugs and glances at me before focusing back on the road.

"You've got that pinched-face look again, and now your eyes are squinty. Lighten up." He smiles.

"You lighten up." I continue to glare at him. I'm being childish, but his words twist in my brain.

Next thing I know he has his bicep in my face and is flexing his muscle, making it pop up and down. "Besides, y'know you want to get some more of this. You can't resist." Laughing, I push away his arm.

"You know you want to get some of *this*." I tell him, pointing to myself. We laugh together, and he reaches over and picks up one of my curls and begins twisting it between his fingers.

"Seriously, Hank. You've been my friend for my entire life. I don't want to lose you."

"You won't. I promise. Think about it. It's a win-win situation. We make some basic ground rules. If we sleep together again, we'll address any awkwardness right away. If we should sleep together again and then with someone else, we tell each other right away. Full disclosure. No more hiding out either. We're adults. If we happen to be in Lakeland at the same time and want to hang out, we hang out."

I'm sure his smile is meant to be encouraging, but I'm glad when he turns his gaze back to the road, afraid my face will show my doubt and hurt his feelings. He slides his hand from my curl to the back of my neck and begins caressing my jawline with his thumb. Instinctively, I turn my face toward his palm. He glances at me and winks.

"I dunno, Hank. So much can go wrong." I can't believe I'm considering it. I make a mental note to go see a shrink immediately when I get home to have my head examined. I must be, unequivocally, out of my mind. Because right now he's rubbing my jaw and I want to jump him. At the very least kiss his palm.

"You know you want to do this," he tells me.

He's right. I do.

"Besides, I'm a sure thing. A safe bet. A fun guy. You don't have to do the whole awkward, get-to-know-me dance. We can get down to having a good time."

"And what if there's no more sex? Or what if there's lots of sex between us and between me and some other guys. Can we be two friends getting together with no expectations?"

"Stop worrying. Have some fun. Good grief."

Maybe I should get some meds, too, because I have to be delusional to think this will work. I'm heavily engaged in my mental argument when Hank moves his hand from my neck, snatches up my coffee, and finishes it.

"Hey. You're a jackass."

"So you keep telling me." He grins, both dimples peek out, and hands me the empty mug. "About next weekend. You free?"

I smile back, resisting the urge to touch him. "No, but the weekend after, I am."

7

AGAINST MY BETTER JUDGMENT, I agreed to let Kenley set me up on a blind date, and today it's going down. It's why I couldn't make plans with Hank.

We're meeting at a local casual-dining seafood restaurant so I drive myself. I'm not experiencing the nervousness I'm usually crippled with when preparing for a date. I'm more laid-back with this planned arrangement for several reasons. One, Kenley and Doug will be there to buffer the situation should he turn out to be a weirdo or something.

Two, I figure it's time to get my feet wet and what better way to start than with someone who I have no initial interest in?

Three, my intention is to use this date as practice because he doesn't sound like someone I would pick for myself based on Kenley's description. Yesterday, I cornered Kenley for some specifics thinking I should at least have *some* information.

"Who is this person you feel driven to set me up with?" I asked her. She's happily married, in that disgusting, true-love sort of way, and probably can't rest until all women have what she has.

"He's a pilot," she told me. "Has one of those big houses in the Fly-In."

The Fly-In is an exclusive subdivision in Daytona Beach. Most of the houses have private hangars for private planes. A runway bisects the subdivision and finding pilots is as easy as throwing a stone. Daytona is a mecca for aviation aficionados, boasting an assortment of aviation schools and one of the nation's best aeronautical universities, Emery Riddle.

"What does he fly?" I asked. A pilot, wouldn't Momma be proud? I'm not interested in anything long-term with pilots, or military guys quite frankly. I can guess what goes on out of town.

"Big jets for one of the major airlines. I don't remember which one. He and Doug belong to the same tennis club."

"You know I'm not crazy about blind dates," I reminded her.

"I know, but we have to strike while the iron is hot," she stated matter-of-factly.

I wasn't even going to dignify that remark with a comment. It was clear Kenley thought my time was running out. For whatever reason, I wasn't sure.

The drive to the restaurant takes ten minutes. The breeze from the ocean pushes my hair around so I pull it into a loose and bouncy ponytail and I grab a light jacket in case the ocean breeze decides to get cooler or stronger. It's doubtful, but at least this once I'll be prepared.

I find Kenley and Doug sitting at a table on the outside deck with no sign of my guinea pig.

I make my way to the table and plop down next to Kenley, leaving the chair across from me empty.

"Hi." I smile at them both. They are the perfect couple. A yin and yang. Though both tall and athletic, he is blond with milky skin and she has dark brown hair with cocoa skin.

Since my divorce, I'm more watchful of my friends and others in their relationships. I figure my failed one is an indication I might need some mentoring, tutoring, or at least guidance in the relationship department. Maybe that's why Hank's idea has such appeal or why I allowed Kenley to set me up.

I aspire to have a relationship like Kenley and Doug's. They are always affectionate with each other, courteous, and considerate, and it's obvious they love each other. I figure an interracial marriage in today's world is far easier than it was sixty years ago but probably still has its moments. There are assholes everywhere. But Kenley and Doug seem undaunted. They have each other. Can one ask for anything more?

"You look great, Paisley. Ted went to the restroom." Doug smiles at me and flags the waitress so I can place my drink order.

Ted arrives as the waitress delivers my drink. He isn't bad-looking. He looks like a pilot with his tight, crisp haircut and graying temples. He's tan, has a nice smile of capped teeth, and hazel eyes. He's ten-to-fifteen years older than me, which isn't a problem, and right before he arrived, Doug told me Ted is thrice divorced. A potential problem? Maybe. I'm not one to cast stones, but how could a relationship reject like myself get together and make something work with such an obvious relationship klutz like Ted?

"Wow, is this her? You are one foxy lady." He smiles, oozes into the chair across from me, picks up my hand, and kisses my knuckles.

Foxy lady? Is it the seventies? I wish more than anything at this moment I could raise one eyebrow like Gigi or Hank. I was never able to master enough control over my facial muscles. I give Kenley and Doug what I hope is a quizzical look. This is who they picked out for me? Good thing I don't have high expectations.

I pull my hand from Ted's, introduce myself and try to spark up some conversation. My marriage to Trevor taught me one thing: if you ask a man the right questions, he'll talk nonstop about himself, requiring only an occasional nod followed by a "mmm-hmm," or "right."

Ted is easier than most. I ask one basic question, "So, you're a pilot?" and he launches right into his personal curriculum vitae.

I learn about Ted, his aforementioned three ex-wives, his bank account, and his golf handicap. He tells me he's raising the last of his three sons. It's the one redeeming quality I can find, though I wonder how they'll fare in the relationship department. Throughout the conversation I manage to read the menu, nod at the right times, and place my order. A couple of times I glance at Kenley, who is now giving me a pleading look.

She is *sooo* in trouble.

As Ted orders the fourth round of drinks, Doug tosses back the remains of Kenley's beer. He's drinking more than his usual two beers. His voice has been slowly going up in octaves as the evening progresses and the drink order climbs. It's none of my business until Kenley decides to share it with me, but she's hardly spoken and is fidgety, two things uncharacteristic of my typically chatty and hard-to-fluster friend. After dinner is finished and the table cleared, Doug staggers his way to the restroom. Kenley excuses herself and follows him.

Ted is still going on and on.

Not one to let an opportunity go to waste, I decide to try some dating moves, hone my skills. I lean back in my chair, cross my legs, and pull up my iced tea, having switched to the alcohol-free drink three rounds back. To give me something to do, I use a straw to sip my tea, and play with it as I listen to Ted droning on.

"Lord," he leans in and whispers to me, "I'd do anything to be that straw."

"I beg your pardon?" I do a mental shake of my head and question my own hearing. I take another sip.

"I'd love to be that straw you are sucking on." He winks at me and leans forward even farther.

In a flash, I'm angry. The sounds of the restaurant are muted as is Ted's voice. His mouth is moving but the thumping sound in my ears makes it impossible to hear. I tremble from the adrenaline rush and my palms itch to smack his face or, at the very least, the table. Ted has shown little to no interest in me and he thinks it's appropriate to make sexual innuendos? Who does he think he is?

I bare my teeth, bite the straw, and pull it from the drink where I spit it on the floor. I slam my glass onto the table and stand. Ted looks surprised and confused, and my anger flares, spreading heat through me like a bush on fire in a drought.

"Is there something I did or said to make you think I want to be talked to this way?" I put my arms akimbo, lean slightly forward, and stare at him.

"Uh...no...but I uh... Aren't divorced women looking for some fun? If you know what I mean?" His smile is more a leer. I blow out a huff of disbelief.

I scan the crowd for Kenley and Doug and find them arguing over by the restrooms. Uh-oh, trouble in paradise.

"Thanks for dinner, Ted. I have to leave though." I snatch up my purse and jacket, berating myself for thanking him when I should have slapped his face. Kenley and Doug stop their heated words when I approach.

"Thanks, but no thanks," I tell them. "I have to leave."

"I'm sorry, Paisley." Kenley reaches out and squeezes my arm and promises to call later and explain. I wave off her apology and leave as fast as my feet can take me without actually running from the building.

When I get home, I take a shower and dress in my comfy pajamas. Do men actually think a woman likes to hear those things? Yuck. He didn't even bother to get to know me before he made his creepy pass, thinking I'm different than the average single girl, something more or something less, all because I'm divorced.

Too furious to do anything, I lie on my bed and watch the ceiling fan go round and round. I promise myself no matter what, I will not settle for just any man. Once was enough. I would rather be by myself than shackled to some idiot like pilot Ted. Trevor used to talk to me the same way. I thought it was because he found me pretty, even sexy. What I learned was he talked to all women like that. Women were objects to him, a means to an end. I was nothing more.

The hardest thing about divorce, for me anyway, was the sudden change of life. One minute I was getting married and buying a house and the next minute I was out of the marriage and living in an apartment only slightly better than the one I'd inhabited in college. I don't like being single, but if my track record with men is a testament, I'm not very good at being married either. Where does that leave me?

Single. Alone?

I feel the tears before I realize I'm crying. I pull out my phone and stare at the screen. I guess I need to know someone is out there. Someone who cares.

I text Hank. *Hi.*

I wait a few heartbeats, and he texts back. *Hi yourself. I like that it's late at night and you're thinking of me.*

Don't let it go to ur head. I'm just saying hi.

You OK?

I hesitate. *Yup.*

R U sure ur OK?

I sigh. Do I want to share with him? *Yeah was going to bed and thought I'd say Hi.*

What r u wearing?

OMG! Never mind. I'm going to bed now:-) LOL. Sweet dreams.

I hold the phone close to my chest and fall asleep.

8

THE LAST FEW weeks of school are some of my favorite times in the school year and a highlight of my job. Being a school-based occupational therapist can be frustrating because it can seem the progress the children make is slow or the weeks appear to repeat, though the last week of school everything is different. No one stands out more than anyone else on crazy-hair day, everyone gets to go on the field trips, and who doesn't love watching movies instead of doing classwork?

With only a week of school left, I have spring fever worse than the kids. I'm ready for unplanned days, no obligations, and sleeping in on weekdays. When Josie calls mid-afternoon in a panic, I'm more than ready to change my scenery.

"Can you meet me at the Tea Room?" she cries without returning my greeting.

"Now?" I look at my watch. I've just come back from a field trip and need to finish my notes and clean my room.

However, I never turn down an opportunity to eat out and the Tea Room is one of my favorites.

"Yes, now. Get your ass over here. I already ordered your favorite." She hangs up before I respond.

Josie Woodmere and I met when Trevor and I separated. She clerks for the attorney I hired and while taking my information to prepare for my divorce, we formed a friendship I knew would span time. She's also part of the group of girls I hang with on a regular basis.

I throw my paperwork and work toys into the back of my car and drive, barely within the limits of the law, to the Tea Room. I find Josie at the table with several magazines spread out before her.

"Hey." I take the seat across from her and pick up the iced tea she's ordered for me. We've done this before.

I look at one of the magazines and am not surprised to see it's a bridal magazine. Josie is getting married at the end of summer and has the tendency to obsess in general. Wedding planning is fertile ground for twenty-four-hour obsession. I pile up the magazines so the waitress can deliver our food.

"You bringing anyone to my wedding?" Josie digs into her salad.

I don't have an "anyone" and can't think of who I want to bring as a date other than Hank, and I'm not sure he'll be in town or interested in going. I know how men are about weddings.

"Probably not." I shrug.

"Good, because you won't be wearing the bridesmaid dress we picked out."

"What?" Josie, the other bridesmaids, and I spent

hours picking out dresses we all liked and thought we might wear again.

"Yeah, apparently there's a back order on the dresses and my pain-in-the-ass mother thinks this is something I planned to stall the wedding. We need to find a backup, quick." She rolls her eyes and takes a gulp of her drink.

This is Josie's third wedding and, if it happens, it will be her first to come to fruition. Her first fiancé was a guy she grew up with, a family friend. They decided to call it off on the eve of their wedding. Not the smartest move, according to Josie, but it was better than marrying a guy who was in love with another girl yet was going to marry Josie out of obligation, friendship. Josie said this guy's life plan would have turned her into her mother, not that there is anything wrong with Josie's mother. To hear Josie tell it, she wasn't interested in becoming a tool for her husband's career nor a charity-running, crash-dieting snob.

Josie tosses a magazine at me. "Start looking for something we both can live with. I'll pay for it since it's unlikely you'll use again." She gives me an apologetic look.

"Don't sweat it." I pick up a magazine, flipping through the pages, pausing on the pages she's dog-eared.

"Thanks, Paisley, you're a true pal." She smiles and uses the side of her finger to dab at her misty eyes.

I know this wedding stuff is hard on her. After running out on groom number one, Josie left her parents with a wedding expense equal to a house down payment and ran off to find herself, moving often. At one time, she ended up at some artist commune. There she met groom number two, a struggling artist who was the extreme opposite of her father. She announced her happily ever after intentions over social media sites and her parents were furious. Halfway to Vegas with the Picasso wannabe, she found herself with cold feet. Though she hadn't cost her parents the expense of another wedding, she'd once again embarrassed them. Apparently, in her hometown, she's developed a reputation for her wedding mishaps.

Josie comes from a wealthy and affluent family and her parents are quite obvious with their expectations of a mate for her. When she became engaged to Brinn McRae, a grew-up-hard, street-smart pilot instructor and business owner, Josie was told she was on her own. If she followed through with the marriage, they would consider reimbursing her some of the expense. If she stayed married for more than five years, they would reimburse her the entire cost.

In her no-nonsense, would-never-guess-she-grew-up-privileged way, Josie told them to stuff it, though the words she used to convey this message were something often heard from a sailor's mouth.

That's our Josie. A beautiful, ebony-haired siren who can make men swoon with her looks and hardened criminals blush with her vocabulary and word combinations.

"This one isn't too bad," I show her a picture of a long, elegant-looking gown with simple straps and an empire waist. "Is it too long for an afternoon wedding?"

"Yes, it's very pretty. I might consider moving my wedding to the evening so you can wear it. Keep looking."

I may have known Josie for only these last eighteen months, but I know how much she loves Brinn. Nothing is going to keep her from marrying him. I also know how much he loves her, which is why he's footing the bill for the whole wedding. He won't let Josie consider paying for anything and tells her he wants to make all her dreams come true. If only her parents knew their daughter is about to marry a self-made millionaire.

I look at the pictures of the brides and grooms in a variety of formal wear and am surprised I'm not bothered by them. In the past, seeing others in wedding garb would remind me of my failure. Today the pictures don't trigger any desire to see Trevor or any remorse over my lost marriage. I suppose I'm getting used to being at odds with where I want to be in my life and where I currently am. I pat myself on the back for having made it this far without self-destructing, there's something to the concept of taking small steps.

"Are you going to Kenley's this weekend?" Josie asks. She holds up a picture of a dress with puffy shoulders and I shake my head.

I groan at the thought of Kenley's party, not just a regular party, a sex-toy party.

She thinks it's a brilliant idea and will be loads of fun. I'd rather be shot out of cannon buck naked, in front of my friends and family, with a YouTube video taken for eternal viewing pleasure.

Who has these parties?

Apparently, lots of people, because I've already been sent a catalog for preorders. Kenley called the day after my disaster date with Ted, begging forgiveness and offering apologies. I was over it by then. I tried to use her guilt to get me out of going to her party.

So far, I hadn't been let off the hook. There's still hope.

"Not if I don't have to." I grab another magazine. "Oh, this is pretty." I show her a dress, hoping to keep her focused on the wedding and not the sex party.

"Oh come on, Paisley, we'll have a blast. And this party is perfect for you. Since you're so selective with who you celebrate your newfound freedom"—she wiggles her brows at me—"you could use a little buddy."

I bury my face in my hands, hoping to hide my blush. Not because she's talking about getting me a toy, but because I rang in my newfound freedom with Hank.

When I look up, Josie's head is turned sideways and she's giving me a quizzical look, similar to a dog hearing an unfamiliar sound.

"What have you done? Did you sleep with the blind date Kenley set you up with?" she asks.

Some people are meant to be friends, and Josie and I are those people. To her, I'm an open book. That's why I spill my guts. First about my disgusting date with Ted, and then about my two weekends with Hank, and how we have plans to meet up the following weekend.

"No shit. You slut." Her voice is loud, her vocabulary unexpected in the quaint, mock-English tea room. Those sitting around us share their glares.

I raise my eyebrows and nod. "Yep, it's true. I'm a tramp," I tell her.

"Ha." She chuckles. "If you're a tramp after sleeping with what, your third guy? I'm... Well, there aren't words for girls like me if three or fewer men makes you a tramp."

"Yeah, I'm a bad friend, right?" It's a thought that's plagued me.

"What did Gigi say when you told her?"

The bite I took hits my stomach like a rock. "I didn't tell her."

She looks at me for a few seconds. "You need to tell her before she finds out some other way."

I groan. "I can't. What if she hates me?"

"She'll hate you more for not telling her. What if you sleep with him again this weekend?"

"I'm not going to. Are you crazy?"

Her look tells me she thinks I'm crazy, stupid, or both. "I don't think you realize how good Kenley's party will be for you. If you feel like a tramp now, dating is going to be difficult. Imagine the relief you can get without having to sleep with anyone. You won't have to worry about this bullshit guilt you seem to love to carry around." She gives me an evil smile with hints of secrets I'm about to learn.

I swallow.

"Was it any good?" Of course Josie would want to know.

"It was better than Trevor on his best day," I tell her, fanning my face.

"Girl, if that's true, you should scoop him up."

I shake my head. "It can't go anywhere. It is what it is or, should I say, it was what it was because it's not happening again. We are just going to be friends who hang out." I stab the tomato on my salad and give her my best matter-of-fact look.

"And why is that?" She's serious now. She's stopped flipping through magazines and stares at me.

"Lots of reasons—"

"Name five."

"That's easy. One, he's been my friend forever and I could lose that."

"He's been your friend forever and knows you so well you don't have to worry about him not liking you. He's seen you, warts and all, and still wants to have sex with you."

I shrug off her words. "Two, he's Gigi's brother. I'm clearly breaking the friendship code."

"Or Gigi will be over the moon—"

"Until it crashes and burns, and then it's awkward and weird."

"Assuming it does," she replies.

"And that brings me to three, four, and five. He's never been in a long-term relationship. He's a sailor who is going to be gone *all the time*, not to mention in danger. Women flock to him like... Well...they just like him. Always have. I've been down that road, Jo, and I can't go there again. And I'll give you a sixth reason. He's my rebound guy. Everyone knows rebound guys go nowhere. You know I'm in no position to be entertaining the possibility of a relationship."

She does an eye roll, but sits quietly with her lips pursed. She looks me in the eye, as if to make sure I'm listening, and says, "You know not everyone is like Trevor."

"I do know that. Hank's a good guy, but good guys still get tempted. Besides, you know I'll worry to the point of being obsessive, which will make me paranoid and jealous and that's when it crashes and burns."

"Do you plan on meeting a guy who will let you chain him to a chair so you can watch him twenty-four, seven?

Don't judge the man on the similarities he has with Trevor. Judge him on his actions. People will always be tempted, Paisley; it's what they do with it that's key."

I give her words some thought, but not much. Josie's marriage false starts can't be weighed the same as a divorce. She doesn't get it; there's no way she could. Divorce does something to you.

"You make good sense—"

"Of course I do." She looks appalled. "Don't close the door on him. If you have a good time together, why wouldn't you hang out? You can stand to have some fun." She sounds like Hank.

"What if I sleep with him again?" I think about it a lot, to be honest.

"Wear protection and enjoy yourself." She grabs a magazine and flips it open.

"Here's the rub, my mother has pounded into my head that good girls keep their legs crossed. Doesn't make much sense, does it? I'm supposed to be an adult, get married, and have children, while remaining a good girl and not having sex."

"Screw your mother. Do you think it's normal she hasn't dated since your father died? I bet she could stand to come to Kenley's party, too. Remember, Paiz, it's not like you've slept with every man you've ever been on a date with."

I cringe at the thought of my mother and sex toys and agree with Josie on my mother's dating status. Her practical approach to my dating life makes sense, and I'm comfortable with her path of logic. I want to believe she's right.

"You feel better?" Josie's smile is open and wide, the light catches her diamond stud piercing in her lower lip and it twinkles.

"Yeah, thanks, Jo. I knew I could count on you." Confiding in Josie brings a sense of relief. I haven't done anything wrong, other than not tell Gigi, and my thoughts move on to other things. Things like Kenley's stupid party.

"Good. Since you're done whining about your problems, do you mind if we get the fuck back to mine?"

We burst out laughing and continue flipping through magazines, agreeing on a few options and making plans to hit up Orlando on Sunday.

9

KENLEY'S "FUN" party consists of twenty women of a variety of ages and marital states, volleying for the most outrageous behavior of the night. Even Kenley's mother is present, wearing a simple skirt and blouse and going around the room tossing up her skirt and showing her thigh-high stockings and garter belts. It's too much for conservative me.

Maybe Trevor was right. Maybe I am a prude. Oh, hell.

My empty stomach roils, and I berate myself for bringing Josie and promising to stay the whole time. If I excuse myself to the restroom and use the one at my place, would anyone notice?

Instead, I sit on a couch and pass various forms of fake male privates around a room. Some ladies hold items up to the light as if inspecting them like diamond brokers. Others ooh and ah and offer personal recommendations.

I focus on spending equal amounts of time giving both Kenley and Josie the stink eye.

Growing up in my house, sex was not something we talked about often, if ever.

Now I'm expected to share personal information with a handful of strangers and some of my closest friends. It'll take a few more drinks and parties to even get me warmed up to the idea.

Babs, our hostess and dominatrix, stands in front of the crowd with her riding crop and pulls a variety of toys and gadgets out of her leather bag. Dressed in what I assume is her finest two-sizes-too-small, shiny, skintight pleather pants and top, she hides her identity behind a matching facial mask. Only her blue eyes and lacquered beehive hairstyle give any indication of the person underneath. She waves items of sin and erotica about, most I've never heard of before. Is it possible to get arrested for owning any of these things? Seriously, the blinds are drawn, the lights are low, and the doors are locked.

Under these circumstances, who wouldn't feel wicked and scandalous, much less outside the law?

"What are you getting, Paisley dear?" Kenley's mom, Clara, asks.

"I'm just window-shopping today." I chase a meatball around my plate and try not to make eye contact with either her or the meatball.

"Oh, nonsense. You need to get at least a personal assistant. If you don't already have one, of course." Unfortunately, I look up to find her arching her brows at me.

When someone mentions a personal assistant, the best scenario I envision is of someone to grocery shop, wash and fold my laundry, and monitor my finances, and the worst scenario is an iPad that dings to remind me of impending appointments. I'm quite certain Clara and I do not share the same definition of a personal assistant.

"Oh yes, she's definitely getting a PA." Josie jumps in with her two cents. I haven't told her yet, but as far as our friendship goes, it's already over.

The fun show lady, Babs, comes to collect orders and Josie asks if she carries any of the items in stock, aside from the ones our group fondled earlier in the evening.

"I always have a few of the PA's," she answers, slapping her whip against her thigh and glaring at my empty order form. "Do you not have a pen to fill this out, sugar?"

She waves the form in my face but I don't take it.

Naturally, Josie intercepts. She grabs the form and removes a pen she's tucked behind her ear. "She's never been to one of these parties, if you know what I mean, she's interested in a PA."

I could smash my wineglass on the table and use the jagged edges to cut someone.

Them. Me. Anyone.

"Do you have a size and color preference?"

Babs doesn't even ask me, runs her questions through Josie. I stare at the rolls of flesh caught between her pleather top and pants.

"Do any come in a paisley pattern?" Clara asks. She cackles and elbows me. I've never heard that one before, honestly. And if there is a Lord in heaven, I hope to never hear it again.

"No, sorry. I only have purple, yellow, and black in stock. Medium, large, and extra-large." Babs's red lips make a straight, no-nonsense line when she attempts a smile.

Please don't make me look at them. I've only seen real ones and a few at that. Just thinking of viewing any more falsies makes my left eye twitch.

"Don't get an extra-large black, dear, they look slimmer than they are," Clara whispers in my ear with a chuckle.

I turn to say something, but find I'm at a loss. My eye twitches, and I guess it looks like a wink because she winks too. My eye continues its spasm, and she winks a second time, her smile faltering. I look away, certain I've entered another dimension of hell.

"Paisley?" Josie asks. "You have a preference?"

I shrug and stare at my hands, eye twitching uncontrollably.

"She'll take a purple medium if you've got it." Leave it to Josie to decide. I get up and make my way to the wet bar. The only stiff thing I need is a drink.

I never pay for the thing. I assume it's a gift. When we leave the party, my new best friend is in the backseat. I question what I'll do with the gel man-piece. Do I take it on vacations with me? How does it go through security at the airport? Does it have a maintenance schedule? According to Josie, I'll never want to leave it, but I seriously doubt it. I'm pretty sure I won't break the wrapping on the nondescript brown box it's packaged in.

"Hey, wanna go to the Fox and Hound for a drink?" Josie asks.

The Fox and Hound is our favorite restaurant and pub. It's owned by Jayne's parents and offers fun British fare.

"God, yes." I pull up to the light, do a U-turn, and head straight for the bar.

"Don't you want to get home to Brinn?" I give her a quick glance.

"Brinn's flown up to D.C. for a meeting. He won't be home till late tonight."

I know she hates it when he flies. Brinn owns his own Cessna and uses it to travel.

I realize, no matter how much she trusts him, she's nervous about him flying at night. I forgive her for her traitorous behavior at the party and offer to buy the first round.

Dodging newly formed rain puddles, which I'm sure elevates Josie's level of nervousness, we run to the pub. Inside, we shake off the rain and make our way through the crowd to plant ourselves at the bar. Josie gets us the first round free from the bartender, Jake. Since she's a former employee, she knows how to get the perks.

"Wanna do Orlando tomorrow instead of Sunday?" Josie sips her mojito.

I shrug. "I may have to be home before dinner. I'm supposed to have plans."

"You're a sly dog. You have plans with Hank, right?" She grins at me.

"I dunno, maybe. He asked if I was free last weekend, but I had Kenley's blind date set up." We both roll our eyes. "I told him I was free this weekend." I shrug. "I haven't heard from him."

"OK, let's leave it for Sunday for now, if you find out you're free, call me. We still running tomorrow?"

"Yes, please." We clink glasses and finish them off.

I'm ordering our second round when I catch sight of a presence behind us and find Brinn standing there, whispering something I assume to be naughty in Josie's ear since she is bright red. I cancel Josie's drink.

"You don't mind if I kidnap Josie, do you, Paisley?" Brinn asks, pulling my friend off the bar stool. "It's been a hard day. My meeting ended sooner than I thought, and I'm ready to go home and snuggle with my girl."

"Nah. Take her. She's no fun anyway, always talking about you." I wave my hand in a flippant manner.

Brinn laughs and throws enough money on the bar to cover our tab including a hefty tip. "Thanks, Paisley."

I don't give Brinn a hard time. He's a genuinely nice guy, and Josie is lucky to have him. We have some weird alliance going on between us. One I'm grateful for. A few months after my divorce, a bunch of us were at dinner and Josie offered to set me up on a date. It was as if mayhem broke out and my friends were jockeying for the right to pair me off.

Brinn stepped in and told them to lay off. "When Paisley's ready to date, she'll let you know. Until then, you let her heal."

It was enough to call off the coyotes and, to this day, only Kenley has persisted on setting me up.

Josie gives me a hug and promises she'll be on time for our run. I'm not counting on it. I give them a brief wave before I return to my drink.

"So you're alone?" Jake the bartender props himself on the bar and smiles at me.

"Yep." I'm usually pretty self-conscious about these things, but since my divorce, I've made a point to do more things alone: go to movies, dinner, and even mini vacations.

It's taken some time, but I'm getting used to it.

"You're in here a lot," he tells me.

"Yikes, really? Guess I need to lay off, huh?" Not a good thing to be a regular at a bar, my mother always said.

"No, not like you think. With your group of friends, the ones who always order martinis, and with Josie." One Wednesday a month Jayne, Kenley, Heather, Josie, and I meet here for girls' night out.

"That's a relief. I was beginning to think I was heading down a path of desperation and becoming a bar hog."

"No, you've got a long way to go." He indicates with his chin for me to look behind me.

I turn. A woman my age is dancing next to the jukebox. Her skirt and shirt are both too tight and too short. She moves to a beat no one else can hear, unless they are next to the jukebox, and makes eyes at the men watching her. If I were to give the dancing woman a quick glance, my first impression could easily be dismissive, labeling her a desperate woman, but I take a few more seconds. I recognize heartbreak when I see it and she's clearly running from it.

I look at Jake and shrug. When I was growing up, my father always told me to either defend people or say nothing. Never say something negative. I take the silent approach. How do I explain to a man that his gender is the precise reason for her display?

"Sad, isn't it?" He empties drinks into the sink and gives me a little smile. I give a slight smile back.

"I know your name," he says, using the world's worst pickup line and stops to lean toward me. He points at me as if the action itself will conjure up my name.

"Patsy? No, wait—" His voice is uncertain.

"No. Don't bother trying to guess. You'll never get it. It's Paisley."

I push my empty glass toward him and feel around for my purse. I get the feeling our conversation has an agenda, and it's making me nervous. Jake is a handsome guy. His brown eyes and sun-kissed brown hair give him a surfer look. He's probably never without a date.

"Paisley? For real?"

Why would I lie about my name? "Yep. It's the name of my father's hometown in Scotland. I count my blessings every day. I'm lucky it wasn't something horrible like Argyll."

"Wow. That's cool. It suits you. Scottish name for the Scottish lass." His attempt at a Scottish accent is pathetic.

It's a strain not to wince. People don't know how to react to my name and some attempt to use a Scottish brogue as a pick up. Is Jake the bartender hitting on me?

He leans forward and brushes a curl off my shoulder, and I have the answer to my question.

"I know this might seem awkward, but I'd love to take you out. I see you in here with your friends and have been wanting to ask you for some time." He flashes me a grin of gleaming, white teeth.

I look around the room and catch sight of the jukebox dancer. Yes, it's time to put one foot forward and go on a real date, not a blind date, a pity date, or a drunk one-nighter. The real thing.

"OK, sure. Sounds good if you promise not to do your poor Scottish accent."

I hang my purse from my shoulder and dig for my keys, too shy to look at him.

Lord, I hate dating. Never liked it in high school or college and if it's possible, I hate it even more post marriage.

He groans. "Bad huh? I promise never to do it again. Let me get your number."

He pulls out his cell, keys in my number, and sends me a text so I'll have his. We make plans for him to call within the next few days to make further plans.

"Until then," I say in my best imitation of my father and grandmother's brogue.

He raises one brow and smiles. "That was great. And sexy." He flirts with ease, a gift clearly bestowed upon the most beautiful people.

I leave Brinn's money on the bar and say my farewell. I'm self-conscious, knowing he's probably watching me walk out of the bar.

In hindsight, I suppose it might not be such a good idea to go out with a guy who I could see the first Wednesday of each month, especially if it goes south. But, what the heck? I have a vibrating, plastic, purple penis waiting for me in my car, what do I have to lose?

10

___

JOSIE BANGS on my door earlier than I expect and I'm still lounging, or as others may call it, sleeping. She comes in carrying two large coffees, and I know I love her. If I ever remarry and have kids, I promise to name one after her.

"Wanna skip the run and go for breakfast? Brinn's gone to Miami so I have all day." Josie's always the voice of temptation.

"How about we run to the café and stroll back?" I'm seriously concerned about my thighs.

She shrugs as she wanders around my apartment opening blinds, then picking dead leaves off my plants.

"Hey it's BOB," she exclaims when she sees the package on my table.

"Who?" I return my focus to the soothing goodness of my coffee.

"BOB. Your new battery-operated boyfriend." She opens the package, pulls the purple eyesore from his place of rest, and waves it around. I almost drop my coffee and die on the spot. I'd been torn last night when I stood at the car. I was afraid to leave it for fear of someone seeing it and reasoned I could hide it in my trash can and take it to the larger Dumpster on trash day.

"Hey." I jump up and snatch it out of her hands. "Keep it down, will ya? I have elderly neighbors."

"As if." Josie yanks it back and walks into my kitchen.

I follow her and watch as she rummages through my junk drawer. "Seriously, Jo, the lady across the street is the nosiest of nosy. I swear she sleeps by her window and has binoculars."

Josie loads BOB with batteries and turns it on. It hums in her hands. I cover my ears.

"Look here, it has a variety of speeds. Who cares if she sees? Maybe she'll get one of her own and find something better to do with her time. Now let's see, where shall we put this?" She taps BOB against her palm and surveys my apartment.

How about the garbage? Because it's been shed of its package, I'm terrified someone will find it there and word will somehow get back to my mother. Maybe I'll throw it in the Halifax River. I wonder if it floats? I suggest nothing. It doesn't matter where Josie puts BOB because he's not staying.

She walks into my bathroom, throws back the shower curtain, and lays it across the rack where I store my hair products and bath soap.

"Here's a great place for the two of you to get to know each other. Now what do you say we walk to the café so we can enjoy our coffees."

"Deal."

I change and we head out. We walk along the Halifax River toward the restored historic district of Daytona Beach and talk about last night. Josie confides in me how Brinn is attempting to put together a deal to open his own commercial airline. Risky business in the wake of September eleventh. He's flying back and forth to D.C. and Miami, meetings with investors. The whole thing makes Josie nervous for reasons she doesn't explain but, if anyone can turn mud into millions, it's Brinn McRae, I tell her.

She gently grabs my forearm and smiles. "Listen, I need a favor."

Uh-oh. "What kind of favor?" Josie isn't one to butter up a person. If she needs something, she asks.

"Brinn's business manager will be here for a few weeks, and I'd like you to join us for dinner one night."

"Huh? Is this a blind date?"

"Yes... No. Kinda. It's more like evening out the numbers so he doesn't feel like a third wheel, while putting two remarkable people together who I think will hit it off."

"Is he a pilot?" I'm not crazy about pilots.

"No, he's a number cruncher. He's moving here, and we want him to have a good time."

I give her a pointed look.

"Not a good time like that. Jeez, I'm not a pimp. I mean the four of us having a nice time together. No pressure."

I do an eye roll. No pressure. I've heard that before.

"You said he's a number cruncher. You mean nerdy accountant?" I sip my coffee and picture a guy who's paper-thin with a bad haircut he probably gave himself.

"Yeah, but hot nerdy accountant." She arches her eyebrows and we laugh.

"OK, I'll do it. What the heck. Oh, speaking of hot. Guess who asked me out?"

I'm nervous telling Josie because she briefly worked with Jake and she's never given him much attention. Meaning, in Josie speak, she doesn't think much of him. I tell her anyway.

"You've got to be fucking kidding me." She throws her drink into a nearby garbage can and stalks ahead.

Stunned, I look around for a camera or someone to yell "psych." Nothing happens and Josie's getting further away. I break into a slight jog to catch up with her. At least I get some running in, and all without spilling my drink.

"What's the matter?" I ask when I catch up. She stops dead in her tracks and I have to stop mid-stride and turn around.

"You give me a hard time about setting you up, yet you go on a blind date Kenley found for you. You make a date with Jake, but you won't give this Hank a chance. If you hook up with Jake, you'll be a two-time loser."

"That's mean." My feelings are hurt. Does she think I'm a one-time loser?

"You're better than he is. All I'm saying is Jake the Snake isn't good enough for you."

"Jake the Snake?" I laugh.

"Yeah. Jake's the player of players. Word is he plays dirty." She plants her hands on her hips. Her expression is straightforward and challenges me to argue back.

Hmm. Jake doesn't give me the player vibe, just that he's comfortable in his skin.

I purse my lips. Trevor was a player. I didn't get the vibe from him either, so there's that.

"What do you mean 'plays dirty'? Never mind, it doesn't matter, because the point here is that I got a date without anyone setting me up."

"It's not a date with potential. You can stop any man here on the street and ask him out and get a date. You're very pretty, and you'll have better odds at finding something with more potential than you'll find with Jake."

"You are missing the point. *He* asked *me* out."

"Ahhh! *You're* missing the point," she takes a deep breath, "OK, fine go out with Jake. See for yourself. He's a sly fox."

"Duly noted."

We are standing there in the middle of the sidewalk, getting odd looks. I'm ready to get this behind us. I indicate with my hand for her to continue.

"Jake only wants one thing." With her chin lifted and squinty eyes, she's gearing up for a debate.

"Ohhh. You think he wants to play hanky-panky with me. Don't you?" I clasp my hands in glee, hoping for some levity.

"I'm positive he does. Jeez, Paisley. He's not the guy for you." She drops her hands from her waist and walks away.

"Who says he has to be and why not?" I ask.

"He'll never give you what you need, and he'll break your heart just for kicks. It's like you want to keep repeating your mistakes." She shakes her head.

"Assuming I'll give him my heart. Maybe this nerdy accountant dude will win my heart."

Josie's look borderlines pity. "You couldn't date him

more than once without giving a part of you. At the very least you'll feel obligated or something. It's who you are, honey."

"I beg to differ. I've had hot, meaningless sex with Hank and seem to be doing fine." Ha. Stuff that, Josie.

She gives me another of her pointed looks.

My temper rises. "I don't have feelings of love or any other sort of attachment for Hank any more than I do the devil himself." I use my haughtiest tone, pull open the restaurant door, and walk in without her. I'm about make an even saucier statement when my cell phone rings.

It's the devil calling.

I gulp and suck in a breath before I accept the call. It's been two weeks since I've talked to him. We've only been in touch through e-mail and text messaging.

"Hello?" Why, with current technology, do I try to pretend I don't know he's calling? Am I able to convey my ambivalence across a fickle and subjective line? No, I haven't been waiting for your call. I'm indifferent to you calling me. My heart is certainly *not* racing. Can he pick up those messages with my one word?

"Hey, Paisley. Sorry I haven't called sooner. I was unexpectedly out of town until yesterday."

"Where'd you go?" I follow Josie to a booth and slide in. She's staring at me with curiosity.

"Oh, just some place dry and hot. Listen, I know we talked about getting together this weekend, but things have changed."

He's canceling. I shake my head at Josie. I knew this was coming. I'm disappointed and vindicated at the same time. Hank Lancaster is like all the other guys.

He only wants one thing, too. Like Josie says Jake does.

"I'd like to get together next weekend—"

"It's OK. You sound real busy." I give Josie an I-told-you-so look. Getting strung along by someone I barely know is one thing. It'll be unbearable for Hank to do it. The last thing I want is to have him cancel on me again next week. How pathetic. I struggle to come up with a reason not to get together.

"Now, Paisley, don't get crazy in the head. I'm coming to Daytona tonight and still want to see you if you're free, but I won't be alone." He lowers his voice. "Work's been rough and we found out today, one of the guys we were at the Academy with was wounded in combat and is in critical condition. Some of the guys need to blow off steam. Someone scored Coke 400 race tickets and... Anyway, I was hoping I could see you again next weekend, alone, to make it up to you. I didn't want to assume you'd be willing to hang out with a bunch of sailors."

"Oh. I hope he's going to be OK." I'm such a master of words. I should make a career of being a wordsmith.

"You wanna meet us for dinner tonight?"

"OK, sure." And I'm a pushover.

"Great. Six o'clock at Hops sound OK?"

"Sure."

Now even Josie throws up her hands in disgust.

"OK, see you then."

I put the phone on the table, look at Josie, and relay the conversation back to her.

"Sounds like fun." She checks the calendar on her phone. "Dammit. I can't go."

I don't point out she isn't invited. It's not like she takes no for an answer anyway.

"Why not?"

"My wedding planner called this morning, and I promised to meet with her to go over a few things. I wonder if I can reschedule her." The last part she mumbles as she types out a text message.

I'm relieved knowing Josie won't be meeting Hank yet. I don't think I'm ready to share him with my Daytona friends. We manage to enjoy the meal and the walk back.

She's easily distracted with wedding talk.

In anticipation of my impending early dinner with Hank, I go clothes shopping. I buy a cute, ankle-length, straight skirt and two-inch heeled boots for the event, hoping the length of my skirt will be a deterrent. I know he says we won't be alone, but I'll take any reinforcement I can get. Perhaps meeting him on my territory, away from our childhood memories, will eliminate whatever pull he has on me. It's a crapshoot, but one I'm willing to take.

11

WHEN I WALK INTO HOPS, I expect to see Hank and a crowd of brawny men. What I find is Hank and two of his friends. They stand like a wall of solid man and more than my attention is drawn to them.

Hank pulls me into a hug and whispers in my ear. "Sorry, babe, this wasn't what I was thinking for this weekend."

"This is great," I say. No chance of me ending up in bed with him. Zilch. I like those odds.

Hank makes the introductions. He stands next to me instead of across from me as if he's showing me off and says, "This is Paisley." He doesn't call me an old friend or his sister's friend. Just Paisley. "Paisley, this is Surge," says Hank.

Surge stands taller than Hank. His head is shaved clean, like his face, and I make no comment about his name nor he about mine. It's friendship at first sight. The other man is Keith. He grants me a mischievous smile and some quick jokes at Hank's expense, and I'm enchanted.

We sit in a corner booth, and everyone orders beer.

"You all went to the Naval Academy together?" I ask.

They start laughing, and the stories begin to fly. Keith is a master storyteller and it's through him I discover Hank's nickname.

"Sister Henrietta?" I look at Hank in wonder. He'd have never allowed such teasing in high school.

Surge jumps in to fill the void. "One afternoon after PT, physical training, Sister Henrietta and I were called on to perform some extra fitness training." The group snickers as they look at each other.

"You see, sweetheart there"—he nods to Hank, who's looking down at the table smiling—"didn't do so well on an inspection and consequently got all of us in trouble for it, resulting in some extra running. Our instructor, a hard-nosed, no bullshit—pardon me—kinda guy, asked Hank to call out some cadence during our run. Except he wanted original cadences and that's not as easy as it sounds."

I look over at Hank, who is ripping the edges off a paper place mat and smiling.

Surge continues, "Your boy, Hank, freezes. Can't come up with anything original, so he starts spouting Bible verses and then poetry." The group starts laughing.

"Poetry? Seriously?" I nudge Hank with my elbow. It's unimaginable.

"Wouldn't my mom be proud to know all the Bible-study group she made us go to came in handy?" He ducks his head and laughs.

At this point Keith jumps in. "Yeah, it started out all right at first but not a lot rhymes with Lord and heaven. So he quickly switched to poetry, something about meat and eat and wanting it and thanking it."

I look at Hank and try to imagine it. "No, you did not. You turned Robby Burns into cadences?" Laughing, I fall over and lean against him.

The guys look at me, questioning. "My family always starts dinner with a toast and a prayer. Sometimes, if my father drank too much before dinner, he'd start reciting Burns. On occasion he would use this one:

"Some hae meat and canna eat,
And some wad eat that want it,
But we hae meat, and we can eat,
And sae the Lord be thanket."

"That's the one," Surge exclaims and we start laughing.

"Hand me a pen, please," Hank asks me under his breath.

I'm curious, wondering what he's doing, but I want to hear the rest of the story.

"OK, why Sister Henrietta?" I ask Surge.

"Because the poetry deteriorates from there. It goes from the Lord, to food, moves to scenery, and ends up about love. The instructors couldn't let Hank's soft, more feminine side disappear. Poetry and Bible verses equals Sister Henrietta."

Keith adds. "Afterward the staff always called upon him to wax poetic. Several times he had to read a poem to the class and the chaplain liked to call on him to read verses at various ceremonies."

Poetry was always a big thing at my house, but I never knew he had an interest.

This is a different side to Hank and I like it.

"What other ones did you recite?" I ask.

"Oh, I don't remember. Some things I made up."

He smiles, hands me my pen, and slips the paper into my purse. "Keep this for me, will you?"

I nod, my focus on his friends. "Tell me more, please."

The dinner flows by at a rapid pace. I laugh until my face hurts and find I'm disappointed when it's time to separate. Hank explains they have race tickets and off they go.

I text Josie to see if she's free from the wedding planner, she is. We catch a movie and decide on drinks afterward. I'm desperate to quiet the nagging thoughts of doubt plaguing me since dinner. I should be happy. It felt so much like the times before we slept together it's as if it never happened. It's not like I really expected him to take me right there on the restaurant booth, in front of his friends. But I did think we'd touch more, or I'd at least have to put up some resistance. I'd expected refraining to be as hard for him as it was for me. Clearly I was mistaken.

In silent agreement, we avoid our usual drinking joint and head to a Mexican restaurant for margaritas. Neither of us knows if Jake is working, and we aren't willing to revisit our earlier conversation.

I finish off my first, miniature-fishbowl-sized frozen

cocktail, when my purse vibrates. I dig out my phone and see Hank's name.

"Paizie." The voice calls out. It sounds like Hank when he is inebriated, but I haven't seen him drunk in years.

"Hank?" The sounds of the racetrack are in the background.

"We have a problem." He hiccups.

"What sort of problem?" I give Josie a look and shrug. She leans in to listen.

"We have a dead battery," he yells.

I hold the phone out so Josie can hear the conversation. He's loud enough that I don't need to put him on speakerphone. A clear sign he drank too much.

"You need me to jump you?" I yell.

Hank growls, "Oh, baby, do I." I realize the folly of my words.

"We also need you to help start this thing," he says.

Josie nods her agreement and is already paying the check. I sigh and give in. Hank tries to give me directions to where they are parked, but for a sailor he does a terrible job. Josie refuses to let me take her home first, obnoxiously curious about the guy who she terms my booty call. I suppose taking her will make it easier for me to find them.

Four eyes are better than two, aren't they? I'll deal with any fallout if I must.

We arrive in under ten minutes and start cruising the racetrack parking lot. The guys aren't too hard to spot. Surge is standing in the bed of the truck, signaling to every passing car, waving his unnaturally long arms in the air. Keith holds a flashlight and waves the beam back and forth as if landing the mother ship. Hank is nowhere in sight.

It's no surprise to see Josie with her cat-ate-the-canary grin.

"I don't want to hear a peep from you," I tell her.

"Where's your Hank?" she asks before we get out of the SUV.

"How do you know he's not the big one on the truck bed?"

"Not your type."

Hank slides out from the truck's cab and appears to catch himself on unsteady feet.

"Ahh. There he is and he's perfect," she coos, practically rubbing her hands together.

I snarl and escape the SUV.

"Hi, fellas," Josie calls out.

"Howdy." Surge stumbles his way out of the truck bed.

"Paizie." Hank shuffles over to me, drapes a heavy arm across my shoulder, and nuzzles my neck.

"You're drunk, mister." I pull away. It's a halfhearted attempt.

"They're all drunk." Josie sweeps her arms wide, pointing not only to Hank and his friends, but to the remaining race fans. Keith is still swinging the flashlight in arcs, and she walks over and takes it from him.

"Who's your friend?" Hank asks.

I make quick introductions and hope Josie will keep her mouth shut. I'm not very lucky in the wish department.

"So you're Mr. Hot and Heavy." Josie gives Hank a thorough inspection.

"That's me." He does a sloppy salute, sways, and I put my arm around his waist, steadying him.

"Listen, boys. You are too wasted to drive home. Why don't I take you down to Denny's for some coffee and greasy food? Hmm?" I guide Hank toward my SUV. "You don't mind, do you, Josie? I can't let them drive home like this."

"Oh no. It's a great idea. This could be real fun." She locks up their truck and pockets the keys.

We round up the drunkards like cattle in a field and load them into my car. Josie squeezes between Surge and Keith in the back.

I drive the short mile to Denny's and steer them to a table closest to the restrooms, just in case. I order everyone a round of coffee and fries. The coffee arrives within minutes.

"Here's to our wounded friend, Kyle." Surge holds up his coffee cup, sloshing some on the table, and takes a drink.

It's clear how this night went down and why they are in the state they're in.

"How's he doing?" Maybe they need to talk about it.

"He'll live," Hank tells me, "with one less limb."

"And a head injury," says Surge.

"And a lifetime of PTSD," adds Keith.

Their mood is somber, and after a few more rounds of coffee and the fries, it's obvious they've sobered up some, though are in no shape to drive.

"All right, fellas," I announce, "looks like you'll have to crash at my place." They snigger and snort while elbowing each other.

"I get the bed," calls Surge.

His remark causes a ruckus regarding who is sleeping where.

I give a shrill whistle, calling a halt to the nonsense before I lay down the law.

"My friend Josie there"—I point and she waves—"currently holds your keys and if you don't hush up, you'll be sleeping in the bed of Surge's truck with the sounds of the racetrack lulling you to sleep. Got it?"

They are as quiet as church mice, with the odd occasional chuckle, on the drive to Josie's house. She passes me their keys before she gets out, gives me a silent look and a wink. I'm surprised she doesn't tell me to get some. Regardless, I ignore her.

I drive the guys back to my apartment and put them to work pulling out my sofa bed and blowing up the air mattress. They speak a silent language, tasking each other with jobs as they move my furniture to make room. They work with military precision, and it's cool to watch. It must be amazing to see when they are not drunk and "in the field" as Hank calls it. They profess they'd be content to sleep on the floor should I only give them a pillow and blanket but I ignore their request. I'm not my mother's daughter for nothing. I pull out my best linens and feather pillows and attempt to make them comfortable.

Hank disappears to the bathroom as I'm sorting pillows. When he doesn't come back I go to check on him. Apparently, he's managed to find his way to my bedroom, an easy task in a five-room apartment, and is passed out facedown on my bed. Shoes and all.

I'm stumped about what to do with the gorgeous guy

spread across my bed. I know I should force him onto the floor, but I don't have the heart. This is the guy who got a special pass to leave the Academy and drove straight through the night to take me to my senior prom when Austin Calhoun dumped me mere days before the event.

I tug off his heavy hiking boots and lay them beside the bed. I pull out his wallet, a pocketknife, and his cell from his back pockets and take a moment to ogle his assets.

Very nice, even at rest. A blush creeps up my neck and warms my face. I'm glad I'm alone.

Pulling a blanket from my closet, I cover him, tucking in his feet the way he likes. I grab my pajamas, change, and wash up in the bathroom. Just a few weeks ago, I was sneaking out of a window, hoping to avoid any aftermath. Now, I crawl into a bed to lie next to him. This time there will be no sneaking out of my own house.

It's nice lying in the dark listening to the sounds a man makes when he sleeps and knowing someone is on the other side of my very large bed.

I snuggle under the covers, forcing myself to stay on my side, and fall asleep watching Hank. I'm pulled from slumber when someone whispers my name and I feel a soft caress on my cheek. I catch the minty smell of toothpaste.

Warm kisses are pressed to my jawline, and I smile.

Mmm, this is either heaven or the best dream ever.

I roll toward a whisper and his warmth and feel the pull of arms bringing me closer. I moan Hank's name.

"Shh." He kisses me long and hard. "Lord, Paisley. I

can't get enough of you." He moves to tease the sensitive spot below my ear.

With only the moonlight and our senses to guide us, we caress, explore, and learn more with each touch. We clutch each other, pressing our bodies together, melding them into one as joint tremors rock us, stifling our cries with kisses. It's the best way to wake up and an even better way to fall back to sleep, snuggled in his arms.

12

I WAKE for the second time with the swirling sensation of need filling me. Hank nuzzles my neck. Is he up for a quickie? Bright sunlight streams through my room and between the warm beams and the feel of Hank against me I bask in my happiness. Even though I don't hear anything from the other rooms, I assume his friends still are out there.

Therefore, I reason, a quickie sounds like the best, most logical, solution.

His arm is across my chest so I snuggle in closer, hoping he'll get the hint, don't want to seem too brazen after all.

"I'm going to jump in your shower, OK?" he whispers, pressing a light, wispy kiss on my neck.

I nod, too disappointed to say anything.

So much for a quickie and my art of subtlety.

I guess it's better to not go there anyway with his friends potentially waking at any moment. I roll to my side to watch a buck-naked Hank slide out of bed, my gaze drawn to his backside. He thinks nothing of walking out into the hallway to my bathroom without so much as a hand covering his bits.

I close my eyes and stretch, satiated by the memory of what occurred last night.

I'm complete, warm and whole. I want a lifetime of this.

My eyes pop open as I contemplate my last thought. Clearly, there's something wrong with me. Nothing permanent can come from this and entertaining the thought is asking for trouble. I repeat my mantra: Hank's my rebound guy, I'm playing the field, gaining experience, and living for me. I'm not settling down. To think otherwise is stupid.

Hank turns on the water and his smooth baritone carries through the wall as he hums. In my heart of hearts, I know I allow this to go on because he would never purposely hurt me, because it's safe. If we got together, I believe, without a doubt, his absence for long periods, the waiting, and uncertainty would destroy us. I'm not a strong enough person.

I take comfort in knowing our friendship has withstood the test of time and when we end this agreement, say good-bye, and move on, we'll be able to remain friends. I need to make sure we don't go too far and cross the line. Not that I'm sure I even know what too far looks like. I hope I'll know it when I see it.

Listening to him hum in the shower is something I choose to simply enjoy and not make too much of. Like Hank said before, I'm not going to let things get crazy in

my head. I'm going to relax, take this experience for what
it's worth.

I roll onto my back and stretch, my limbs limp
noodles. It isn't until Hank's humming suddenly stops,
followed by a burst of laughter, that I remember what's in
my shower.

Hank's found BOB.

I sit up, mortified, and clutch the sheets to my chest.

Ohmigod!

Can I claim it's someone else's? Damn that Josie.
Damn that Kenley.

I'm suspended in time, uncertain about what to do.
The shower turns off and the curtain's metal rings collide
with a tinny sound as Hank slides open the curtain. It
propels me into motion. I leap from the bed, but my foot
is caught in the tangle of sheets, and I fall to the floor,
missing a blow to the head from my dresser by a hair. I
struggle like a mad woman to detangle myself before he
comes back. I tug on the sheet while pulling back my foot,
my hands tremble, my heart races and pounds in my ears.

"Come on, come on, come on," I plead with the sheet.

My foot jerks free and knocks against the side of the
bed. Wincing, I spring up and limp hop to my closet
hoping to pull out my robe in time. Hank flings open the
door, wrapped only in a towel, holding the purple penis.

I scream in horror. Using my hands, I attempt to cover
both my girl parts and my eyes.

"What's this?" he asks with a look of such naughtiness
I know my soul is damned to hell just for owning such a
thing.

"Close the door, Hank," I cry. I'm afraid one of his friends might pass and stop to check out the commotion.

"Don't worry about them. I heard them leave earlier. Probably out for breakfast. I don't think they'll be back for a while." He steps closer. His eyes gleam.

Hank waves the toy around and takes another step. He cocks one eyebrow and turns on the battery end of the penis, making it hum.

God help me. I want to die.

With one hand still covering my girl parts, I pull my robe from the closet. "My girlfriends gave it to me as a gift." I clutch the material to me, stepping back toward the bed.

"Have you used one of these before?"

I shake my head. He stands a breath away and I'm paralyzed.

"Ah. Let me show you." Hank pounces on me before I'm able to process his words. One minute I'm next to the bed with my robe clutched to my front, the next I'm thrown on the bed. Hank, minus the towel, is on top of me, and BOB is discarded.

With a hot, firm kiss on my mouth, Hank brands me with his touch. There is something about the press of his hard body against mine, the ripples that define the muscles in his upper arms, that sucks out all reason and self-control and leaves me wanton and needy. Like a top spinning crazily, I try to touch all of him. To feel everything at once. I nip at his neck and wrap my legs around him, grinding my pelvis into him while he caresses me with the strokes of a hungry man. I slide against him and get as close as possible. I want to fuse our bodies. Our need for each other overflows.

"You're going to kill me," he says.

His words empower me to take control, something I've never done in the past and yet I know just what to do, where to touch. I guide, I lead, and I command. We laugh at our haste, as our bodies collide, and press kisses wherever we can. We can't stop looking at each other as we meet the other's needs.

"Sweet Jesus," he exclaims as I cry out.

It's the best quickie. Of all time. Ever.

Hank rolls me beneath him and we pant in unison. His grin is big, his dimples deeper than normal and without thinking, I rise up, press a quick peck on his chin, and plop back with a laugh. My skin tingles with pleasure and tiny goose bumps ripple over Hank's arms. Moments pass as we search each other's faces. He lowers his head, our lips a breath apart before he gently brushes his against mine.

I close my eyes and think about rocking his world again. If this is the life of a hussy, I'm willing to give it a shot. I'll continue to work and shop. I won't need to eat or exercise, these bedroom activities will be my substitute. I'd probably be the most relaxed I've been in my entire life if I go on a sex-with-Hank diet.

He picks up one of my curls and twirls it around his finger.

"Better get up, babe, fellas will be here in a short time." He rolls onto his back, squeals like a girl, and pops up off the bed. BOB, still humming, apparently poked Hank in the backside. Hank picks it up and grins at me.

"Here I'll... You can...just...ah...give it to me." I reach over and take it, fumble to turn it off, and slide it into the nightstand drawer.

"I'm curious. You're obviously uncomfortable with it. Why do you even have one?" He pulls the towel off the bed and wraps it around his waist.

"It's my new boyfriend until I find an official one. Josie says I may never want to find a real one because I could get too attached." I gesture to the drawer with my head and try to make light of my embarrassment.

Hank stares at me. "What determines an official boyfriend?"

I shrug. "I don't know, haven't had one since Trevor."

I roll out of bed and pull on my pajamas. Though we just made insanely hot love, I'm still shy about him seeing my body.

"Might sleeping with someone count in the boyfriend equation?" His face seems to harden, and he glances at his feet. My mind races, trying to understand where he's going with this. But I feel compelled to remind him this was his idea.

"In the past, I only slept with someone after they were my boyfriend." I hold up two fingers to remind him of my limited experience. "This is new territory for me. What you and I are doing. If this was the past and I went a day without hearing from you. Well...cuckoo." I laugh awkwardly while making crazy signs beside my head.

"So what's—" he starts.

"I don't want to be that person anymore. Maybe it's because I trust you or have known you forever or both. I dunno, I don't feel so crazy about this." I sweep my hand toward my rumpled bed and give him a tentative smile. "I like how comfortable this is. How I don't have any expectations."

My best guess about this conversation is Hank's history of avoiding relationships. In the years I've known him, I've never seen him excited or eager about one. Considering those facts and his recent statement regarding his work life and limited time to invest in a relationship, I'm guessing he's worried I'm going to somehow jack up his ten-year plan or whatever it is he has plotted out.

"Don't worry," I continue, "I don't quite know what this is between us, but I'm not interested in ruining it. Or forcing you into a relationship that either of us might not want. I'm enjoying our time together." I shrug and smile up at him. I hope I've said the right thing.

Gone is the soft, sweet look he gave me moments ago in bed, replacing it is one of granite, the only movement a slight tic in his jaw.

"I mean, this is what you wanted, right? Us getting together to have a good time?" I ask.

His jaw unclenches and he looks at the floor, sighs, and looks back at me. "Yeah, this is what I wanted. You still comfortable with everything?"

I rewind, looking back over yesterday and today and until now haven't been a bit uncomfortable. Does he means am I still comfortable because we've sexed it up again?

"Oh, uh...well I do have a date next weekend so I'll let you know then." My laugh comes out sounding nervous.

Honestly, thinking about it does feel kind of weird. I

search his face for signs that he may find it weird too but he doesn't look at me, instead he pulls on last night's jeans and shirt.

"I'll be waiting in the living room when you're ready to take me to get Surge's truck."

"Wait." I reach out and grab his arm, "Have I said something wrong? I'm trying to make sure we don't cross the line. Are you comfortable with everything?"

He looks at me and sighs again. "We're cool." He picks up his shoes and leaves.

The room, once warm by our energy, has turned cold. I quickly dress in running clothes, pull my hair into a ponytail, and head out to the living room. We ride in silence to the speedway. The trip seems to last forever with Hank sitting like a rock beside me.

Once there, we jump the truck off and he follows me back to get his friends. He doesn't even get out of the truck to say good-bye. I stand on my balcony, watching them drive away and wonder what went wrong.

13

———

MY DATE with Jake falls the week after Hank was in town for the race. I haven't heard from Hank. Usually I get a brief e-mail or text, but it's been radio silence since they drove away. I admit I'm too chicken to send him any text or e-mail. Besides, what would I say? Instead I let it hang there, this awkward silence.

But the heaviness of what happened or didn't happen that morning leaves me unsettled as I dress for my date. About twice a day for a week I've thought about canceling on Jake. Funny enough, it was Josie who convinced me to keep it.

I believe her exact words were, "Oh no, go on a date with asshole Jake. Maybe you'll actually get a fucking clue and wake up."

I hate first dates. I hate that this may have made things awkward between Hank and me. I hate how I'm thinking of him first and not my original goal of dating. I hate telling people about my life, not to mention my dad. I hate small talk and the awkward moment at the end of the evening where you either want them to kiss you or you can't get away fast enough. Not a healthy mindset, I reckon, if I plan to have a successful first date with Jake.

I'm in a bohemian mood so I decide on a wrap skirt, peasant blouse, and use a flat iron on my hair. I weave a braid across the front, pulling my hair away from my face and use a flower clip to bind it. As I put on my makeup, I try and calm my nerves by reciting a Robby Burns poem. It's a trick my dad and Nana always did to distract us. I pick my favorite.

"But to see her was to love her,
Love but her, and love forever.
Had we never lov'd sae kindly,
Had we never lov'd sae blindly,
Never met—or never parted—
We had ne'er been broken hearted."

Reciting the poem makes me think of Hank and his cadence, which reminds me of the folded paper he put in my purse. I stop and grab my purse and pull the paper from the front pocket. As I unfold it, I find he's ripped it into the shape of a heart. Written on the paper is the same poem and scribbled in Hank's slanted writing is, *This is the poem I turned into cadence.*

I stare at the paper, my heart pounding. I pull out my cell, my finger hovering over his number. Should I call? Should I text? What do I say? I don't even know what I'm feeling, other than shaking hands and a racing heart. I sit like a stupid lump on a hump until my doorbell rings and forces me to put it aside.

Jake is handsome in crisp jeans and a light cotton shirt. His surfer look makes him appear relaxed and friendly. Like he's the kind of guy who takes everything in stride and lives to be spontaneous. He looks fun. It's weird seeing him outside of the bar where I never had this perception before. I ignore the poem repeating in my head and focus on Jake.

He takes me to dinner at a local chain restaurant where he knows the bartenders and is pleased to score us free drinks. Over dinner, he tells me he's from Ft. Lauderdale and his father is a pilot. Which is why he is attending Embry Riddle University; he, too, is a pilot and wants to own an airline one day. Says he wants to outperform his dad.

"Do you mind skipping the movie and going to the beach? Maybe we can get a drink and walk the beach a bit?" He almost sounds shy.

"Sounds great." It's always a positive sign when people don't need the buffer of a movie to get through the evening. I don't find being with him as awkward as I thought I would and gamble on it getting better.

We drive over to a popular tourist area and leave his car in a parking garage. The popular downtown pier and boardwalk offer several restaurants that line the beach, thereby making it fertile gathering grounds for locals and tourists. It's a short walk to the beach and the weather is perfect for slipping off my sandals and letting the warm ocean water brush my feet.

Jake and I join others strolling the beach. A volleyball

game is going on about a hundred yards ahead of us, couples are scattered along blankets dotting the sand, basking in the moonlight, and laughter floats across the beach. We walk in comfortable silence.

Jake takes my hand and holds it in his. It's a beautiful night and everything is perfect, but feels wrong. I have the urge to pull my hand away. Even if I promised myself I'd date and not get attached, it's as if I'm betraying Hank. Biting back frustration, I struggle with my opposing emotions and have to push back the negative thoughts and doubts. I'm determined to have a normal date, and by all dating standards, this would be considered a normal date thus far.

"Want to stop for a drink?" He interrupts my thoughts and points to a local hotel with an outside patio crowded with people and wrought iron tables. I agree and we snag the last empty table. Jake places drink orders at the bar without even asking me what I prefer. Bonus when dating one's bartender, I assume. He pretty much knows my repertoire of preferred drinks, although it might have been nice to be asked.

Jake brings me an apple martini and gives me a half smile as he eases into a chair.

His smile seems genuine and not one of a player, which I always imagine to be smarmy, sort of like pilot Ted's leer.

"I can't believe you are here with me, Paisley."

"Why?" I swirl the martini around in the glass. Tonight seems more of a crisp wine night.

"Because I thought you were out of my league. That night when Josie left you alone I thought I'd finally gotten lucky." He raises his glass, and I meet it in the traditional toast fashion. "Here's to taking chances. Sometimes they pay off."

"*Slainte*," I say and take a sip. Jake's words resonate with me. I'm not good at taking chances, Hank's offer being the first in a long time. I'm determined to take more.

A week is a long time for Hank and I not to be in touch. Perhaps I should take the chance and reach out to him. I'm reaching for my phone before I realize what I'm doing.

I do a mental head slap. I don't want to be *that* girl.

"I've told you a lot about me; what about you? Are you and Josie close? Hey, if this works out, maybe we can double date with Josie and Brinn. Have you been friends for a long time?"

Jake leans back in his chair and works his beer. He keeps scanning the crowd.

Does he want to know about me or Josie? It's off-putting and comes out of nowhere.

"Ah... I've known Josie for over a year."

"That's cool. I guess you're going to their wedding?" I nod and take a drink. I let the silence fall around us.

"So are you from here?" he asks.

"No, Lakeland." He gives me a puzzled look. "It's between Tampa and Orlando. In the center of the state."

"Oh yeah, I think I've driven through there once or twice. Isn't it somewhat backwoods?" He finishes his beer and signals the waiter for another one.

"Um... I guess it can be. No more than any other town." I'm a tad defensive.

"I bet you couldn't wait to blow out of town. Your folks

still live there?" he asks and quickly scans the crowd again.

"Yeah, my mom, grandmother, sister, and her family are still there. Actually, I like it. It's a nice community to raise kids and pretty convenient to everything."

"Where's your dad? Back in Scotland? That's super-cool by the way. Do you have a dual citizenship?"

Talking about Scotland reminds me of our yearly family trips over there to visit Nana and of course always leads to memories of my father. I try to keep it simple. "My dad died over ten years ago and yes, I have dual citizenship."

I take a swig of my drink. The sweetness of the cocktail is strong and I have to force my swallow. I push my glass away and shift in my chair so I'm able to look out at the beach. Thinking about my dad makes me sad. Thinking of Lakeland makes me want to call Hank and go hang out with him instead.

"Man, I'm sorry. Must've been hard."

I nod. Sometimes when I'm alone and I look at a picture of my father, I cry. A deep gut-wrenching cry, too. It still hurts like hell. I don't know how I would have gotten through any of it without Gigi or Hank or even their mom and Poppy. I don't know what prompts me to tell Jake my family's business. Maybe it's the mood on the beach or the mood I'm in.

"My dad took a job at the Cape. Working for NASA. He was an engineer. My mom was real resistant to moving because I was in high school. They decided my dad would drive home every weekend. He was killed driving back to us one Friday."

"Wow. How old were you?" he asks.

"Fifteen. Can you imagine the guilt my mother must have for not moving there when he took the job?" I'd never thought of this before. My mind always goes back to the dark days of her struggle, when she stopped getting out of bed or caring about anything, including her two teenage daughters.

"Your parents still got along? Before your dad died?" He seems amazed it's even possible.

"Yeah. She's never dated or remarried." I'm struck with a new appreciation for my mother and my parents' marriage.

"My parents hate each other," he tells me. "They are still married, but man, can they fight. It's nice to be on my own." He tips back his beer and finishes it off.

"Hey, let's walk down to the Deck. I didn't mean to get you depressed and the music there should pick you back up."

He gestures to my unfinished drink, and I shake my head. Jake finishes it off and reaches for my hand to pull me from my chair.

We make our way to the Ocean Deck, a bar even the tourists know to visit. It's a local icon and a favorite for the college set and the recently graduated. We enter the bar from the beach side. It's overcrowded and obnoxiously loud with a local reggae band playing.

Jake turns me around and we head back outside where the volume is more conducive to conversation.

"You want another drink?" he calls out over the bass.

"Just a water please."

Before he can walk away another guy joins us. The two guys fist bump and Jake turns back to me.

"Paisley, this is John Tolliver. He's my roommate. John, this is Paisley McAllister. Keep her company, man, while I run inside for drinks." And he's gone.

I smile at John.

"Paisley, is it? Your parents named you after one of those amoeba-looking fabric patterns? Were they hippies or something?" He doesn't smile back and his eyes never leave my chest.

"Your parents named you after a toilet. Were they custodians?" I widen my smile.

I did it. I managed a retort right when I needed one. I look to pass off a high five to someone, anyone, but I'm alone.

He sneers and walks off to talk to a very short-legged, large-chested girl. I scan the crowd. Even in college, I hated the bar scene. Now I hate it even more.

Alone on the deck, I look into the bar through the plastic windows. Jake is talking to another girl. He hands her a drink, wraps an arm around her, pulls her close, and nuzzles her neck. She laughs in response to something he says and as they separate, I watch him hand her his keys. They walk to the front door holding hands.

I know I'm a social reject when it comes to dating. I also know as innocent as it seems, it probably isn't. I look to see if I know anyone else in the crowd who can give me a ride home and come up wanting. I thank my lucky stars I still have my purse and haven't left it in the car as Jake suggested. At least I've done something right this time.

I skirt around the side of the Deck and climb the

outside stairs to the front of the building in hopes of finding a taxi. I expect I'll have to walk to the main drag to find one. Scanning for Jake, I'm relieved to not find him in the crowd at the front of the building.

If this was a date with someone other than Jake, I'd call Josie. I turn my cell over in my palm, picturing the I-told-you-so look she's sure to give me. I decide to call Jayne, who is never one to judge. She might be able to get here faster than Josie because she hangs out at her parent's pub, which is nearby. I dial her up, give a quick explanation, and she agrees to come pick me up.

Crossing the street toward Burger King, our rendezvous spot, I focus on looking straight ahead, afraid if I look over my shoulder I'll see Jake. I pick up my pace when he calls out my name.

Damn.

"Hey, Paisley." He runs up. His sweet smile makes me look away. "I'm sorry if I worried you. A friend needed to use my car so I walked him to it. You didn't have to come looking for me."

"You mean her."

"What?"

"You mean you walked *her* to your car. And how am I supposed to get home, Jake?"

I keep walking to the Burger King but he jumps in front of me, bringing me to a halt. I look past him, trying not to make eye contact.

"Yeah, him, her, whatever. She'll be right back. I didn't think we were going anywhere soon. I don't know what you saw but I was just helping out a friend."

Either he doesn't realize I'm upset, or he chooses to

ignore it, but either way causes me to suffer the fleeting sensation that maybe I'm overreacting.

"I have to go, Jake. My friend Jayne called and is having a personal crisis." I start to walk toward the fast-food chain. "I'm meeting her here. She called while you were walking your friend to the car."

Coward. I lie because it's easier than starting a disagreement here in the middle of the road. I experience a pang of self-loathing because I don't confront him about what I saw.

Jake is silent for a moment. He continues to walk beside me.

"I'm sorry you have to go. I had a good time tonight, even if you were going to ditch me without saying good-bye." His smile is all lip and no teeth.

Jayne drives into the crowded parking lot and honks. I face Jake but take a side step toward Jayne's car. I guess being married to a man who thought oral sex with his female colleagues didn't count as an affair since there wasn't penetration, has left me somewhat gun-shy. Maybe I've been hasty in writing off Jake. Maybe she really is only a friend.

I give him a smile. "I enjoyed the night," I tell him. I mean, I enjoyed it up until now.

"I'll give you a call." He gives me a sweet kiss on the cheek.

I run to the safety of Jayne's car. Unfortunately, my thoughts, fears, and paranoia follow me there.

14

WHEN I GET HOME, I check my e-mail. I think it's rude to text and check e-mail when on a date. I also think it's rude to nuzzle a girl's neck when on a date with a different girl but, according to Jake I misinterpreted it. The more I replay it, the more I begin to question myself. Maybe he's right.

Still nothing from Hank, the silence tells me he's mad. I've replayed the morning he left with his friends, ad nauseam, and I hope it's not because of my date with Jake. I was honest with him. Wasn't that part of the no-strings-attached agreement?

Jake doesn't contact me either throughout the rest of the weekend or the beginning of the week. Wednesday is my standard girls' night out and I'm nervous about seeing him, if he's working. On the drive to the pub, I find myself going through the dater-remorse cycle. I kick myself for overreacting to what I witnessed inside the bar and how I handled it.

One minute I find myself praising him for his calmness because I basically abandoned him without so much as a see-ya and the next I'm cursing my stupidity and lack of trust in my instincts.

I'm still stumbling around in my head as I make my way into the pub and bump into Josie's back. She's talking with Jayne and they step apart, neither meeting my gaze when I say both my apologies and hellos.

One look at Jayne tells me she's sharing my date escape with Josie. I cast an irritated look her way before I head to the table. Jayne may never judge, but I guess she'll gossip. I avoid the bar and say hello to Kenley, already seated.

"Where's Heather?" I ask.

"Heather is having some problems with Tyler and Justin." Kenley doesn't elaborate further and takes a long drink from her very large double cocktail. It's been a hard journey since Tyler's seizure a few weeks back, lots of doctor appointments and hospital visits. What's made it worse is Justin, Heather's dirt-bag husband, hasn't participated in any of it.

"Anything I can help with? Do they have a formal diagnosis yet?" When the waitress passes, I order a whiskey sour.

"No, definitely a seizure disorder. They're still ruling out other things. I tried to talk to her again today about letting me help more, but she shuts me out. She may not come tonight because of me." Kenley orders another drink and I make a mental note to cut her off after this one.

These days Heather's life must be awfully difficult. It

makes my woes seem silly. I'm reminded to keep things in perspective. My dad used to say, regardless of how bad you think you have it, someone always has it worse.

Jayne and Josie join us with their drinks and the conversation regarding Heather continues. I decide it's time to look to see if Jake's working. It's stupid to act as if I don't know he works here. I readjust in the seat and scan the bar.

Jake's working. He stands at the end of the bar and smiles at me followed by a finger wave. I smile and wave back. He winks, and I forgive him for the misunderstanding. He looks good in a tight Tommy Hilfiger T-shirt with his muscles pronounced. The dark blue of the shirt sets off his sun-kissed brown hair and tan. He turns away and goes to the other end, to help a customer I assume.

My cell phone rings, and I pull it from my purse. It's Jake.

"Hey, Paisley." I look and see him on the phone. We both laugh.

"Hey, yourself."

"I was afraid you weren't talking to me, I waited to see if you'd even look at me tonight. I'm glad you did."

I look down at the table and trace a scratch in the surface. It bugs me Jake waited until now to reach out to me. I guess he, too, might have been nervous or uncertain.

"Think maybe you'll go out with me again?" he asks.

"I think you'll have to ask and find out."

"Whad'ya say? Wanna go out Saturday?"

I purse my lips, trying to visualize my calendar.

"Mmm, Saturday? Sorry, I have plans for Saturday." I'm supposed to go to Lakeland this weekend.

"Seriously?" His voice tells me he wasn't expecting that response. "You don't have to play hard to get. I said I was sorry."

I'm taken aback. "Yes, seriously. I have to be in Lakeland this weekend for a family get-together. I'm not playing hard to get. I'm being honest." The girls are trying to appear as if they aren't listening but they are. No one is talking, and Jayne leans toward me.

"I'm sorry, Paisley. Jeez, I say that a lot to you. I'm not used to girls being honest with me. Usually they play games." He smiles sheepishly.

I totally understand. "That's OK."

"OK, how about sometime next week? I'm off Thursday."

"Me too." I laugh. "What time?"

"Noon?"

I'm surprised, and I guess it comes across because he laughs when I ask, "Noon?"

"Afraid to spend a full day with me?"

"No, I try not to be up before noon but OK, noon sounds great."

We finish making plans and say our good-byes, watching each other across the room. When I return my attention to my friends, they are staring at me and Josie is making a retching face.

"Thanks, Josie," I bite out.

"Look, after what he did, I can't believe you are going out on a second date with him."

I glare at Jayne, who has the good sense to look contrite, before I reply, "It's only a date or two, Josie. It's not marriage. How am I supposed to know what I want if I don't have these experiences? Isn't that what dating's about? Finding what you like?"

She shrugs. "You're too stupid to see what's good and what's not. Good keeps bumping up against you and you still push it away."

"Gee, thanks a lot. I didn't know you felt that way." I jerk up my purse and begin digging for money.

"That's not what she means, Paisley, and you know it." This time Jayne joins in. "She means you're too trusting and romantic and more often than not it skews the true picture." Jayne reaches out and clasps my hand.

It still doesn't take the sting out of Josie's words. I look at Josie, and she has tears brimming in her eyes.

"You're not *stupid*, stupid, but Jayne is right. You'll look too hard and miss what's right under your nose. I want you to be happy. I'm sorry. I could've said that the first time."

I guess if your friends can't tell you how they feel and want what's best for you, then what kind of friends are they?

"It's all right, Josie. Can't you let me experiment here for a while?" I squeeze Jayne's hand and she releases it. I guess now she feels certain I won't bolt.

Josie begrudgingly nods her acceptance, "OK, but you cannot, and I mean it, you *cannot* bring that asshat to my wedding." She points to Jake.

"OK." I shrug. I wasn't planning on it. I'm about to order another round when my cell rings again. This time it's Heather. I tell everyone at the table and they become quiet as they wait for me to answer it.

"I'm sorry, hon, I don't have a sitter for Tyler. I won't be able to make it." Her voice sounds raw, as if she's been crying.

"Is there anything we can do for you?" I ask.

Heather starts sobbing, and I can't understand a thing she says. Something about her life going to shit.

"Are you up for company?" I ask. "We can bring the party to you." I give my friends a look. Everyone is nodding their heads.

"Really?" She seems surprised.

I give her our estimated time of arrival and disconnect. We make a list of items to get. Josie and I are to cover the booze portion and Jayne and Kenley head to Publix to get comfort food.

Thirty minutes later, we find Heather dressed in grungy sweats, her face pale, and eyes red. She repeats to everyone what she tried to tell me on the phone. Justin has left her, on a permanent basis.

"It's Tyler," she wails. "You know he's always been demanding and now with these doctor appointments, things are harder. We constantly argue about who should be taking care of him. How he should be taken care of. I can't do it all. I need help." She throws herself on the couch and begins to cry again.

Unfortunately, Kenley and I thought Heather and Justin were heading down the path of no return. He was always absent, busy with his friends and his job. What kind of man leaves a woman with a special-needs child and tells her he's done with the both of them? Justin Michaels is that kind of man.

I experience a surge of panic and fear. What if this were to happen to me, again? I don't know if I could take it. It's a selfish moment, and I try to hide behind the blender and martini mix as I go cold and clammy. No matter how many times I rub my hand down my skirt, the sweat clings to my palms.

Kenley rushes over to comfort Heather. "You're not alone, sweetie, you have me and the girls."

"You have your own problems, Kenley. I can't trouble you with mine." I witness a shared look between them after they hug.

"Wait, what?" I stop mixing drinks to look at Kenley, remembering her odd behavior and their fight during my blind date with pilot Ted. I knew something was off then.

"What's going on?" I sit on the ottoman in front of them.

She shrugs but won't meet my eyes. Heather whispers an apology to her.

"Kenley?" I press.

She sighs and clutches Heather's hands. "Doug and I have been trying to have a baby, and it's not going well." She turns to Heather. "Let me help, please. I need the distraction."

"What do you mean, it's not going well?" Having been responsible for the cocktails, Josie puts a tray of drinks on the coffee table and plops into an armchair.

"I mean we can't get pregnant because of some motility issue with Doug, who takes it as a sign of failure, drinks more than ever. He spends lots of time at the club. The strain and friction are exhausting." Her shoulders sag as she punctuates the sentence with a large sigh.

"It's a good thing we have each other," I say because it's true.

"We're a hot mess, huh?" Heather laughs for the first time tonight.

We gather into a group hug and, once we break, the liquor starts flowing. I try not to think of my fears. How will I ever find a nice guy? One who believes in "till death do us part." At one of the hardest moments in Heather and Justin's life, he bailed.

Do men stick around? Do they share their part of the responsibility or when times get tough, do they help make a burden look more like an obstacle?

I don't know. My father was a part-time dad right before he died, commuting between his family and his job. I try to take some of Hank's advice and not let it get crazy in my head. But I know the time will come when I'll succumb to the fear.

———

When I get home, I'm still shaken up thinking about Heather's experience and Kenley's disclosure. Even though it's hours past late, sleep remains elusive. I indulge in a cheap version of therapy by taking a hot bath and having a good cry.

When my fingers are shriveled and the water is cold, I get out. Still unable to sleep I lie in bed and check my e-mail. Hank sent one. The time stamp was an hour ago.

Hey, just got home. Maybe we should talk tomorrow. Give me a call.

. . .

I pull the sheets up to my chin and try to withstand the loneliness surrounding me.

Watching Heather's dreams crumble reminds me of my own losses and, though I'm much happier without Trevor, I still like the idea of being one half to a whole. Of course I know a person needs to be whole to be a half of something, but I don't know what more I need to do to come to terms with my single status. I'm trying. I really am.

I roll over and, on impulse, call Hank. It'll be nice to hear his voice even if he is mad at me. He answers on the second ring.

"Yep."

"Hey. It's me." I try not to cry.

"Hey, Paisley." The way he says my name, his voice lifting slightly on the last letter, tells me it's followed by a smile. "What are you doing up at this time of night?"

It's not what I expect, considering, the last time we saw each other, he left taciturnly.

"I could ask you the same thing."

"I just got in from my trip and was unpacking, sorting my mail, and watching some TV. I guess my clock is off. I'm not too tired."

"Where did you go?" I stretch back onto my pillow and try to breathe. Holding back my tears is causing a lump to form in my throat.

"Off to take care of business." He sighs and the TV clicks off in the background.

"Is that code for you can't tell me? You go out of town a lot."

"Nah, it's code for nothing interesting. Traveling is part

of the job. I work for one of the admirals, so when he goes out of town, so do I. In this case it was a conference in D.C. You haven't answered my question. What's got you up?"

I pause and tears break lose. "My friend's husband left her. Left her and their child. I just found out today."

"I'm sorry to hear that."

"It's my friend whose child had the seizure. I guess he couldn't take it. Truth is neither can Heather, at least she can't alone."

"I'm sure it's a hard thing to deal with. I can't imagine. People react in different ways to these things." He pauses. "Are you surprised he bailed?"

I don't give it a moment's thought. "No, not really."

"What else is bothering you?"

"I dunno. I guess it's hard to watch people hurt."

"And?" he prompts.

My pangs of fear expand and bring with them anger. "Do marriages last anymore?"

"Yeah, I think so."

"I look around me and see marriages falling apart all the time."

"Who else's has fallen apart?"

Feeling defensive, I give a quick shrug. I know he can't see me, but I have nothing more to say.

"You've seen only yours and your friend's fall apart. Sarah Grace and Dan are still married. Gigi and John have been married five years, my parents almost forty. I bet your parents would still be together."

"Yeah, but Gigi and John aren't happy."

He laughs abruptly. "Aren't they?"

"Have you seen them lately? They fight all the time." Obviously I know them better than he does.

"Do they? Maybe you should take another look." He sounds smug and all knowing.

Why did I even call him?

"Never mind. I thought you'd understand," I snap.

"I do understand, Paisley, more than you think. Not everyone is upstanding or will react the way *you* think they should. People are flawed. That doesn't make their actions unforgivable. Sometimes you have unreasonable expectations."

I gasp and am about to launch into a rant when he interrupts.

"Take this guy, for example. You seem bent out of shape because he left, but you just said you aren't surprised. When his kid had a seizure, his wife doesn't even call him. She calls her sister-in-law. No one expected him to rush home and help. Either he's already let everyone know he's the unreliable sort so his actions now shouldn't be any surprise, or he's never been given the chance to step up, so why should he bother now?"

I sigh with exasperation. How can he possibly understand? When was the last time he watched his marriage fall apart? Oh yeah, I forgot. Hank's never been married. What was I thinking to call him?

"How is being responsible, loving, dependable, and trustworthy an unreasonable expectation?"

"People you love will let you down. It's where you go from there that makes the difference. Now don't hang up. I can tell you're angry. I only want you to think about why you're really upset."

"And just what makes you think this isn't the real reason why I'm upset?" My tears have dried up, replaced with bolts of anger flashing through me.

"Because I know you."

What Mr. Henry Shane Lancaster the Third doesn't realize is I've changed. I'm no longer the teenybopper who used to hang out at his house all the time. I *have* changed.

"So why do you think I'm upset?" I'm a natural glutton for punishment.

He's quiet a moment except for a grunt that tells me he's choosing his words carefully. Hank has always been deliberate about his words.

"Let me ask you this, Paisley. Are you one of those people who needs to be married, or are you OK by yourself? For the rest of your life." He yawns as if our conversation is prosaic.

"Of course I don't *have* to be married. If I *had* to be married, wouldn't I still be with Trevor?" I counter, emphasizing each word. I'm positive of my response and feelings.

"OK, but who initiated, who pursued the divorce?" he pushes.

"I don't think it's relevant whose idea it was. I think it shows who was the quitter and who was willing to make it work." I'd taken my wedding vows seriously and didn't appreciate any implications otherwise.

"I'm not an advocate for divorce, Paisley, which is why I've yet to marry. I also don't need to be married to complete some life goal."

"Do you ever want to marry, Hank?"

"Yes, when the time is right and the girl, too. Which

may be never." He sounds calm and blasé. "Just think about what I've said."

It's bullshit, in my opinion. Since when did Hank think he'd become the resident expert on Paisley McAllister? Sleeping with someone doesn't lend itself to insider information.

"I'm sorry I called so late." If he can't give me what I want, if he doesn't want to understand then there is no point to continuing this conversation. Frustrated, I jerk my covers to my chin and make a great production of snuggling in my bed, hoping the sound is coming across on his end.

"Don't get angry. I want what's best for you."

"Are you going to Poppy's party?" I'm rethinking my weekend plans.

"I don't know. I may have to head out again. Paisley?"

"Good night, Hank." I try to sound friendly.

"Night." He sighs and hangs up.

I slam the phone on the bed and surrender my urge to scream.

"Asshole." I yell and turn over in a fit of vindication. I start to cry and don't stop until my body gives in to exhaustion and I fall asleep.

15

I DRIVE to Lakeland early Saturday morning with plans to stay the night at my mother's and see Gigi. Her dad's birthday party is this afternoon. It's a large family event, and I haven't missed one yet. Last I heard, Hank won't be there, leaving me feeling the weird combination of disappointment and relief.

I head straight to my mother's house, use my spare key to let myself in, and find no one home. Momma's preferred mode of transportation, her golf cart, is not in the garage. I toss my bag into her spare room, jot a quick note, and drive the ten minutes to my sister's. Sometimes on Saturdays my mother takes her little cart to my sister's for breakfast with her grandchildren.

When I arrive, Sarah Grace is manically sweeping her front porch. She pierces me with a glare and I rack my brain, wondering if maybe I offended her.

"Hi." I hope I've read her mood wrong.

"You've been to Momma's yet?" She doesn't stop sweeping.

"Yeah, I just left there and neither she nor Nana was home. I thought maybe they were here." I walk onto the porch and try to avoid her broom.

She huffs, throws down the broom, and stalks inside, leaving me to follow. My mother and sister have this crazy love-hate relationship and living close never helps matters much. It's because they're alike, independent and stubborn.

"What's happened?" I know the minute I ask I'll regret it. I also know if I don't ask I'll regret it more.

Backing out of the kitchen, Dan gives me a curt shake of his head and mouths, "Good luck."

Coward. I want to yell it at him.

"Your momma," Sarah Grace says it with clipped words. "Your mother... Oh, I can't even say it." She pulls out a baguette and begins to slice it into wide pieces.

"Momma what?" I want to snap at her but I know doing so will get me nowhere.

Instead, I mentally count to ten, three times. One day I'm gonna drink on the drive into town. Maybe then I'll be able to cope with my family's madness.

She stops cutting, pinches up her face, and turns to me. "Momma went on a date last night."

"Oh, phew. I mean, you had me worried for a minute."

"What do you mean, 'Oh'? Momma has been with another man and Daddy's been dead only a few years."

"Ten." Ten very long years.

"What?" She gives me another annoyed look, for talking out of turn, I suppose.

"Daddy's been gone ten years, Sarah Grace."

"I know how long Daddy's been gone, Paisley. That's not the point. The point is Momma is already out there dating and can't even bother to talk it over with us, and don't you think she's a bit too old for this?"

She pulls eggs and milk out of the fridge and begins to mix the two. I know she's making French toast and my sister makes the best French toast. However, there is no doubt this conversation is leading me down the path of no breakfast at the Mitchell House.

I don't know what to say. It's great my mother went on a date and, frankly, it's about time. I don't understand why Sarah Grace is this upset. I try to choose my words carefully.

"Are you ever too old for companionship? Maybe she needs some male attention. She's the one who's alone." OK, maybe those weren't the best choice of words, but I couldn't help it.

My sister throws her whisk into the sink and turns her fury toward me.

"Don't tell me what momma needs and doesn't need, Miss-come-only-every-few-weekends. I see her almost every day. I stand in a better position to tell you what she needs." She dunks bread into the egg mixture and slaps it onto a griddle. "Besides, you'd think she'd give me the courtesy of telling me about her plans instead of letting me stumble on them unaware."

Ahh, therein lies the real problem. Sarah Grace does *not* like surprises, of any kind.

"You stumbled upon them?" I have visions of Sarah

Grace walking in on Momma and some strange man in bed and I shudder.

"We went to dinner last night and there they were. Snug in a booth, laughing." She flips her French toast and is about to say more when we are interrupted by her kids.

"Aunt Paisley's here," Jackson says as he runs to me, arms open for a hug. Jill right behind him. I wrap them both into a tight hug and squeeze them until they squeal before I let go.

"Are you staying for breakfast?" Jill asks.

"No," my sister answers.

"Sorry. I have to go see Mimi and Nana. What's happened to your hair?" I ask Jill, who until recently sported very long hair. Now it brushes her shoulders.

Jackson erupts with laughter, and Jill gives me a sad face.

"We were playing with Pete and he stuck gum in my hair," she says and follows it up with a pout.

"Oh, honey, don't you know peanut butter can get gum out?" She's wanted long "princess hair" forever.

"They took it upon themselves to solve the problem," Dan calls from the couch as he's flipping channels.

"I cut it." Jack puffs out his chest.

"You went to Gigi's to play?" I ask Sarah Grace.

"Yes, we've set up a weekly play date for the summer." Her look dares me to challenge her. I won't. It makes sense for them to do play dates. Though it's hard to imagine Gigi adding booze to her tea in front of Sarah Grace. If she wasn't in such a foul mood, I might ask her if she thinks Gigi is happy, but it'll have to wait.

"Time to eat," Sarah Grace calls and looks away. Dan

walks by, giving me a shrug. He walks over to Sarah Grace and hugs her from behind, she sinks into him before stepping away to finish her French toast. This is what a happy couple looks like, even when one is being a miserable cow. I give the kids a good-bye hug and get out fast. I figure it's worth swinging past my mom's one more time.

This time she and Nana are there and making a fancy breakfast of crepes with fresh fruit.

"Paisley," they call out in unison, raising champagne glasses filled with what looks like orange juice.

At least I'm wanted somewhere.

"Would you like a crepe?" my mother asks.

"Please." My stomach is growling something fierce.

"Did you get my note?" I pour a glass of orange juice and giggle when my grandmother adds champagne.

"Aye, we knew ye wouldn't be there long. We were giving ye ten minutes more before callin' ye." Nana lifts her glass. "To Helen's date."

We raise our glasses to toast. I take a good swallow and finish it in one toss. So far the day isn't going well for me.

"Tell me about this date, Momma."

She flips the crepe, using the pan only, and turns to me.

"You aren't upset, are you?" Her tone tells me it doesn't matter at this point.

"Actually, I think you're long overdue."

"Hear. Hear." Nana fills up our glasses again, raises hers, and takes a drink.

"You're sweet, Paisley. I think it's time, too." My mother smiles at me and comes over to give me a kiss. She's not one for affection, so when she dishes it out I'm always surprised. My dad was the touchy-feely one. It makes me realize how much I miss being affectionate with my family, with people I love.

I'd never thought of my mother as a single person who might be lonely, desperately missing her husband, until I was in the process of my divorce and in a similar position, without a husband. At one time, she'd been half of a well-oiled, smoothly running whole. I can't remember my parents arguing. Something they must have worked out early in their marriage.

I scan my mother's kitchen and living room. The pictures of my father and all of us are scattered throughout. I'd always assumed my mother did that for our benefit. I realize now it's been for hers too. Losing a husband because you are not compatible is difficult. Losing a life mate unexpectedly must have been devastating.

"It's time for you, too." She hands me a plate of perfect crepes with a scoop of mixed berries on top. "Marriage is hard work, Paisley. Make sure you pick someone who can do the work. Who wants to do the work."

"Hear. Hear." Nana cheers for the second time.

As if I knew Trevor wasn't going to work on our marriage. It's not like he was a slacker. He was a medical student for crying out loud. I'm not a complete idiot. But her words dig and cut me open. I focus on my plate, grasping for composure. What if I smash the plate against the counter or cram the crepes in her face? Will she hear me then?

It requires some serious mental deep breathing before I'm able to say anything. "I know it's hard work. I gave Trevor everything, and we were fine until he got into med school." Which, in all honestly, was the first six months of our marriage.

I know what I need to say but my courage to say it is waffling. "When you say those things, I take it personally. Like I'm a failure." I'm pleased I remember to use the I statements my shrink taught me.

"I don't mean it, honey. I don't want to watch you get hurt again." With a wave of her hand she dismisses me yet again and turns back to focus on her crepes. The mood deflates faster than a balloon.

"That's what I'm talking about, Momma, you're insinuating I'm going to fail again." Hell with "I" statements. Once I start, the rest bubbles up and over. "The comments about my hair, telling Hank I'm divorced and not many people want to date me. Those things hurt. Just now you blew me off. Yes, my marriage failed. Yes, I didn't pick so well in Trevor, but I'm sick of you defining me by this one incident."

When she doesn't look at me, I look over at my Nana. She's smiling and gives me the thumbs-up. I wait for my mother to say something, do something. She stares down at her crepe; the only things moving are her blinking eyes and the slow rise and fall of her chest. I wait, running my lower lip over my teeth.

She sighs and moves the pan over to the other burner before she comes to me. She takes my hands and looks me in the eyes.

"Paisley, I think you're a bright, funny, beautiful woman. You've been in hiding since the day you found Trevor with that girl." She raises her hand to stop me from interrupting, "Yes, you've been getting out. Yes, you're dating." She emphasizes the word dating as if I've been calling sitting next to a stranger at the movies a date. "But you're still not really present. It's getting better. The last few months I've seen bits of the old you. When I said those things, I was trying some of the reverse psychology Dr. Phil talks about on his show. I wanted to get you angry so you would see how much you have to offer. I never meant to hurt you, only wake you up."

What she's saying takes the sting out of her words, somewhat. It still hurts and was embarrassing, but perhaps there was a method to her parental madness.

"I spent the last ten years grieving for your father, and I probably always will. It took your Nana to get me to see my life isn't over. I don't want you to get stuck in the same rut I did. I'm sorry. I'll try to choose better words next time." It's all I can ask.

When I smile Nana hoots and refills everyone's glasses, then raises hers for a toast.

"Here's to two lovely women who deserve true love and happiness. *Slainte*." She hiccups and drains her glass. My mother and I follow suit.

We spend the rest of the morning talking about my mother's date, eating crepes, and sipping mimosas. It's wonderful and the guy my mother went out with sounds pretty nice, too. She promises to introduce me if they make it to date number five. It's heartening to know even fifty-five-year-old widows have dating criteria.

With my day perking up, I do a quick change and head out to Gigi's house. We plan to ride together to her father's party.

16

I ARRIVE at Gigi's to find kids running around the front yard. The neighbor parent is standing around chatting with a different neighbor. There's no sign of Gigi. I know John's home because his government car is parked in the driveway, crooked.

"Hey, Pete," I call out. "Where's your mom?"

"Inside, wrestling with Pop," he yells, without breaking stride as he chases his neighbor, Eddie, around the yard. I watch him take aim, throw the ball, and bounce it squarely off the back of Eddie's head.

I walk through the garage and bang on the door. Does Pete mean fighting? Could John be roughing Gigi up? The thought stops me in my tracks, but I shake it off. If John was manhandling Gigi in any sort of fashion, Hank would pound him onto the dirt. I figure Pete must mean they're arguing. If I'm right and they are, as I think they often do, I don't want any part of it. I had my rumble for the day.

No one comes to the door. I knock harder, waiting a few beats before I pull it open.

"Yoo-hoo," I say.

Gigi comes running around the corner looking flushed and unkempt. How do these people fight? Is it really a wrestling match in the Matthewses' household? I'm not about to ask.

"Sorry, Paisley." She's out of breath. "I'll be ready in a minute. You'll have to move your car 'cause John has to go to work. We'll take mine."

She leans out the kitchen door and hollers, "Pete, get your backpack. We're leaving in five minutes."

She bustles off toward her room, and John comes around the corner with a cigarette dangling from his mouth. A holster wraps around his shoulder and tucks under his arm. It's weighed down with a gun. I see what Gigi likes about him. Physically, I mean. Back in the day when they were dating, he was pretty fun for the quiet sort. Of course, they dated for only six months before they married. Everyone's fun the first six months. But how can a girl like the guy who obviously makes her best friend miserable?

I move my SUV onto the side of the road, load Pete into Gigi's SUV, and honk the horn. She comes running out, loaded down with bags and presents. Looking at her now makes me wonder how she manages a household. She's always been the organized and methodical one, but today she's disheveled and appears weary, or simply beat down, not giving off good vibes about the whole marriage-and-kid thing. I suppose it's harder when a single parent runs the house. John's an FBI agent with the Tampa office and stays busy. Before they had a child, it didn't seem to be such a big deal if he was gone for few weeks at a time or the occasional overnight. Now Gigi voices her concerns about Pete being without his dad for extended periods and her role as both parents. I want to point out perhaps drinking while doing housework isn't necessarily the best example either, but I figure my life is jacked up enough and I should stop while I'm ahead.

"You OK?" I take a juice box from the loaded soft cooler Gigi keeps in her car and hand it to Pete. She looks a bit...frazzled. Her blond hair is pulled back into a haphazard ponytail, only half of it was pulled through the band, and she has a noticeable makeup line under her chin.

"I'm fine. Just...preoccupied." She shrugs and turns onto her parents' street. I resist the urge to lean in and sniff for booze. I don't think it will go over well, her being my ride home. Plus, I don't think she would drink and drive with her kid in the car.

We pull onto the driveway. Even though I know Hank isn't expected, my whole body sags with relief when I find his truck isn't among those in the driveway.

"You might want to fix your hair and you have a...." I rub some of her makeup line in, trying to blend it before I jump out, moving to the back to free Pete from his car seat. I laugh at her expression when she realizes how disheveled her appearance is.

Like a herd of noisy kindergartners, we head into the house and are greeted by the gathering. Gigi's younger sister, Joanna, is inside with her current boyfriend. She doesn't have much regard for me. Guess she thinks I suck up her sister time with Gigi and leave her nothing. The party is a festive family event with fond jesting, good food, and unconditional love. I'm in complete heaven and am enjoying myself, talking with some of their cousins, when Ms. Becky calls out.

"Hank."

I'm mid-adjustment on a stool when she says his name, causing my foot to slip out from under me. I grip the counter but my seat still misses the stool, which elicits a "whoops" and "oops" from me as I slide down, bang my chin on the countertop, and reseat myself. Thankfully, not many people see my fall, except the two cousins I was talking to and the one person I'm avoiding. Hank.

I try hard not to make a big deal out of it but my face burns. I pick up my glass of iced tea, take a drink, and turn my back on him. Wrapped in the fold of his family, Hank is busy giving his gift to his father and getting caught up with relatives.

After what I hope is a normal amount of time, I make my escape to the bathroom, forced to use the one by the bedrooms because the guest bath is occupied. I pass the room of sin and desire on my way, keeping my eyes focused on the bathroom door for fear of making any inadvertent suggestions to Hank.

Inside, I try to figure out a way to escape and get back to my car and spend a few minutes of wasted time kicking myself for not driving. I'm sporting a nice red area on my chin, which will bruise.

I could call my mom, but I imagine her picking me up in the golf cart, seeing Hank and beginning her match-making machinations again so I nix the idea. Besides, she's probably still tipsy from imbibing too many mimosas. I could run over to Sarah Grace's house but she's likely still in her snit. It comes down to picking the least of the two tortures, leave or stay, and clearly staying here is it. My bruised chin and I are doomed, destined to stay until Gigi wants to leave.

With my bruised chin up and nerves steeled, I exit the room and seek comfort in knowing he'll never make a move with his parents nearby. I pass the guest room, thinking I'm in the clear, when a hand snakes out and grabs my arm.

It's Hank. He drags me into the room, closes the door, and backs me up against it. "Hi, Paisley." He brushes his lips against the red area on my chin.

In one breath, I'm gone, lost in the headiness of Hank's touch. My knees buckle, and I sway against him. Hank moves the kiss to my lips and deepens it. Logical thoughts evaporate. The merest touch from him spreads delicious warmth through my body and I pull him closer.

"Mmm," he purrs. "But no." He pushes back. "I hoped I would see you. I also hoped you weren't mad anymore." He kisses his way down my neck.

"Mad about what? Oh, the night we talked about my friend's husband. That's long forgotten. I'm not mad."

I'm distracted and ravenous for him. It feels as if a life-time has passed since we last touched.

I try to pull his shirt from his pants, but he grabs my hands and pulls them to his chest, clasping them between his.

"What's the problem?" I grin.

"I don't think we should do this." He groans. "Lord knows I want to."

"So I ask again, what's the problem?" I sneak a finger in between the buttons on his shirt and stroke a tiny patch on his chest.

"I want to stop." He laughs and wiggles away, though he doesn't drop my hands.

I don't want him to stop. I don't want to stop. I don't care if everyone walks in on us. OK, I do because picturing his mom walking in sends a flash of common sense through me. His lower half is still pressed against me, and it takes every stupid ounce of discipline I have to not wrap my legs around him but to focus and hear what he's saying.

"OK, I'll stop, only because your family is on the other side of this door," I say. "You're still holding my hands."

He rolls his eyes. "I know. I've got something I want to say and I want you to listen." His face gets serious.

"OK. But if you want me to really hear it you should take a step back because...well." My cheeks tingle as they flush.

Hank chuckles, lets go of my hands, and takes a step back.

"We should go on a date," he tells me.

"A date?" I'm baffled.

"Yeah, a date. You know. One of those things you've been doing with other guys."

"Oh, ha-ha." Now I'm annoyed. "Why a date?"

"Why not? We've totally skipped a step by going to bed together. I think we need to back it up and start over with a date."

"I don't know, Hank. What would our families say?"

"Argghhh, Paisley. Who gives a... Why are you so worried about what people will say? It's not as if I'm married or anything." He stops, I assume, to compose himself. He takes a deep breath before continuing. "Why is a date with me such a foreign concept to you?"

I shrug. I guess I never thought of it before. It's kind of weird imagining an actual date with Hank, weird and kind of exciting. My giddiness comes out as a snicker.

His brow furrows.

"Because sometimes I remember things. Things you might not want your date to know," I say.

"Like what? I'm an open book." He crosses his arms.

"Remember when you were in fifth grade and were totally crazy for *Star Wars*?"

He closes his eyes, and nods. He knows where I'm going with this but he hides it with impatience. "What's this have to do with us going on a date?"

"Well, you used to make Gigi and me dress up as Princess Leia and Luke Skywalker. By the way, I did not enjoy being bumped to Chewbacca to save Joanna's feelings when she wanted to play." I giggle and snort when I try to compose myself.

"Maybe I'll be thinking of those things or like when you crashed your bike into the side of Poppy's car or like the time I caught you looking in my bedroom window or I'll think about the bowl cut your momma gave you...."

"Why, you." He laughs, swoops in and picks me up, then tosses me on the bed and sits on top of me. "I get the picture," he says. "You think of those things when we're making love?"

I laugh and push my skirt down in the open spaces between his legs. "Yes, sometimes I want to do a Wookie cry just for you."

"If you're thinking about Chewbacca, I'm doing something wrong." He shrugs sheepishly.

"You know I'm teasing. Being with you is like being with a Jedi master," I tell him. It comes out without me thinking about it. It's true, so I let it go.

"Wow, high praise indeed."

"OK." I smile up at him. "I think you can get off me now. I know you say your family won't care if we date but they might not want to walk in on us."

He gives me a bright grin and it takes my breath away. Why I never noticed how downright stunning Hank looks is beyond me.

He's always been a fixture in my life, it's not like I never had the opportunity.

Perhaps having a crummy marriage made me appreciate more of the finer things. He's all ease and fluid movements, which is hard to imagine on a guy who stands six foot two. There is something very manly about the heavy silver watch on his wrist and ink of a tattoo peeking out from under the sleeve of his T-shirt.

"You haven't said yes, yet." He rolls away to sit on the bed's edge.

"You know I might be more inclined to answer your question if you actually asked me," I tell him.

"All right. I reckon I can do that. Wanna get together later, sometimes it's called a date, and do something safe and harmless in the presence of others to guarantee it?" His lopsided smile opens up.

"You mean today?" I assumed we would do this out of Lakeland.

"Yes, today." He looks me in the eye and holds my hand. "Trust me."

It's a leap of faith for me. "OK, what time are you thinking?"

"How about four? You're staying at your momma's, right?"

I nod. "Sounds good."

He stands, helps me off the bed, and I smooth my skirt. When I look at him, the expression on his face makes my knees wobble. He takes a step toward me, and I run out of the room as fast as humanly possible. His laughter follows me down the hallway.

This will be fun, I reason. A date. With Hank. And since it's "technically" our first official date, we probably won't end up in the sack.

"Right," I mumble, forgetting I'm once again in the bosom of my surrogate family. Gigi gives me a quizzical look, but before I can explain, Pete throws up all over my lower extremities.

It's a quick ride back to Gigi's with Pete puking all the way. I use the excuse of needing a shower and a change as my reason to not return to the party and make my way to my mother's. Excitement for my impending date makes me giggle.

17

I WALK into my mother's house to find her and Nana lying in the living room, watching old movies.

They're drunk. Or as my dad would say, pissed.

The blinds are drawn and the lights off. Nana has one hand over her eyes, moaning, and my mother is holding a cold pack to her temple.

"Jeez, what kind of role models are you two anyway?" I start laughing.

"Shh," Nana whispers. "I've the queen's marching band harpin' on in me head and it's killin' me."

"What's that smell?" My mother eases up into a sit.

"Ye mean it's not ye, Helen? I thought ye'd tossed your haggis."

"It's me," I tell them. "Pete threw up on me." I do smell a bit putrid. Even with a quick rinse off, the smell lingers and permeates.

"Go get cleaned up. You're making your grandmother and me sick." My mother lies back with a groan.

"Or maybe the mimosas are what's making you sick." I beat feet to the shower anyway.

When I finish they are still lying about, moaning. I flip on a light and start the Keuring. I make two cups of coffee, taking one to each of the lushes. My mother asks about the party and the Lancaster clan. I give her a brief rundown of what went on and who was there. They purr when I mention Hank's name.

"Ye ken, Paisley, I've been thinking. Since ye've had a man and now dinna have one, you're free to run amok."

I look at my mother for translation.

"What are you saying, Annie?" she asks.

"I'm sayin' Paisley needs to do some shagging." She raises her coffee cup and does a silent toast to me.

"Nana." My mother and I call in unison.

Where did she hear the term shag? What does she know?

The doorbell rings, and I bolt to get it.

Speaking of shags. "Hank's here," I call as I let him in. "Let's continue this conversation never again."

My mother and Nana laugh. I don't have to explain why the lights are low and they're drinking coffee. The empty champagne bottles on the kitchen counter tell the tale.

"Ceud mile failte," Nana calls out to him. Not one welcome but one hundred thousand. Only Hank can get such love from my family.

"Tapadh leat."

I'm surprised he remembers the simple phrases of politeness my father taught us years ago.

Nana beams at him and I narrow my eyes in suspicion. What a brownnoser.

"How about we walk the lake and stop for ice cream?" He gives my mother and Nana a kiss on the cheek and gives my bare feet a pointed look.

Lake Hollingsworth is the lake of choice for the exercise enthusiast. It boasts a paved, oversize sidewalk and markers so people can clock their distance. It's one of my favorite places to go for exercise and right around the corner is my favorite ice-cream shop. In high school, the lake was always a popular place to go since opposite of the country club is Florida Southern College, known for its baseball team. In particular, the fine college boys who play on said team.

I dash off to get my shoes and put them on in the living room, afraid to leave him alone with Nana for fear she might bring up the shagging business again. Hopefully, I've been able to hide our recent...indiscretion. Could Hank? And from my all-knowing, all-seeing granny?

Hank drives and for a moment I'm lost in time. As if I'm sixteen again and, like I've done a million times before, I'm going to the lake with Hank. Except this time it's a date. I try not to fidget or chew my thumbnail. I want him to find me interesting but can't find any intriguing topics, everything suddenly sounds stupid or frivolous. So I let him make the small talk and listen as he compares what it was like living in Japan.

We start out with a comfortable stroll. The afternoon is still sweltering but hints at relief with the fading sun. Late June isn't known for its breezy evenings, it's known for its daily rain, which came earlier today and helped cool the earth a degree or two.

"I haven't been here in years." Hank drops a casual arm around my shoulders.

"Me either. I used to come here with Sarah Grace and walk the twins when they were younger. Seems like an eternity." Life seemed much simpler when I was making those trips home from college. I was young, dumber, and in love with Trevor.

Sometimes I wish I had a magic wand and could go into the past and try my life over again by choosing a different path. Would I have married someone else, or still be single?

"I remember you and Gigi coming here. Poppy used to send me out looking for you two all the time. Drove me nuts. If I couldn't find you two hanging out at McDonald's, I came here." He chuckles at the memory.

My thoughts go to that day in the past, when he came here to tell me my dad had been in an accident.

Gigi and I watched his old truck come barreling toward us and were caught off guard when he came to a stop with half his truck still in the traffic lane, half on the grass.

I could tell by his ashen face something was wrong. When he turned watery eyes to me, I almost fell to my knees. Hank ran to me, scooped me up, and carried me to his truck.

I don't remember the ride home, only pleading with God to let my dad be OK. I remember tears of fear running madly down my face and not being able to catch my breath. I remember walking in my house and knowing my prayers had not been answered.

It wasn't until I lay in bed, Gigi zonked out beside me and Hank sleeping on the floor, that it hit me. I rolled over on my stomach and looked toward the floor where he slept. Only he was awake.

He reached up and took my hand. I was comforted by his touch and desperate to be held. I slid from my bed and lay next to him as he wrapped his arms around me and held me. It was then I wailed for my father.

Remembering makes me tear up. I would have never gotten through the days following my father's death had it not been for Gigi and Hank.

I face him. He tightens his arm around me, his expression soft. He remembers too, and I wrap my arms around his neck as we continue to walk, me backward. I've shared lots of memories with this guy. My mind rolls over the time we've spent together since I woke up next to him in Gigi's bed. I have to be honest. It was inevitable we would get together, since we share so much. We did flirt a lot in high school. There's no point denying everything, anything, anymore. Knowing I want to be here with him more than anywhere else is telling. Maybe this isn't as harmless as I think. Maybe he doesn't think so either?

The moment wraps around us, binding us together with a firm knot.

"Maybe this wasn't a good idea." He returns the hug and brushes a kiss on the top of my head.

"It was a fine idea. I never thanked you for that night, Hank."

"You never have to either."

I smile up at him as the pain of the memory eases. "Fine. I won't feel compelled to buy the ice cream today." I flick my head, swinging my ponytail in his face.

He gives it a playful yank, spins me around, and gives me a push in the back, sending me stumbling forward.

Some things never change.

I catch my balance and laugh. Then I stick out my tongue, before I take off at a run.

"Hey," he yells, footsteps slapping behind me.

I pick up my pace. Glancing over my shoulder, I gauge how much of a lead I have. When I look forward again, I notice the sidewalk has a raised corner. But it's too late. One minute I'm running and the next my toe catches and in a ball of limbs and hair I go ass over teakettle. I land, thankfully, in the grass, on my back, my arms spread wide beside me.

"Jeez, Paisley, you OK?" He leans over me.

I'm too busy wheezing to answer him. All this air around me and I can't seem to get any of it. I gasp, wheeze some more and manage to nod my head. I stay on the ground for a few more minutes and once Hank is assured I'm fine, he moves out of my line of vision.

When I manage to sit up, I look for him. He's standing about fifteen feet away with his back to me, his shoulders shaking. He's working hard at holding in his laughter. "You think it's funny." I ease myself off the ground.

Laughter erupts from him. He turns once, sets his eyes on me, starts laughing uncontrollably, and has to turn away.

"All right. Ha-ha. It isn't that funny." Apparently, it is, because now he's bent over with his hands on his thighs, overcome with hilarity. His backside, the only portion of him facing me, presents quite the opportunity and the urge is impossible to resist.

Maybe it's because I'm embarrassed or being spiteful, because I walk over to where he's still bent over, wheezing from laughter and, using the right amount of force and my foot, I push him forward. Face-first.

He goes sprawling onto the grass.

I burst out in laughter.

"It's funny now." I call to him as he rolls onto his back. The look in his eyes tells me I have a few seconds head start. I stop laughing and take off running. Not jogging.

Not a sprint. A true dart for my life.

His breath is on my neck and his presence looms over me, yet I can't make my legs go any faster. He swoops, then lunges and tackles me at the waist. We both catch air and go rolling, part on the grass and part on the pavement.

I scrape my knee, but manage to flip to my side so as not to belly flop onto the ground. Together we skid on the grass and come to a stop near the water.

Both laughing, we roll onto our backs, my head pinning his arm beneath me.

"Man, you can run fast." He pants.

"It's my long legs." I hold them up for inspection. Blood trickles off my right knee.

"You OK?" He points to my knee.

"Yep. You?

"Yep. Truce?"

"Truce." I hold up my hand and lift my head so he can pull his arm out from under me. He takes my hand in his and we shake. We lie there panting, catching our breath, and I'm reminded of our hot nights of sex, very similar to this moment, only without clothes and spectators. I must have turned red because Hank chuckles beside me and tells me he's thinking the same thing.

"Come on. Let's go get some ice cream." He sits up and pulls me with him. We're only halfway around the lake, his truck is on the other side, and I'm ready for the ice cream now.

"Go ahead and get the truck. I'll wait here on this bench," I tell him, trying to milk the situation, and hobble toward the bench.

"Oh no, you don't. Here, climb on." He gives me his back and I jump on. I haven't had a piggyback ride in years.

We don't make it very far before he whines, "Mercy girl."

I slide off him and swat at his arm. We laugh and link hands. I don't care. I don't care if people see us or what they might say. It's as if I'm living on the edge. It's been a good day, minus Sarah Grace's tantrum and the vomiting on me, and since Hank offers to buy the ice cream, I decide to get the largest one they offer with my favorite toppings.

We drive to a different lake with ducks and benches and pig out as we watch day give way to evening. I lick the last of the butterscotch syrup off my spoon and think about what Nana said about me "shagging" some guys. Hank is sitting close, our legs touch, pulled together by a force bigger than I can comprehend. I'm overcome with a hard to define need. It's strong and simple and will only be fed by being with him. I throw my spoon, cup, and napkins in the trash and come back to stand in front of him.

I guess he feels it too because he reaches out and places his hands on my hips and pulls me toward him. Energy twists off us in a frenzy, and I expect the air surrounding us to pop and snap. He pulls me across his lap and nestles me in the crook of his arm, snuggling me in close.

"No sex," he whispers. "Just a date."

Though we sit in the shadows, the fading light allows us to look into each other's eyes. His stare rivets me. He leans in and kisses me on the nose.

"*An toir thu dhomh pòg?*" His voice is husky. I do as he requests and press my lips to his, all my sense goes in the garbage can with my discarded spoon and cup.

He holds the kiss before slowly moving away.

"Thanks for coming out with me tonight," he says.

"Thanks for asking me."

I'm certain he feels the pull like I do, and I know we're about to have sex. I'm OK knowing every time we get together we end up in bed. It's simple; I want to be with him. Besides, even my grandmother gave me permission to do it.

Yet nothing happens. We sit here. I'm jittery with need but too afraid to make the first move. Hank shifts on the bench and leans back, his arm still around me, the space between us a little wider.

"Um... I thought maybe...." I begin.

"I don't think we should," he tells me. "To be honest, I'm having a hard time sleeping with you and knowing when I leave, you go on dates."

"I've been on two dates and one was set up before anything happened between us," I say. I have the need to explain.

"And you have another one planned?"

"Yes, but I'm not going to sleep with him. It's just a date. A way for me to get back into the thick of it." I try to explain but it seems to come out wrong. "There's no place I'd rather be right now than here with you. This, right here, right now is fantastic." And I mean it. Spending the afternoon with him was easy and fun.

"You're a cheap date. Ice cream and a park bench." I hear the smile in his voice.

I lean my head on his shoulder. "This is nice," I tell him as I try to keep my thoughts from going to naughty places. Sitting next to him fills me with a sense of femininity I've never experienced before. He's solid and warm and I want to burrow into his side and breathe him in.

"Hank?" I whisper, my voice hoarse.

"Please, Paisley, I'm working super-hard at restraining myself. I'm trying to show you we can get together without having sex." He looks away, toward the lake, and strokes my shoulder with his thumb.

I look around, not a car in sight. It's dark and trees seclude us.

"To hell with that." I shift to straddle him. Sure, it's a good idea being together without falling into bed, but I need him to need me.

He pulls me toward him and burns me to my center with a kiss, one with such intense heat I'm surprised it doesn't disintegrate my clothes. I reach for the button on his pants.

"No." He grabs my hands and looks at me.

"Yes," I say.

"No." He stands and pushes me off his lap.

"Come on. I'll take you home." He grabs my hand and pulls me toward his truck.

"Hank," I cry with frustration and tug my hand back.

He turns to face me and throws his hands in the air. "What do you want from me? Sex? We can't even go on a simple date. Jeez, I can't believe I'm saying this." He runs his hand through his hair before stuffing it in his pocket.

"Maybe we could try another date," I suggest. My heart flutters with the anticipation of a second date. The weight of time hangs between us as I wait for him to decide if he wants to be with me again.

"You know, I've heard of worse ideas," he answers. He links his fingers with mine and walks me to his truck.

Now I see the line we aren't supposed to cross and, of course, I think I'm straddling it, with a tenuous toehold on both sides.

18

I'M TEMPTED to cancel my date with Jake. It doesn't feel right anymore after last weekend with Hank, but I push forward because that's the plan, dammit. Besides, I hate canceling on people unless I have a good reason. If I made something up, I'd stammer through the lie.

Jake picks me up around noon with a picnic basket in tow and drives to the airfield where he houses his plane. I'm shocked to find out he owns a small plane and flies, by himself, to various places. Like Brinn.

I relax and let the good time happen. We fly across the state to Cedar Key, where we devour our picnic lunch and walk the small, eclectic tourist town. It's a pleasant day, an enjoyable date with an easy vibe. As we fly home, he suggests getting takeout and watching a movie. I agree without a second's hesitation. If Jake's a player, he's very smooth. He hasn't even touched me today. I guess I'm expecting some old cliché in his conversation or premature claims of undying love, even someone like pilot Ted and his creepy innuendos. Jake is different. He's funny, proper, and attentive.

We pick up beer, Chinese food, and I make popcorn before we settle in to a scary movie. My personal favorites are the gory flicks. I like to scare people afterward, especially Sarah Grace, who is super-susceptible to after-movie mind games.

Jake props his feet up on my coffee table as he pulls me close. I fidget, trying to get comfortable and relax but the ease I experienced earlier is gone and there's something about Jake that makes me uncertain. Maybe it's because we barely know each other and this is the awkwardness that comes with the early stages of dating.

I tuck my feet up under me so I'm not sitting snuggled in his arm. I like the way he smells, a bit like the sun and a whole lot like sin, sort of a musky, coconut, manly smell. It's so different from Hank who smells like the out of doors, kind of like evergreens, cedar, and with a hint of citrus. I mentally berate myself as I try not to think about Hank but move back a tad anyway.

"Josie is getting married soon, right?" He scoops up a handful of popcorn.

Our legs are touching and he keeps brushing his hand against mine as he reaches for more popcorn.

"Yeah, in a few weeks. You used to work together, right?" I probe for a reason for his interest in Josie.

"Barely. She was leaving as I was just coming on. We maybe overlapped a few weeks."

I laugh at a campy, supposed to be scary, part in the movie. Seriously, who runs toward the dark, scary area and away from the light? Even bugs fly toward the light. It's instinctive, except, apparently, in dumb girls.

I look at Jake and laugh. "These movies are the best."

"May I kiss you?" He catches me unaware and lowers his lips to mine.

It isn't the best kiss of my life, rockets don't go off, my heart doesn't race, and the earth stays on its path. It's pleasant enough. He's not one of those guys who kisses like a lizard, flicking his tongue in and out. But the strongest reaction I muster is "eh." He picks up speed, moving to my neck, right below my ear. This is my sweet spot, yet something about the way he teases it is annoying.

A nervous giggle escapes, and I press my lips together hoping to stop any more from getting out.

"Do you like it when I do this?" He tugs on my earlobe.

"Mmm." I stifle another giggle and close my eyes.

"Why don't you tell me how much you like it?" He nips my neck.

My eyes pop open. Uh-oh. I don't do dirty talk. I close my eyes again and choose to ignore it, hoping to distract him by running my hands over his back.

Jake lowers me flat onto the couch and stretches out on top of me. He pulls my top from my shorts and makes quick work of the buttons, laying my shirt open.

He goes for my breast and asks, "Do you feel dirty, Paisley? Do you need me to clean you up?" He runs his tongue up my belly, starting at my navel, traveling to my neck. Little goose bumps cover me and not in excitement.

I must have tensed up because Jake stops to look at me. "Are you OK?"

"Uhh, yeah." I go for broke. "I'm inexperienced with the dirty-talk stuff and uh…a bit nervous. Could we ease our way into this?"

I smile and hope I don't look terrified. I'm baffled how he can go from asking for permission for a kiss to dirty talk.

He pauses, his dark head bent in front of me, and shrugs. "Sure, I guess."

Nobody moves. The way he rests against me, pushing his weight into me, reminds me of Trevor and I'm taken aback by the sudden sense of a power struggle. It's stupid but I don't want to be perceived as prudish. Inexperienced but willing is one thing. Priggish is another. Frigid is what Trevor used to say and I sometimes wonder if he was right. Because I want to push Jake off me. Am I not being open-minded enough? Yet, my hands tremble and my knees twitch and not from the uncertainty that anticipation brings. This is rooted deeper in doubt and discomfort.

I don't want to kiss him anymore. Honestly, I want to call it a night but he's staring at my boobs as if he's expecting them to do something and that makes me apprehensive. Jake is suddenly very unpredictable. How will he react if I push him off?

Ask him to leave? I haven't felt this vulnerable since Trevor.

"Are you OK?" I ask.

He doesn't immediately answer. "I'm used to being with more experienced women. It's refreshing to be with someone as innocent as you. You may lack imagination, but I can teach you how to please me."

He smiles and unsnaps my bra, the whole time staring into my eyes. He moves his mouth to the side of my right boob and begins to suck it, still not breaking eye contact.

I don't know what to do. I'm far past nervous and my mind races, muddling my thoughts. I don't consider myself naive by any stretch of the imagination. I was married, for fuck's sake. Isn't there a purple plastic, albeit unused, penis in my dresser drawer? And he can teach me?

I hate myself for lacking the instant courage I need to force him off me. I close my eyes, trying to bank my fear and draw on my anger. His sucking begins to get uncomfortable. I arch toward him, hoping to ease the contact between his mouth and my breast.

"Jake." I squirm as panic fills me. Jake digs his hands into my hips, pushes me back down, and he grinds himself against me. I try to steady my heart, control my trembling. My mind races, desperate to remember some sort of self-defense move Josie taught me that I could use against him.

He breaks free. I peek through my lids and see him coming in to kiss me. Any ounce of harlot in me has packed up and moved on, replaced by the Paisley I thought I left behind in my divorce. I'm seconds from a full-blown panic attack when his cell phone rings.

"Sorry, babe, I have to get this." He sits up and reaches for his phone. I grasp my shirt and tug the two sides together, avoiding the glaring red mark on the swell of my breast. I button my shirt, not caring if the buttons line up or that my bra isn't fastened. I roll off the couch and side-step around him.

He reaches out and catches my legs, pulling me back to stand in front of him. I try not to shake and steady my breathing. My heart is pounding in my ears. The burning of his hands on my thigh holds my attention, making it impossible to focus on his conversation. My mind screams, asking me where's my self-respect? But I have no answer, I'm a pliable shell of a person.

Jake disconnects the call and yanks me toward him. He buries his face in my stomach, nips at my flesh, looks up, and says, "I have to head out, girl. I'm sorry we were interrupted."

I'm not.

I shrug as if there isn't anything we can do about these things. He pushes me away, gets up, and gathers his keys, phone, and shoes.

"Can I take the beer?"

"Sure." Take whatever you want. Just leave.

"I have to go to Ft. Lauderdale for at least a week. I'd love to see you when I get back."

A lock of brown hair flops over his eyes, and he looks nothing like the guy I spent a fun day with, the one who asked for permission and seemed to take things slowly. He looks like the player Josie warned me about and worse.

"Um, it's going to be hectic soon. I've Josie's wedding and... I'm in the wedding, um, so I may be out of town." My goal is to avoid a confrontation that could get ugly quick. Instinct tells me I'm no match for him.

"Oh yeah? Let me know what day and time and I'll make sure I'm free to escort you."

Did he just invite himself? It doesn't matter. Just leave! I want to scream it at him. Leave already!

"We'll talk about it when you get back," I say. I'm such an idiot. I know I should say no, that I already have a date, or make up some other reason. The idea of spending the weekend out of town with Jake has absolutely no appeal. Shoot, spending any time alone with Jake has no further appeal. But I'm hoping once he's gone I'll have the advantage of distance to help me avoid the problem.

He gives me a kiss and leaves, oblivious to my unease. I bolt my door and go around checking the windows. I want to call Josie, but am too ashamed. Gigi? I can't bring myself to pick up the phone, much less dial.

I start a hot shower and sit on the tub floor, letting the water wash over me until my skin is shriveled. I ignore the welt on my chest, even though common sense tells me I should put a cold pack on it. But, I can't face it. I can't face myself and my inactions.

When I was married to Trevor I used to stand up for myself, try to set limits but he always wore me down. Even a simple disagreement was exhausting. Tonight, I saw the same mannerisms in Jake, the desire to manage me. I'd thought I'd moved on from those days and that person I use to be and it's a devastating crush to my soul to know that I haven't entirely done so. I cover the welt with a baggy T-shirt and leggings, and climb in bed, where I channel surf for several hours until sheer exhaustion forces my eyes closed.

19

I NEED to accessorize my new bridesmaid gown and the best place in town to do is Jayne's shop, the Daily Mirror.

I'm still unnerved from my incident with Jake. Every time I think about how I handled the situation, I get angry. I have a talent for finding fault with myself first, rather than assigning the responsibility to the person who deserves it. In this case, however, that person is me. The last time I was overcome with self-loathing because of another's actions, I was with Trevor.

Jayne's shop is always busy. Lots of people drive from all points around Florida to get her exclusive, European-style clothes. She carries both high-end and off-the-rack fashion. Jayne is incredibly talented with putting together outfits for every body type and accessorizing with a flair original to her.

I carry my shimmering navy blue gown in and wait for Jayne to get to me.

"Give me fifteen more minutes, love. Mrs. Anderson

needs a little more reassurance." She winks and moves into the area separated from the off the rack shoppers like me.

In the back private dressing area, Jayne offers her clients tea, coffee, or wine, and fresh scones. She also has a woman on hand to complete tailoring. Out front, we poor peasants are subjected to mints, Walker's butter cookies, and our choice of water with lemon or cucumbers. Point is, it's still water.

Stains must be avoided at every cost because, clearly, we spill things.

A classic eighties song comes on overhead, and I walk around the shop, trying on hats, scarves, and costume jewelry, singing along.

Jayne walks by and unwinds a lavender scarf off my head. "Go put your dress on, Paisley, and stay away from this shade of purple. It does nothing for your skin. I'll be with you in a minute."

I look at my eggplant tank top and grimace.

"Darker purples with blue tones are fine." She walks into the back with an armful of clothes.

I move to the changing room with my gown. It's a simple dress I like better than the original one we picked out. Strapless, with a sweetheart bust and tea-length, since it's an afternoon wedding, the gown tightens right below my breasts and goes straight out in what Jayne would call a conservative A-line. The length makes me looks leggy. I hope Jayne can hook me up with the right shoes and jewelry. Maybe even suggest a hairstyle.

I slide the dress over my body and admire how well it fits. I may not have the most becoming of faces, unflattering hair, and pale skin, but I did inherit my mother's fantastic legs and running keeps me lithe. It also keeps my boobs on the smaller side, and with the right garment I can go braless without flopping everywhere.

I try to zip it in the back, but I'm all elbows and keep bumping the stall walls. I wait for Jayne, holding it up until she's free. I poke my head out of the dressing room and she's there so I turn and let her work the zipper.

"This is quite lovely on you, Paisley." Jayne stands back and studies the dress. Together we take in the shimmering navy blue with threads of silver running through it.

Peeking above the gown line is the red bruise.

Jayne raises an eyebrow and smiles to encourage me to spill the story.

I shake my head in disagreement. "It wasn't like that, Jayne."

"Oh please, you don't have to be shy with me. It can be however you like."

"No, really. It was a bit...." Jayne fusses with my hair, twisting it into various updos. I struggle to find the right word and shudder with the memory.

"What happened?" She brings me to a cozy seat and pushes me in it.

I wonder if I might get a scone. Jayne's mother makes the best scones. I smooth the folds of the fabric, tracing a thread down the length of the dress. Better not get a scone. I'd probably get a stain on the dress.

"I don't know what happened. One minute he's trying to get me to talk dirty and the next he's doing this." I look at the angry red mark and cover it with my hand.

"Just tell Hank you don't like it."

"This wasn't Hank." He'd never do something like this without the girl's explicit consent. I don't want to tell Jayne it was Jake, afraid of the lecture she might give me. But I do anyway.

Jayne is quiet for a moment, and stands abruptly. "It sounds to me like you both have different sexual energy and you'll have to come to a compromise before you go any further. If you want to go any further that is." She leaves the room, comes back with a tray of scones, and holds them out to me for selection.

"Bless you, Jayne." I bite into one full of cranberries as she spreads a napkin over my lap. "You may be right." About the sexual-energy part, how we are on different wavelengths. Though I don't see myself talking to Jake about it. There's no possible compromise in our future. How do we meet halfway on this?

"Make sure you don't do anything you're uncomfortable with in the future. Be honest with him and see where it takes you. Now, I bought some lovely silver sandals from Italy a few months ago and they'd be perfect with your dress."

She vanishes into the back room and comes back a moment later carrying a small shoe box. She pulls open the lid and pulls out a shoe bag.

These must be some shoes, wrapped up better than Waterford crystal.

She slides the shoes out of the bag and I'm stunned. The silver of the shoes looks almost translucent and they sport a three-inch heel. Thin straps cross over the foot, swirling around to finish as they wrap around the ankle.

I "ooh" like Nana and my mother always do. The shoes are breathtaking.

"Try them on." Jayne hands them to me.

I slide them on, stand, and feel like a princess. I walk to the full-length mirror and like what I see, minus the red mark. I'll try to cover that with makeup if it isn't gone in three weeks.

"OK." I brace myself. "How much are they?"

"I'll give them to you for a bit over cost." She smiles, names the price, and I sway. They come pretty close to the cost of my dress, but since I didn't pay for my dress and I'm in love with the shoes, I go ahead and buy them.

"Are you taking anyone to the wedding?" She rewraps them.

"Well, no. Jake volunteered. He's not an option." She gives me a face to indicate she agrees. "And there isn't anyone who I could take up to Amelia Island anyway and spend the whole weekend with."

Jayne snorts in disbelief. I narrow my eyes, remembering when I bumped into her and Josie huddled together at the bar.

"And who are *you* taking to the wedding?" I know it's a mean thing to say since she's been on an even longer dry spell than me. Apparently, Jayne is pickier than I am because I know she's turned down several men.

"I'm not taking anyone, and I chose it to be so. You, on the other hand, have a secret man named Hank who sounds absolutely lovely and you should take him."

I shrug at the mention of Hank's name. "I think he'll be out of town. Maybe I choose to go alone, too. Ever think about that?"

She rings the shoes up, along with a classic simple silver choker, earrings, and three-quarter gloves in silver, and hands me the purchase. "It's quite possible you're being a dolt where this man is concerned."

"Which one?" She ignores my sarcasm.

"Both. Give me the hunky Hank. He sounds like a keeper."

"You can have him. He's like a brother to me anyway." A flare of jealousy streaks through me as I picture Jayne with Hank.

Jayne looks off as if daydreaming; she purses her lips and crinkles her delicate British nose. "Hmm, isn't it against the law to do those type of things with one's brother?" She smiles.

Damn Josie and her very large, fat mouth.

I snatch up my bag and walk off in a snit.

"Have fun at Josie's tonight. If you don't want this hot nerd, throw him my way," she calls to my back, chuckling.

I give her a flippant wave and huff out of the store, anxious to give Josie a piece of my mind.

***

"Oh my God, you aren't wearing your hair like that, are you?" Josie inspects me, scanning from top to bottom.

"You're lucky I'm even here. I saw Jayne today and it seems someone has been telling her things about Hank." I push my way in and throw my purse on the bench in her foyer.

"I haven't said anything other than what you've told them. Just giving them my perspective. Nothing more.

Come on, let's do something with your hair. Brinn and Stacy haven't landed yet, we have time." She heads off toward her master bedroom, dragging me behind by my hand. It's a complete mess with clothes and makeup scattered everywhere, so unlike Josie.

I've done nothing different or special with my hair and am wearing it au naturel, loose and curly. She pushes me onto the little bench in front of her vanity and starts fussing with my hair. But she's mumbling and sighing impatiently and I as I watch her in the mirror she keeps glancing at her watch.

"Josie, how are you going to be married to Brinn for the rest of your life if you're a nervous wreck every time he's out flying?"

She shakes her head and starts gathering small sections of hair around my forehead. "I'm not nervous because he's flying. It's this start-up he's doing. He's competing against another company for the same area and with similar routes and it's gotten ugly. There's been more 'accidents' than normal at the hangar, things that could set us back or take us out of the running for good. Until this is behind us, I don't think I'll be OK."

"Holy shit, Josie. I didn't know. I'm sorry." It explains a lot with her edginess and mood.

"Brinn wasn't telling me. He was acting weird. I did a little digging and started putting the pieces together before I confronted him. He's starting to fill me in now, though I know there's more he's not telling me."

I grab her hand and our eyes meet in the mirror. "Tell me how I can help."

She laughs. "You can help us have a good time tonight. We need a few laughs."

"Did you say his name was Stacy? You know you aren't painting a good picture here. I believe you've used words like nerdy, number cruncher, and his name is Stacy."

She pulls the sides of my hair back and clips them with a small mother of pearl barrette. I like it.

"I believe I also used words like hot and...."

"Yeah, you used only hot. Hot could go either way. As in smoking hot to look at or excessively sweaty."

We laugh and Josie busies herself touching up my makeup.

"Stacy is crazy nice. He's been here a week looking for a house to rent. He's funny—"

"Looking?" I ask.

"No, funny like ha-ha. One of those honest-to-God nice guys. Who happens to be good looking."

"You do know calling them nice is the kiss of death for men? Nice guy, nerdy, carries a calculator... His pluses and minuses aren't equaling out here, Jo."

"Just wait and see. You'll like him." She twirls a brush in blush and lightly sweeps it across my face. She's going back for a second sweep when we hear a door bang closed.

"Honey, we're home." It's not Brinn's voice.

Josie smiles and her shoulders relax. She tosses the brush on her vanity, grabs my hand, and drags me out of the chair and through the house to the kitchen where Brinn and his business manager, Stacy, are standing.

"I thought you guys were stuck circling the tower waiting for clearance." She gives Brinn a hug and a kiss.

"We got clearance right after I texted you. We stopped and grabbed some beer, too," Brinn tells her.

"Yeah, we would've been here sooner, but genius can't figure out how many cans are in a six-pack. I told him to grab about three varieties so we'd have enough beer." Stacy shakes his head and smirks.

He's very good-looking, dark brown hair, bright blue eyes, and an easy smile. He stands as tall as Hank, though his lanky frame makes Hank look stocky.

"Stacy, this is my friend, Paisley. Paisley, this is Stacy," Josie says.

We shake hands. Something about the softness in his eyes, the way they stay crinkled in the corner, and the gentle but firm way he shakes my hand puts me at ease.

"Thanks for joining us, Paisley. You being here will give me someone to talk to when those two get lovey and forget someone else is in the room."

"Oh, they ignore you, too? I thought I was the only privileged one." We laugh when Josie takes a playful swat at me.

"Come on, everyone in the car. We have reservations." She steers us into the garage and drives to one of my favorite restaurants on the water. We sit outside and enjoy the Atlantic breeze coming off the ocean.

The evening goes remarkably well. I spend dinner getting to know Stacy better.

He doesn't have a wandering eye or a wandering hand. His attention is on us, the people he came with. He's easy to be around. It's as if we've been friends for a long time. He tells me about getting his MBA and how he's always been a supernerd—his words—for numbers and math. I tell him about occupational therapy school and dissecting cadavers.

"Oh, Paisley," Josie says, "Stacy needs to know which area has the better elementary schools." She turns to him. "Your daughter's going into third grade right?"

He nods. "That's right. Where I look for a house is based on the school. I want to give Cordie as much stability as I can, considering everything is going to change for her."

"Cordie?" I ask.

"Cordelia, I didn't name her. Her mother did." He gives me a smile and picks up his beer. "No, I don't have a wife waiting for me at home. Or any other kids. I'm going to have to tell you the story aren't I?"

I pause. "You don't *have* to tell me the story, but I'm curious. Or plain nosy. Depending on who you ask, and it might be better if you do tell me, or else I'll be forced to create my own story about your life."

He laughs and clinks his beer with mine. "Who wouldn't be nosy about this? OK, I dated Karen, Cordie's mom, briefly in college. As these things sometimes happen, she ended up pregnant. As the guy in this scenario, I didn't have too many options. It's not like we're given much say in these matters. I wasn't going to marry her, but I was willing to date and see where things went. She wasn't. She thought she could be a single mother. Two days after she delivered Cordie, she left her with me and took off. Haven't seen her since."

"Holy cow. You raised a newborn, alone, while in college?" I'm certainly impressed.

"I wish I could say yes. I'd look like a hero stud, but my

parents helped. I moved back in with them and my mom stayed home with Cordie. I couldn't have done any of it without them." He pulls out his phone and shows me pictures of a cute eight-year-old with blond hair and his blue eyes.

"She's beautiful," I say.

"Yeah, she's pretty spectacular. This move is gonna be hard on her with leaving my folks."

"I bet it's going to be hard on your parents, too." Even when Momma and Sarah Grace are fighting, Momma still gets the twins for a full day and overnight. She starts missing them when she goes three days without seeing them.

"It'll be hard on everyone. My dad is a photographer for *National Geographic* and it's been my mom's life dream to go with him on some of his assignments. Now's the time for them to fulfill their plans. Now's the time for me to start this adventure." He nods to Brinn. "It's all good stuff."

I reach into my purse and pull out my phone. "What's your number? I'll text you some school names." I send out names of the schools I think are the ones I'd like to see my kids or Sarah Grace's twins go to.

Josie's right. He's a tad nerdy but in a hot way. I almost wonder if the nerdiness comes from his clothes and bad haircut and not so much his mannerisms. He's laid-back and easygoing, has a good sense of humor, and can be quite wry. It's attractive and I like him. Just not in the way Josie was hoping.

His leg brushes mine and I feel nothing. No spark. Stacy is the kind of guy women call a keeper, and try as I might he's not for me. But he's perfect for Jayne.

"Let's get ice cream and head back to our house and sit on the beach," Josie says.

We agree and Stacy picks up the tab. We're getting up from the table when he asks, "Hey, anyone got a calculator? I can't figure the tip on this bill."

Brinn and Josie walk away. I look at him and snap my mouth shut.

"It's a joke," he tells me. "Nobody gets my math humor."

I laugh. Not because he's funny, but because he's nice and I have a great idea.

"Hey, Josie?" I call. "Would you mind if I give Jayne a call and invite her? I know she's home alone tonight."

"Oh, OK," she says.

"You won't be offended if I invite another girlfriend to join us? Give these two"—I indicate Brinn and Josie—"ice cream and a lounge chair, and the end of them is near. Plus, you'll have two girls to entertain you."

"I like those odds." He smiles.

"See, I got your math joke."

"I like you, Paisley. You're all right."

"Wait till you meet my friend Jayne. *Prepare to be entertained*," I say in my best game-show-announcer voice. "By entertained I mean clean wholesome fun, just so y'know."

"Sounds great, but I'm not dancing or singing karaoke," he says.

"Well hell, now you've gone and ruined it." We laugh as I pull out my phone and dial up Jayne.

20

I HAVEN'T SEEN HANK; he's been working fourteen-hour days so our contact has been limited to casual e-mails and text messages. I haven't given Jake much thought other than he's still out of town. My days are my own, and I enjoy the stress-free time spent being a lazy cow. I've spent today sitting by the pool, under an umbrella, of course. As the sun prepares to kiss off, I head inside and place a pizza-delivery order. There's a good book and a bottle of wine calling my name.

A knock on the door surprises me and with a spring in my step I fling open the door. My smile turns into a lip curl and I swallow a dry heave. Jake is holding a bag of Chinese takeout and waving a movie.

"Hey, babe, I thought we'd pick up where we left off."

My stomach turns and with nerves steeled, I conjure up my resolve. I refuse to let him manipulate me.

He pushes his way in and kicks the door closed, kisses me on the neck, and heads toward my kitchen.

I scramble to come up with a reason why he can't stay. I'm still in my swimsuit with a towel wrapped around me. I go to my room and toss on my cover-up, the one that hangs to my knees.

I want Jake to leave but no viable excuse is coming to mind. Think, I scream in my head. I remember what Jayne said about being honest. It's not rude or unreasonable to ask him to leave even if I have no other plans. He may argue back, but I'll stand my ground. I repeat this several times, hoping to make it true. I head to the kitchen, my speech prepared, when someone else bangs on my door. I scramble to get it.

Please be Josie, I pray. She'll know how to handle it.

I swing the door open to see Hank standing there with his lopsided grin and his hair mussed. A motorcycle helmet hangs in his left hand.

"Hey." His smile broadens.

My body tingles and I smile back, "Hey—"

"Hey, babe, where do you keep the forks?" Jake comes in, pulls the door open farther, and gives Hank the once-over.

"Who are you?" Hank asks.

"Her boyfriend. Who are you?"

"Wait. What?" I ask Jake. I shake my head and look at Hank. "He's not—"

"I've caught you at a bad time. I'll get going," Hank replies. His shoulders slump as he steps back and winces. My heart breaks, leaps, and then freezes in panic.

He walks off. I face Jake and throw my hands up in question. Words escape me, and I dart out the door after Hank.

I follow him down the hallway and have to skip steps on the stairs to catch up with him. We reach the parking lot, and I stretch out trying to touch him but he's just out of reach. He stops suddenly and turns toward me, causing me to skid to a stop.

"This is exactly what I was talking about, Paisley, at the park. On our date." I give him a puzzled look.

"Sleeping with you and sharing you with others. It goes against my nature."

"It's not—"

"Answer me one question. Are you sleeping with him?" He sets his jaw. If he would shut up for a second, I would answer all his questions.

I turn my face up to him and try not to twitch or blink so he can see, without a doubt, I'm telling the truth.

"No. This is like only the third time I've seen him and I did not plan nor ask for this. He showed up uninvited. He is not my boyfriend." His eyes search my face. "Scout's honor."

"Didn't you get kicked out of Girl Scouts?"

"No, I left voluntarily. Do you remember everything?" I ask.

"Why did he say he was your boyfriend?" He turns and walks to one of the most spectacular motorcycles I have ever seen.

I stare at it in awe. "I dunno. Maybe he thought you were gonna brain him with your helmet." I nod toward the full-face black helmet. "You being the tough biker and all."

We grin. I look at the bike and run my hands over the tank.

"I showed up uninvited," he says.

"Yes, but you have a standing invitation."

He pauses. "Seriously, what's his deal?" He's not snarky, just curious.

I shrug, "I dunno. Totally caught me off guard. I was about to ask him to leave when you knocked. How long have you owned a motorcycle?" I walk over to Hank, push up the sleeve on his left arm, and trace a tattoo of the Navy insignia with my index finger. "You, sir, have hidden depths."

He smiles his crooked smile I love so much. "What are you doing with that guy, Paisley?"

I shrugged. "Nothing, I hadn't planned on seeing him again. Besides, who needs a boyfriend when I've got BOB." It's my attempt at a joke.

"BOB?" He quirks a brow.

"Yeah, you remember BOB." I do some awkward hand gestures and stop when realization dawns and he smirks.

Hank comes from around the bike, puts his helmet on the ground, and backs me up against my SUV, which is parked next to his bike.

"Yes, but can BOB do this?" He lifts me up, presses me between the car and his body, and kisses me thoroughly. I lose all sense of time and space. He breaks the kiss, hovers his lips over mine as he lowers me slowly to the ground. My knees buckle, and I give a nervous giggle.

He brushes a second gentle kiss on my lips, takes a step back, pulls on his helmet, flips the faceplate up, and straddles his bike.

"You let me know when you get BOB to do that." He

winks and starts the bike up. The vibrations of the bike echo the tremor in my body.

I'm rooted to my spot, like a dullard, with what I suspect is a goofy look on my face. At least I manage a small wave as he rides off.

A reflection of light from an apartment across the way catches my eye, and I look over to see Mrs. Cranston, the nosiest neighbor this world over, watching me through binoculars.

Ha. I knew she used them. Wait till I tell Josie.

"Hi, Mrs. Cranston." I wave before heading back to my apartment. Jake is standing on my balcony eating Chinese food out of the container and looking down at me.

Holy hell. My left eye twitches.

I climb the stairs to my apartment, my mind a total blank, at a loss for what to say.

I swing open the door and brace myself. He continues to stand there and eat.

"Ah..." Yep, it's all I got.

"I was going to ask if you missed me." He gives me a wounded look. Like I missed a cold sore. "I can see you had a distraction. Guess I need to step up my game."

He puts the Chinese food on my coffee table, without a coaster, and I stare at the food box as the gummy gravy oozes out from the bottom. He steps closer and tries to pull me into an embrace, but I put my hands up on his chest to stop him.

"Listen, Jake. I'm sorry, I have plans. I appreciate the spontaneity, but the timing is off." I don't want an ugly confrontation, convinced if we get into it he'll just twist my words until I'm confused and the message is lost. I don't have the debate skills to go up against guys like Trevor and Jake. I want him to leave. I try to take a step back, but he wraps his arms around my waist and pulls me toward him.

"I won't lie and say I'm not hurt. I know you're giving me the brush-off but you're making a mistake." He weasels his hands under the bottom of my bathing-suit cover and pinches my bum so hard I yelp and jump closer. He locks me in tight. "Don't you understand, Paisley? Don't you think we can have something good?" His voice is low, almost a whisper.

Never in my life have I been this unnerved and scared shitless. I nod, afraid to do anything other than agree.

"Great. I'll let you come up with something for our next date. Make it good." His kiss is rough; his lips push against mine with such force it hurts, and I taste the metallic flavor of blood in my mouth. He pulls away, pushing me backward, and I fall onto the floor. He steps over me and scoops up his keys as he heads toward the door.

"Oh, what color is your dress for the wedding? I'll try to coordinate it with my suit." He turns back and waits with an impatient look, as if I'm a petulant child.

"Navy." It comes out a whisper.

"Great. Navy. I expect to hear from you soon. I enjoy being with you. You're a cool chick." He winks and walks out.

When the door closes, I jump up, throw the lock, and slide down the door, my back resting against it. I bite my thumbnail as I listen through the door, afraid he may come back.

There's a soft shuffle on the other side and I press my ear closer, straining. I jump when someone knocks.

"Who is it?" I demand in what I hope is my sternest voice but there is no denying I'm rattled.

"Pizza delivery."

I look through the peephole and let out my breath.

It's the pizza guy.

I grab my money, open the door, snatch the pizza, toss him my cash, very large tip included, and slam the door, throwing the bolt again. I lean against the door, holding my pizza, shaking.

Jake has made me afraid in my own home.

"Wow, thanks lady," the kid yells through the door. Clearly, he is pleased with my tip.

My trembling is no longer generated by fear but anger. I'm pissed off. Who the fuck does Jake think he is? I have a flash to Trevor. Toward the end of our marriage he used to play the same type of mind games and he nearly broke me. I don't like the parallel.

Jayne's words about honesty and Josie's about feeling obligated resonate with me.

And then there's Hank's kisses. Even when hurried, they never cause pain. Ignoring what needs to be said between Jake and me won't resolve this problem. I was stupid to think it would. I'm tired of being a victim. I may not have changed as much as I originally thought but here's the opportunity to make more of that change happen. I've come this far, and I won't be held down by anyone, including me, anymore.

I snatch up the Chinese food on my table, wipe up the gravy square, combine them with the container in my kitchen, and drop them in the trash. There is no way in hell I'm eating something Jake brought. For all I know it's laced with a date-rape drug. I wouldn't put it past him.

I uncork my bottle of wine, grab a napkin, the pizza box, and my book, and head out to my balcony. I toy with the idea of texting Hank, asking him to come back. But then he really would be my booty call. I stick to the original plan.

Tonight is going to be what I originally wanted, an evening with only myself for company.

21

"He's pretty good, huh?" I ask Josie without taking my eyes off Hank.

"Freakishly good," she says. "Has he always been a good dancer?"

I grab her arm, snort with laughter, pull her close, and say, "Don't tell anyone. Hank took dance lessons."

"Seriously? When?"

"Last half of middle school, beginning of high school. Our parents' grand idea. We were in the same class together: Gigi, me, Hank, and their younger sister Joanna. I took a blood oath to never tell." We laugh and continue our observation of Hank.

"It's definitely paid off for him. Guy's got moves."

We stand in the crowd, watching the people on the dance floor. It's typical to see mostly women dancing together though tonight some of the good old boys are out there making it happen, Hank being one of them. Of course, he's making it happen with Melinda Bane, which has me grinding my teeth.

Why I agreed to come to this stupid event is beyond me. Between the guilt laid on by Gigi and Sarah Grace, I was in poor shape when my own mother started in on me.

The Swan Ball is held every summer. It's a fund-raiser to help local kids with new school clothes, school supplies, and even establishes scholarships. Any extra money goes toward a Christmas festival for the same group of kids. Under normal circumstances I like it because it's held outside, is for a good cause, and promises a good time. I don't like it right now because I have to watch Hank and Melinda.

Earlier, I counted seven booze tents and as I watch Hank spin Melinda around the floor, I decide I need to need to partake in some of the free wine.

I admit I'm jealous. Not jealous because Melinda gets tons of attention, like in high school, or because she seems so unflawed. Honestly, who can two-step in those heels? I bet she's stepping all over his feet. I'm jealous because I don't like seeing Hank with another girl. Any girl. Certainly not one who's as schooled in the arts of man wooing as Melinda.

This is a whole new emotion for me.

"Come on. Let's move before he sees us," I say and head toward the wine booths.

The song ends, and Hank calls my name. Josie looks at me but I pretend I'm too distracted to hear him and order a white wine at the nearest booth. I'm sipping it, giving her dirt about the local vendors I know from high school, and hopefully, emitting an air of indifference when he approaches.

"Hey." He's out of breath from whooping it up on the dance floor. "Josie, right? How are you?" His smile is warm as he gives her his attention.

"That's me. It's nice to meet you sober," she says, and they both give a quick laugh. She cuts her eyes to me. "You know, I'm gonna go use the restroom." She backs away from us, not giving me a chance to stop her.

"When did you get here?"

I swear, if he smiles at me, I will lose my mind.

"A while ago." I set my teeth, unable to even fake a smile.

"You OK?" He orders a glass of white wine.

I narrow my eyes. In a crowd like this, Hank's a beer guy.

"You getting one for Melinda?" My words come out biting.

He looks at me, puzzled, "Yeah, is something wrong?"

"Oh, no. Nothing." My sarcasm isn't lost on Hank. He's known me too long. I take a sip of wine and raise my eyebrows.

"What's with the attitude?" he asks.

I don't want to fight, but my blood is boiling and refraining is no longer an option.

"Really? Melinda Bane? Seriously?" I walk off in a huff. I get about two steps when he grabs my elbow and steers me to a space between two tents, trying to avoid a scene.

"I'm not sure what you're implying. I didn't bring her. Not that it's any business of yours."

"We've been sleeping together. Don't you think I should know if you have a date?"

He snorts and gives me a scathing look. "It's nothing you haven't done to me." OK, he's got me there.

"I don't flaunt my dates in front of you," I say.

"I'm not on a date." He throws his hand up in disgust. "What do you want from me?"

His question gives me pause. What do I want? My thoughts wander to places I never imagined they would go nor could I have imagined the small ache in my heart accompanying those thoughts.

"You're right. I lost sight of our deal. We don't have a relationship. We're clear we both don't want one." I can't stop the accusatory tone that carries my words.

"I never said I didn't want a relationship; I said my job makes it a hard. You're the one who wants to 'try a few guys on for size.'"

He throws my words at me and they hit like a slap on the face. I suck in my breath and toss my wine in the trash can.

"You said you weren't interested in Melinda," I say.

"It was one dance. You're overreacting."

Maybe. Maybe I am. I know there are suppose to be no strings with our deal, but if he's going to go on dates, why does it have to be with Melinda? He knows I hate her.

He knows she's always been a cow to me.

"You know what, Hank, this"—I point to him and then myself—"is a great idea. Things aren't awkward between us at all. Nothing's changed, either." I lean in. "Brilliant, isn't that the word you used? Yeah, brilliant." I walk off.

This time he doesn't catch up with me. This time I'm on my own.

I find Josie near the art tents. I snatch her glass of wine and down it.

"Are you OK?" There are a thousand other things she could say to me and be right about all of them.

"Yeah, come on, I'll introduce you to my sister." I steer Josie toward the tents of various vendors. One of which is my sister's and Dan's, both peddling their respective companies. She and Gigi appear to be in an animated conversation.

"Hey, how's it going?" I start with a hug to Gigi before moving to my sister.

"Paisley, I'm glad you came." Sarah Grace leans over the table, and we kiss each other's cheeks.

"Sarah Grace, this is my friend Josie, who is getting married in two weeks." Gigi and Josie already know each other.

"Ohh, Paisley sent me a picture of her bridesmaid dress. I love the color. Beautiful." Sarah Grace can be very easy to get to know.

"Thanks. I'm getting a lot of flak from my mom about not having the men in tuxes. She thinks the navy suits are understated."

"Well, I think it's beautiful," Sarah Grace says. "Very elegant. How are you holding up? Not getting nervous or anything? Not like Paisley who spent the whole night before throwing up and crying."

I groan. "I had food poisoning."

"Mm-hmm, so you keep saying. Remember how Nana said she'd give you ten thousand dollars and buy you a plane ticket to Scotland if you didn't go through with it?"

Josie's mouth drops open.

Gigi laughs. "Remember she told me to go get the car and bring it around?"

"I bet you all think I was stupid for not taking it and running," I say.

"At the time yes, because he seemed too perfect to me. Almost one-dimensional. Now I'm glad you married Trevor." Sarah Grace continues when I gave her a glare. "I wish he would have been the man you needed and I certainly didn't enjoy watching you go through your divorce, but I see something in you now I haven't seen for a long time. Something good and if going through everything with Trevor is what's making it come back out, then I guess it was worth it in the end. Because now you can really find true happiness."

"I agree," says Gigi. "I hope now you're more intolerant of BS. You sure put up with a lot."

I'm caught off guard and about to ask more, when a tall, middle-aged man steps up to the booth and smiles at Sarah Grace. This is clearly his first Swan Ball because he's dressed in a three-piece suit with a monogrammed handkerchief and cuff links to boot.

Doesn't he know clogging and square dancing may break out at any moment? Or most of the men here think being dressed up is having their jeans starched? Lakeland should call their Swan Ball the Swan Shindig. Or Swan Hoedown. Certainly not ball. I mean, there are two boiled-peanut booths here for Pete's sake.

"Excuse me? Are you the interior designer who decorated the Townsend property?" His voice is nasally, with a nondescript drawl.

"Yes, I am." Sarah Grace smiles.

"You did a magnificent job. I'm the architect in charge of renovation and revitalizing the downtown area and I would like to speak with you at length regarding the possibility of us doing some work together." He reaches into his breast pocket, pulls out a business card, and passes it to Sarah Grace.

"You're not from around here, are you?" Gigi asks.

"No. Oregon." He gives her a curious look.

"We can tell. It's the suit," I say.

"I was told it was a business-dress affair." A flash of irritation crosses his face.

We nod. Someone is pranking the new guy.

"Honey," Gigi says, "blue jeans are the business attire for these guys."

He nods as he absorbs the information.

Sarah Grace hands him her business card. "Thank you for thinking of me. I'll talk to my business partner and see if it's something we might be interested in."

"Please do. Call my office for an appointment if you find you're interested." He nods to us all. Lord, he must be hot as a fire poker in that suit. A small bead of sweat rolls down his temple and he pulls out his hankie and dabs at it. "If you'll excuse me. Have a nice day."

We watch him leave. He's a good hundred yards away before anyone says anything.

"Poor bastard," Josie says and we all laugh.

Sarah Grace snort-laughs.

"What's so funny?" Hank wanders over.

"How long have you been there?" Gigi swats at her brother.

"Long enough. I came over to see if anyone wants to get out on the dance floor and two-step with me." He dares one of us to be a taker.

"Not me. That's just too weird," says Gigi.

"Paisley?" he asks, extending the metaphoric olive branch.

"Actually, Josie would love to do it." I'm extorting reparation for a long list of injustices, the most recent being BOB.

"I don't even know how to two-step. Paisley was gonna teach me." With a tentative hand, Josie reaches out and takes Hank's, and she gives me a shrug.

"Well then, let me be the first to show you how it's done. You're gonna be a pro when I get done with you. I'll teach you the right way, not some half-assed McAllister way." He whisks her off and heads to the floor.

"Hey," Sarah Grace calls out to him, "I'm deeply wounded by your words and utter lies."

Gigi huffs. "Lies you say? We all know Lancasters have moves and McAllisters have two left feet."

"Hang on," I say, "just who do you think taught you Lancasters any of those moves?"

"Ms. Lisa at Lakeland Dance Studio, that's who," says Gigi.

It's on now. The friendly competition between our two families, spanning decades, is rearing up once again.

"There's lots of trash-talking going on here," John says as he and Dan walk up.

He puts his beer on the table and grabs Gigi's hand,

pulling her toward him. "We heard you all way over by the beer booth. I say, no more posturing, we go out there and show 'em."

"Wanna put your money where your mouth is?" Dan reaches for Sarah Grace, pulls her over the booth's table, and rushes her toward the dance floor, trying to beat Gigi and John.

"I'll just stay here and watch the booth," I say. "Don't mind me."

My phone chimes, and I pull it out, looking at the face. One missed call from Jake and now a text message.

Why haven't I heard from you? Let's get together. Soon.

Like the other messages and calls since he pushed me to the floor, I ignore it and wish for the umpteenth time this phone had a block-caller option. My day with Jake is coming. I just have to work up to it.

Gigi said she hoped I was more intolerant of BS. I think I may be. I sure hope I am. I look out at the dance floor. My family and friends are out there laughing with each other, having a good time. I turn my phone off and tuck it into my back pocket.

Right here, right now, this is darn near perfect, fight with Hank notwithstanding.

All I need is a dance partner.

Mr. Suit-and-Sweaty walks by and I call out, "Hey, architect guy."

He wipes his brow with his hankie as he chugs a beer. He looks at me and points to himself.

"Yeah, you. Do you know how to two-step?" I don't even know why I'm asking him, except this guy has got to be miserable and hot, yet is still trying to make a good impression and network. Plus, it never hurts to be friendly, Southern hospitality and all that.

"Preston and no, I'm afraid I don't." He walks toward me and I move to meet him.

"Well, Preston, you know how to follow directions?"

He nods and takes a long swig of a beer.

"Good, take off your jacket and tie and hand them over."

He does as I ask, and I toss them behind the table at Sarah Grace's booth. "Roll your sleeves up. The designer you were chatting up is my sister, who is on the dance floor. You being out there dancing will go a long way with her and these people."

He rolls up his sleeves and gives me a smile. "Lead the way...."

"Paisley. This is a great way to get in with the good-old-boy network running rampant in this town. That and buying a large truck and jacking it up on some Super Swampers."

"Super Swampers?" He steps onto the floor and lets me take the lead. He's a quick study.

"Tires. Relax your arms." I pull him around the floor and point out people he'll likely work with. Many are guys I went to school with who've taken over for their fathers. We do two laps before he takes over and begins to lead me.

"Hey, I just took this novice here and taught him to two-step with only two turns around the floor," I say to Gigi and John.

"Prove it." She grabs Preston's hands, leaving me to dance with John.

"Let's see some of that McAllister Magic," John says. We dance off.

One song blends into another and the competition continues. Who can outdo whom? I dance with more people than I can count and laugh nonstop. It's during the fifth song that I find myself in Hank's arms.

My face freezes, and I tense. I don't want to fight with him. I don't want things to be awkward between us and there's no question I don't want him dancing with Melinda anymore either.

He twirls me around once and I step on his toes twice before I smile at him.

"You feel better now?" he says when I grind my foot against his.

"Actually, I do." I relax against him and follow his lead.

"About Melinda," he says.

I groan. "Please don't ruin the moment."

"You totally blew it out of proportion." He moves me into a pivot step.

"Kind of like you did when you came to my apartment."

"The difference is Melinda isn't at my house. It was one dance, and before I danced with her, I danced with Michelle Jones."

"Oh." He's kind of got me there. I did overreact. He's staring at me with a raised brow.

"What? You want an apology or something?" I ask.

"That would be a good start." He waits.

"Hmm, not going to happen." Time to change the subject. "How many turns around the floor did it take Josie to pick it up?" I watch Josie take a misstep with Dan.

"About three. Maybe four. Why?"

"I taught the suit over there how in two and now look at him." I nod toward Preston, who is twirling Sarah Grace around. "That's right, sucker. McAllister Magic strikes again. I'm the Ginger Rogers of Central Florida." I beam up at him. Hank laughs and draws me in closer.

"I haven't seen you this happy in a long time. It's nice," he says.

"Don't get a big head. I like to dance."

"How about that apology now?" He's tenacious at best.

"How about you give me one." I turn the tables on him.

"For what?"

"Exactly. Why should I give you an apology?" I duck under his arm as he turns me through the steps.

"Just once it would be nice to hear you say you're sorry." He slides his hand down, resting it in the hollow of my back.

"Never." I step closer.

"We'll see."

We smile at each other and my heart leaps.

Uh-oh.

22

———

I ARRIVE at the Fox and Hound early, head straight to our usual place, and toss my heavy bag full of bachelorette party plans and tentative agendas onto the table. It's an impromptu get-together on a Thursday night, mainly to discuss our plans for Josie.

Jayne's talking on her cell phone. She blushes when she sees me, and I surmise she's talking to Stacy. She insists they're just friends, but I see how they look at each other. She quietly ends the call and flips open the ideas book I've created for Josie's bachelorette party. Dinner service hasn't begun and the place is quiet. I'm nervous about seeing Jake, dread a confrontation, so I naturally avoid looking at the bar. But I know I can't sit with my friends and make chitchat while this hangs over me. Irritated, I pull from that emotion rather than my fear. I remember those feelings of intimidation and powerlessness. It's now or never.

"Paisley—" she starts.

I hold up my hand. "Hold on, there's something I need to do first before I lose my nerve. Do I have any lipstick?" I bare my teeth. If I'm going to do this, I'm at least going to look good doing it.

She shakes her head, looking at me with a wide-eyed gaze, questioning. I take a deep breath, stare at my fingernails, take a second breath, and do a quick scan toward the bar. Part of me hopes he won't be here. When I see him, my heart stutters, races, and I dig what nails I have left into my palms. Jake's back is to me. I'm pretty confident he hasn't seen me come in the door. He's too busy leaning over the bar toward the same blonde he nuzzled on our first date, his hand on her shoulder. She's sitting sideways on the stool and when she laughs, which is frequently, she tosses her hair over her shoulder and leans toward his arm.

It's taken me three days to gather up my courage and proceed with my plan. If my divorce from Trevor and over a year of therapy has taught me anything, it's how well I play the role of victim, how willing I am to be manipulated, even if it's subconscious. I'm not going there anymore. I'm not burying my head like I did with Trevor. Call it naïveté or being foolhardy, it doesn't matter. The fact is I let this fuck stick Jake manipulate me while my intuition was screaming in protest. This is reminiscent of Trevor and that's not OK with me.

I'm different now. At least I hope I am. Or trying to be.

There will be no burying my head this time, no more wishing it away. This one requires confrontation, something I'm not very good at. I used to be. Back when I was a kid, before my dad died.

I vow never to be in this position again. Wouldn't it have been easier to not make a second date with him than to be in this current situation? I suck in a breath, curse my trembling hands, and make my way to the bar. I take a seat behind him, on the other side of the bar. Jake doesn't hear me approach, but he does hear me pull out the bar stool.

"Be with you in a minute," the creep says over his shoulder, not turning my way. He continues to flirt with the blonde, twisting a lock of her hair around his finger like he's done to mine.

Asshole. What's with men? Do they have a list of moves and this is one of them?

I'm infuriated and it helps settle my nerves. Not only has Jake done this move on me, so has Hank. This pisses me off the most. Is it a move, a play? A way to reel women in?

Because that's what twirling a girl's hair does. It makes the girl think the guy is completely into her and is sweet enough to do something as girlie as twirling their hair.

Next time I see Hank Lancaster I'm punching him in the gut. Hard.

From my position at the bar, the breathy sound of their whispers reaches me, but not the words. The blonde gets red-faced and even more flirty. I look back at Jayne and see both Josie and Kenley have arrived and are watching me. I put my finger to my lips.

Jake is slow to move away, letting her hair slip through his fingers. The player Josie was talking about is so obvious now. His moves are smooth and perfect. He flirts like a professional. The blonde gets up and heads toward the restrooms. That's when Jake turns around.

"Paisley. Baby." He glides toward me in the hip-thrusting way gigolos do and leans over to give me a kiss. I turn my head in time for it to land on my left cheek.

"Who's your friend?" I keep my question mild, not that I care. Not that I don't already know. What I'd seen on our first date and today is enough information for me.

Yet, I want to see how he reacts.

"Where? Who?" He gets doe-eyed.

"The girl you were just talking to. I could swear I've seen her before and am trying to place it." I gave him what I hope is a quizzical look, while I tap my left temple as if I'm struggling.

"What girl? I don't know what you are talking about." He attempts what I'm guessing is a quick diversion. "What's the plan for this weekend? You come up with a surprise for me like I asked? Hey, you talked to Josie, right, about the wedding?"

It's pretty astounding, his audacity. I suppose I should introduce this guy to my ex. They seem to have some things in common, one being they think I have the intelligence quotient of a doorknob. Anger takes over. It fuels me.

"There is no plan this weekend, Jake, and your surprise is this: I don't want to see you again and you aren't going to Josie's wedding. Surprise!" I smile and do jazz hands beside my face.

Damn, I should have ordered drinks first. What if he

jacks them up or does something terrible like spitting in them?

Jake's eyes get squinty as he stares at me. He reaches out and grasps both of my upper arms and wrenches me up and against the bar. Only the tips of my toes touch the bar-stool rung.

"I thought I told you I wanted to go to Brinn's wedding." His words are a snarl. He twists his hands, causing my arms to burn.

"I can't imagine why. You don't even know Brinn." I try hard not to flinch, and I curl my left hand into a fist. If I hit upward, my left will have to do the work because he's leaning toward my dominant arm. It's a choice of damage over power should I decide to punch him. He leans in closer.

"Everyone knows Brinn MacRae. I've been trying to get hired on with him for a year now. I want to be in on this company from the start-up. This is my one chance. My last chance." He squeezes harder.

Ahh. Now I know what this is about. I'm such an idiot. I'm a pawn in a game, a way around an obstacle. I want to kick him in the man bits.

"You want to let go of my arms before I clobber you?" I say it as if it's a light request of no consequence, though my heart is racing and nothing about this moment feels remotely light.

"You want to rethink not taking me to this wedding."

Whoa. Did he just threaten me? I jerk my arms up, break free, and slide back onto the stool. My arms burn from his release. I continue to hold his stare, refusing to blink.

"You come near me or my friends again and so help me God—"

"What are you gonna do?" He pulls out a tea towel and begins to wipe down the bar, casual-like.

"I'll turn your nut sack into an evening bag, and I'll take it to Josie's wedding. At least a part of you'll get to go." I don't crack a smile. "Push me. I dare you."

He breaks eye contact first. I slide off the stool and walk away. I want to run to the bathroom and cry. I want to call Hank and have him beat up Jake. I want to kick myself for being stupid. I don't know what I'm going to do if he does push me, but it sounds good. Can you even make a purse from a nut sack?

On wobbly legs, I walk to the table where Kenley, Josie, and Jayne sit waiting, and take a seat facing the bar. I want to see if the guy spits in my drinks. On second thought, I don't think I'll be ordering drinks. Regardless, I'm too afraid to turn my back to him.

"Are you OK? What happened there?" Kenley leans in to ask.

"I had to hold Josie back," Jayne says.

"I think I'm going to be sick." I tell them with a smile, putting on a brave front in case Jake is looking. "He was only going out with me to get to Josie's wedding. It seems he is...desperate to work for Brinn and he thought if he went to the wedding, he would be able to get in." Boy, I could use a drink. My hands tremble. I push them under my legs to steady them and look at Josie.

"Desperate. Ha. He's been trying to buy into the company. Even started some rumor about shoddy work at the hangar and tried to ruin Brinn's reputation. He crashed Brinn's meeting in Ft. Lauderdale last week."

I stare openmouthed at her. Is she, or is she not my friend? "Why didn't you fucking tell me this?"

"Now, Paisley, calm down." Jayne is always the mediator.

"No, I won't calm down." It's difficult keeping my voice very low. "He's crazy and you let me go out with him." Incredible. Well, she can be one bridesmaid short.

"I told you he was crazy right off the bat. I didn't know about this stuff until yesterday when Brinn told me. He wasn't sure it was Jake until he showed up in Ft. Lauderdale. He wouldn't have said anything except he knew I worked with him. When I mentioned you were seeing him, he told me the whole story. I was gonna tell you tonight," she says in one crazy-long breath.

We reach across the table to hold each other's hand.

"I'm sorry, Paisley, had I known sooner, I would've said something. You know I would've, right?" Josie says.

"It's all right. I—"

"Oh, dear. Look at your arms." Jayne covers her mouth with her hands.

Large red welts are rising on my arms. On the back, there are clear finger marks.

"I owe you an apology as well. That...that..." Jayne points to my chest. "Mark he gave you. I thought you gave him permission." She looks horrified. "Oh, Paisley, I'm so very sorry, darling. Now I realize what he was doing. Jake's not only a creep, he's a sexual predator. I have to tell Mum."

Jayne leaves before I'm able to stop her. I explain the

details to Josie and Kenley, and we decide to move our get together to a different place. If I don't leave soon, I may lose my ever-loving mind.

Jayne comes back after a few minutes. "They're going to sack him," she explains. "We should leave."

We gather our stuff and walk out. I don't even look back. I take in a deep breath once we get outside and try to calm myself.

"You know, I have an idea." Josie pulls out her phone and begins to dial. "Listen up, girls. You're going to like this. And if not, too bad. It's my last wish as a single girl."

————

We circle the apartment complex for the third time, and Josie giggles.

"Shhh," Kenley whispers.

"Who's gonna hear us? We're in a car with the windows up," says Jayne. "Move your elbow, Heather, it's in my side."

My three friends sit scrunched in the back of Josie's Porsche. After hearing Josie's plan, we tried to talk her out of it, but she can be quite convincing. The others capitulated. I was the most resistant. I used Heather as an excuse, saying it would be unfair to leave her out so we should scrap the idea. Because stars line up for Josie Woodmere, a few quick phone calls later, Doug is watching Heather's son and Heather is crowded in the back of a Porsche coupe.

"Remind me why we took your car again?" Heather asks.

"These things weren't designed for people to ride in the back." Kenley shifts to allow Heather, who is sitting in the middle on the hump, more room.

"Not three people," Heather says.

"No, it's made for shopping bags. I told you we should have stopped for Brinn's SUV." Josie gives me a pointed look.

"It doesn't matter now, does it? We're here." I point to the row of cars parked in front of the apartment. I was the one who pushed to do this sooner than later. I like to get my purposeful acts of stupidity over early so I can spend the rest of the day beating myself up over it.

"Which one is his car?"

"Kenley, honestly, you don't have to whisper." Jayne sighs.

"The black one is the douche bag's car," Josie chimes in. She circles past it a few times.

His license plate reads NO1BETR. It can't be denied. I'm a dumbass.

I look at my watch and at my girlfriends. We're dressed in black and have dark hats covering our heads. Camouflage paint streaks Josie's face.

Perhaps we're out of our minds. It's way past the witching hour, some of us have drank way too much, thankfully, they're in the backseat, and I've spent an obscene amount of money on toilet paper, shoe polish, eggs, shaving cream, and glitter. The more time passes, the more this idea smells.

Josie eases the car into a spot about a block away and we sit. No one speaks as she turns off the engine.

"Make sure you take your foot off the brake," Kenley whispers.

"Duh," says Josie.

"We stay together, cross the grass patch there in front, and it's the third car on the left," Josie tells us. "Got it?" In a past life I'm guessing she did military ops.

"The jeep?" asks Jayne.

"Your other left, Jayne, the Mercedes," I tell her.

"When can we go?" Heather asks.

"I have to pee." Finally, Kenley uses a normal voice.

"A few more minutes, ladies, and it will be all systems go." Josie reaches across me to pull a Swiss Army knife out of her glove box.

"Judas Priest, Josie, what do you plan to do with that?" I ask.

She shrugs and gives us what I assume is the signal to go. We scramble from the car; some of us fall out. Kenley and I make our way to the hatchback and pull out the supplies. I hand out items to each of my friends and we follow Josie up the side of the parking lot, across the grassy patch, stopping every few cars until we reach the one we want.

Jake's car.

Kenley snags a roll of toilet paper out of my arms and disappears around the side of another car. I'm confused for a moment until the sound of liquid hitting the pavement gives me clarity.

Josie and I grimace. She begins to shake a can of shaving cream and writes something on his windshield. I blush when I read it. We roll, we crack eggs on the car, we glitter, and we spray shaving-cream profanity on the glass before we take a step back to admire our handiwork.

I walk to the back of the car and see Josie squatting by the rear driver side tire, Swiss army knife open and poised to strike.

"Holy shit, Josie!" I cry in my loudest whisper. I reach out and grab her wrist.

"I'm not that mad."

"This isn't for you. This is for Brinn," she whispers.

"Look, I know you're upset, too, but this moves into serious vandalism. Don't stoop to his level."

I let go and walk away. She folds up the knife with a *click* and picks up her shaving-cream can. She walks to the windshield and places a Ziploc bag with a white note inside under the wiper blade.

"What's in there?" I ask.

"Insurance," she says.

"Insurance?"

"So there's no retaliation." Her face is deadpan.

Somewhere in the distance, a door to an apartment opens and five girls go running for their lives.

I jump over Kenley's puddle of pee, and Heather runs through it with a cry of disgust. Josie slides across the grass, wet with dew, and still beats us to the car. It's a free for all as Heather, Jayne, and Kenley fight each other to be the first to get in. I jump in through the hatch we left open and hold it down but not latched. Josie pulls away, with the lights off I hope, as I pray we get away.

Josie pulls into a parking lot about a mile away, I let go of the hatch when she says my name and jump out of the back, run to the passenger door, and squish up front with

Jayne. We're about five miles away when someone starts laughing.

"It smells like piss in here," says Kenley.

"You couldn't have gone around the building," Heather cries in disgust.

More laughter fills the car, the tension breaks, and someone questions Josie on her colorful language.

23

I SIT BACK in my beach chair and readjust my umbrella so only odd angles of my body catch the occasional ray. I enjoy the beach. I like to swim. I don't like sunburns and freckling, a common downside for redheads like me.

"This bachelorette party rocks." Kenley runs up from the beach and flops onto a lounge chair, seawater glistening off her dark skin, sand clinging to her feet and calves.

"Great idea, Paisley," Heather mumbles. She sounds half-asleep, lying there on her stomach, absorbing sun.

"It was a collective effort between Jayne and I. Plus, I wanted to make sure we don't run into Brinn and his buddies who, I'm told, are staying in Daytona. Welcome to Fernandina Beach." I spread out my arms and smile at my friends.

"You are aware I specifically said no strippers, so the most excitement this event will get is if one of you gets drunk," says Josie.

Everyone boos her choice of limiting our debauchery, but I'm relieved. I think most of us are, yet pretend otherwise.

We're a pretty tame group. Besides the usual suspects, we've added her boss and my divorce attorney, Samantha King, and Gigi. Gigi came up late last night and stayed with me.

The plan is to enjoy the sun, have a nice dinner, and hit the town for some pub fun. I scan the faces of the people walking the beach and sunbathing, looking for Hank. I know he lives nearby, and it would be pure coincidence to see him here, yet I keep scanning. I don't even know if he's in town.

"Hey, Gigi, we aren't going to run into Hank here are we? Isn't he out of town?" I want to punch myself in the face for asking. It's been a week since the Swan Ball. And we've texted twice.

"No, I believe he got back the other night." She sips an iced tea. It's odd she's not drinking. Being away from John and Pete, isn't this the prime opportunity to do so?

"How's John?" I always inquire about Pete, never about her husband.

She continues to read her book as she answers me. "Fine. Hates his job but is a workaholic like my father. What did I expect? They say women marry their fathers, and I'm living proof of that."

I'm glad she isn't looking at me because I'm pretty sure disbelief shows on my face. John is nothing like her father. Poppy is warm and affectionate to his children and his wife. He's a dedicated family man who'd rather spend time with his kids than time at work. I'm having a hard time seeing him as a workaholic. John is a quiet man who appears to be irritated by the slightest thing. I can't recall a time I've seen him do activities with his son, and I always seem to interrupt a fight between he and Gigi.

"You said John is keeping Pete this weekend?" I ask.

"Yeah, he took some vacation time and is taking Pete camping." This time she does look at me and laughs, pointing at my face.

"Really?"

"Yes, really."

"Do you think it will go over well?"

"Yeah. Why? They camp out all the time." She turns back to her book.

I must have sat gape-mouthed for some time. My conversation with Hank is a resounding reminder that I may not know John at all and if I want to change my strong opinion of him, I should probably base it on fact not just experience. But my experience shouldn't be discounted.

Of course, to Gigi and Hank, things seem normal because they are too close, unable to gain perspective. Though close to the entire family, I'm able to observe Gigi's relationship with a divorced eye and know when something is wrong. Lord knows, I love her like a sister, but something in her relationship is rotten for sure and denial is going to get her nowhere. Just like it got me.

As for her remark about how women marry men like their fathers. I'm an exception to the rule. Large, intimidating Scotsmen are hard to find in Florida. Trevor was nothing like my father. He was wiry and secretive; my father had been broad and warm and open. I run through a mental list of men I know and come up with no one remotely similar to my dad. Men like him and Poppy aren't made anymore. OK, Hank is sort of like my dad. He's funny and serious, warm and smart. He's dependable like my dad. He's trustworthy.

I shrug to no one as my thoughts run wild. OK, the sex with Hank isn't boring, or the conversation, but if I was in the market for a relationship, Hank still wouldn't be a candidate. He'd never be around, moves every few years, and he's my friend. Because of Hank, I'm going to be more prepared and observant so next time I will choose wisely.

He's shown me a new standard for which to measure men and that it's not overreaching.

I look at the other girls, spread out alongside me on the beach. Heather is the only one looking up at me.

"Was Trevor like your father?" she asks.

"Nope. Is Justin like yours?" It will be interesting to do a poll among our group.

Heather looks over at Kenley, who isn't making eye contact with anyone. She's squishing her toes in and out of the sand and staring at the pattern. Heather looks at me and nods her head.

"Justin is just like my dad. Of course, my dad mellowed more with age and became more of a family man after us kids moved out." She turns to look at Kenley again and it prompts me to ask.

"How 'bout you, Kenley?" Since Heather's dad is Kenley's father-in-law and if women married men like their fathers, was the same true for men growing up to be like their fathers? I wouldn't have guessed Heather's dad was anything other than superb.

The gang is perking up and joining the conversation. We wait for Kenley to answer. Finally, still staring at her toes, she shakes her head and looks over at Heather.

"No, but he wants to be like my father."

"Ha. Please tell me you aren't trying to change him," Josie says. "We know that's an effort in futility."

Kenley shakes her head. "What I mean is Doug was raised by an absent father." She reaches out and takes Heather's hand. "He wants to be more like my father. He has the potential, something I've seen since the beginning."

I know they're still struggling with the fertility issues and it does seem as if Doug is coping better. He's the reason Heather can be here this weekend. He's keeping her son, with the occasional help from their mother.

"How about you, Josie; Brinn like your dad?" Heather asks.

"In some ways, I guess. I like to think Brinn has the positive traits of my father and none of the bad. More important, I hope I'm nothing like my mother."

"Whoa. Stop there, you're starting a whole separate conversation," Samantha calls out.

"I think I'd need my shrink if we go there." Kenley laughs.

"I'd consider myself lucky to find a man like my father. He's lovely and treats my mum wonderfully." Jayne sighs.

"Is Hank like your father, Paisley?" Heather asks. All eyes swivel to me.

As soon as it's out, I feel rather than see Gigi sit up straight and I give Heather a large-eyed look of warning.

"My Hank?" Gigi asks.

My smile quivers, and I shrug my shoulder. "Maybe," I squeak.

Everyone is watching us. Heather's hands are clasped over her mouth.

"What's going on with you and my brother?" Gigi leans in toward me. There is no telling which way her emotions are swinging.

"Nothing much." I strain to smile wider.

Josie snorts. Gigi looks from Josie to me.

"Nothing but hot sex," Jayne chimes in with her two cents.

I groan and close my eyes, as a wave of nausea hits me. I've been dreading this moment.

"I can't believe you didn't tell her," Josie says, sotto voce.

"You slept with my brother? Were you drunk or something?" Gigi's voice starts to climb.

"Yep," says Josie

"Just the first time," I say to Josie with attitude.

"There was more than one time?" Gigi chokes.

"*He* was drunk the second time. Hmm, Paisley. Have you two ever had sex without drinking?" Josie is smug.

"For your information, we actually *have* had sex without any alcohol being involved whatsoever." I lean back against my chair and cross my arms. Ha! Put that in your pipe and smoke it.

I realize what I've said and glance at Gigi, who is staring at me openmouthed.

The others are snickering.

"You've slept with my brother repeatedly?" she asks. Her voice is low, quiet.

I gulp and nod. "I wouldn't say repeatedly, I mean we...uh... Please don't be mad."

"I'm not mad because you and Hank have been playing house. I'm mad because you haven't told me. When did this start?"

I blow out a puff of air. "Right after you canceled going to the surf competition." She pauses three beats. Is she lining up the events, figuring out the timeline?

"Oh my God! You mean to tell me the day you came to my house and turned redder than a beet when I asked who you were sleeping with, it was my brother?"

I nod.

"Why didn't you tell me?" Her brow is pulled in, her nose scrunched up, and the hurt I've caused is reflected in her eyes.

"I was afraid you would think I crossed some line. I never intended for it to happen—"

"Or continue to happen," Kenley says.

"Shut up." I point to Kenley but keep looking at Gigi. "I'm sorry I didn't tell you. We aren't serious or anything. Please don't be mad." It's like bailing water out of a sinking boat.

Everyone is quiet, and I bite my thumbnail, waiting for Gigi's next move. She stares at me for what feels like an eternity, and I know she's processing it.

"That's too bad, Paisley, because I can't think of a better person for you than my brother. You already fit into my family, and I'd love to have you for a sister." Gigi reopens her book and leans back.

"Now wait a minute," I say. "Let's don't take it too far. I don't think Hank is looking for a girlfriend. I know I'm not looking for a boyfriend, and it wouldn't work out between us because he's kind of been my rebound guy."

"Stupid, isn't she?" Josie asks.

There's a round of agreements before Jayne starts filling Gigi in on Jake, the parts I conveniently forgot, and she shoots me a look of disappointment.

"Have you not learned anything? You should snap up my brother and run." She looks back at her book, irritated.

"What exactly do you mean? I've just begun dating again and yes, some have been epic fails. Would it be fair to start a relationship with Hank because we have a good time together and are comfortable with each other?" I shake my head. It's a sound argument.

"That's why people start relationships. Some even start them on less," says Jayne.

"And Hank's got even more going for him. He's trust-worthy and honest," says Gigi.

"Not a shitbag. A good dancer, and sexy as hell," finishes Josie.

"Hell, I'll take him." Heather raises her hand.

"Don't hurt Hank, Paisley," Gigi whispers. "That's when this will have gone too far."

"As if I could, honey. Trust me. Hank has no more interest in me than I do him."

I reach out to hug her and am relieved when she returns it. It's good to know she doesn't hate me.

<h1 style="text-align:center">24</h1>

I WAKE UP, mouth dry and feeling heavy as if I'm covered with a weighted blanket. It's hard to lift my head from the pillow. My brain feels as if it's pressing against my skull, desperate to be free. Any sudden movement and I may spontaneously explode. At the pace of a turtle, slower than a sloth, I roll onto my back and crack open one eye.

The annoying streams of sunlight invading my hotel room make me wince in pain and close my eye. Do Gigi and the others feel as bad as I do? I reach blindly for the night table and pat it, searching for my glasses. I ease them on and open my eyes one at a time to scan the room. The drapes to the balcony are open and Gigi's sitting out on there, enjoying the sun. She's drinking something, hopefully the magic elixir for this hangover. I would give up my nana for the pain to go away. I roll out of bed and ease my way to the sliding door.

"Is there anything medicinal in that drink for me?" My voice is husky, too much hollering the night before.

"Straight up coffee." She smiles. "I ordered you some breakfast and a gallon of coffee."

I move out onto the patio and recoil in horror at the bright light, hissing as it burns my eyes. I glare at Gigi, who is laughing.

"Why are you so perky?" I snarl.

"Maybe you shouldn't have drank so much." She hands me a mug of coffee and the vapors boost me up, a bit. With deliberate steps, I ease into a chair. Gigi's sunglasses are lying on the table and I put them on over my glasses to help cut the glare.

"And has your tolerance gotten so high those drinks didn't affect you?" This is my friend who laces her iced tea with whiskey.

"I had one drink." She lathers cream cheese on a bagel.

The thought of a dairy product makes me gag. "What? You lie. You had just as many drinks as I did." I tear a bagel into quarters and toss one piece in my mouth.

"Nope, only one drink and I switched to club soda. Our dancing made me thirsty." She wrinkles her nose at me with her silent "so there."

I try to wrap my mind around what she says, but I'm still a tad drunk, thereby making cohesive thought difficult.

"Huh?"

Gigi laughs again. "It's not like I'm a lush." She hands me an orange and I peel it, breaking off the skin bit by bit. Nothing is making sense anymore. Isn't she a lush?

Doesn't she drink because of her horrible marriage?

"You pour Jack Daniels in your tea at home." Gigi burst out laughing and I wince at the noise.

"It was sweet tea. Pete's pre-K teacher thinks he has ADHD, and, before we hop him up on drugs, we're changing his diet to see if it makes any difference. One of the things we've cut is sugar drinks, including tea. As his role models, we've cut sugar out of our diet too. Though sometimes I sweeten mine when he's not around. I hide it in the Jack bottle." She shrugs.

My mind cycles back through the other things I've witnessed and possibly misinterpreted. I'm about to ask more questions when she sobers me up in instant.

"I called Hank and I thought we could swing by before heading back to Daytona."

I drop the orange on the table, where it bounces and lands on the floor. I grab at it, the sudden movement causes my stomach to turn. I pause mid-position and rest my head on my knee.

"Does he know I'm coming?" I mumbled from below the table. Last time I saw Hank was at the Swan Ball, where I purposefully stepped on his feet when we were dancing and denied him an apology for my jealous snit.

"He knows we're together. Is there some problem?"

I grab the orange from the patio floor, dust it off on my shorts, sit up, and finish peeling it.

"Nope. No problem." I shove orange pieces into my mouth, avoiding her stare.

We take our time with breakfast, and I take a long shower before we check out of the hotel and head to Hank's. The others are still sleeping in or have already left for home. Gigi drives since I'm still loopy.

Turns out Hank lives close to our weekend party haven, in a nice neighborhood with large trees covered in Spanish moss. The houses are older but updated, and many are on the water. Old-fashioned street lamps line landscaped sidewalks, and a park sits in the middle of the neighborhood.

Gigi pulls up to a small ranch on the water. Hank's truck is parked in the driveway. I'm assuming his motorcycle is tucked in the one-car garage.

We get out, and I let Gigi lead the way. I'm nervous and jittery. I wish I could blame it on last night's booze but it's because something has changed between us. What does he think about my jealously toward Melinda? Will it be awkward with the three of us being in the same room and Gigi knowing about our sexcapades?

Gigi rings the doorbell several times in succession as she smiles at me. I smile back and, if possible, feel more self-conscious because she won't stop smiling or ringing the bell.

Hank jerks open the door. "Knock it off, Gigi. One time will suffice. Leave your shoes at the door." He points to a mat just inside the door and walks away, the door left open.

We kick off our flip-flops and pad our way into the cozy living room.

I admit to having preconceived ideas about men and their bachelor pads. I guess Trevor set the standard since I conjure up visions of his college place and prepare to compare it with Hank's.

Hank's place is a complete surprise. Instead of concrete blocks or bricks and boards holding up his television, Hank's is encased in distressed armoire. An over-stuffed couch and chair are centered around a fireplace and the armoire.

Signs of his travels are scattered throughout. I stare at two identically framed cartouches, hand painted on old yellowing papyrus paper, as Gigi flops onto the couch and begins to pester her brother for a drink.

"What's this say?" I stare at the beautiful hand drawn symbols.

He stops midway to the kitchen. "The one on the right is my last name, and the other is my first name."

I step further into his living room to see other pieces of art on his walls. The collection is breathtaking. In addition to the Arabian art are oil paintings of Italian villages and watercolors of French bistros. An Egyptian camel saddle sits next to a Japanese apothecary cabinet, standing close to four feet high.

Seeing the proof of his travels sends a thrill of excitement and fear through me.

There are so many places I've never seen, my travel experience being limited to the United Kingdom and back. Real croissants in Paris? The Coliseum in Rome? Exciting until I think of leaving my family behind. Not watching the twins grow up would make me sick to my stomach.

"Have you been to all these places?" I ask.

"Yeah," he mumbles as he hands me a glass of iced tea before shuffling away.

"He has more Japanese stuff in his bedroom. You should go see it," Gigi says.

For a man, Hank has extraordinary taste. Yeah, he has

stacks of DVDs along a wall and serves my tea in a beer mug, but overall, I admit I'm impressed, right down to the Persian rug gracing his living room floor.

I want to sit but Gigi's sprawled on the couch, leaving the love seat to Hank and me. I go to the couch anyway. She tries to put up a fight but I sit, forcing her to scoot down before I plant my butt on her head.

"Your place looks great, Hank. I would love to see the places you've seen." I smile and take a drink.

He doesn't acknowledge my words with anything but a nod and a yawn. He looks tired. He's dressed in navy shorts and a yellow T-shirt emblazoned with the US Navy logo. His hair is tousled, and it's longer than normal. He has dark circles under his eyes and at least two days' worth of beard on his face. Gigi kicks him, and they give each other a brief look.

"Sorry, Paisley, I'm just tired and jet-lagged."

"That's OK. Where'd you go?" A basket sits next to the couch, stacked with magazines. I sort through several *National Geographics*, *Smithsonians*, and a variety of foreign ones with their native script scrawled on their covers.

"We went to the Middle East."

His words catch my attention and I swing my gaze to him. Middle East? Where there's currently a war? It makes sense with him being in the Navy, but I never put the two together.

"Is it safe?" I look between the siblings. It's a stupid question but it comes out anyway. Hank shrugs.

Knowing I'm not going to get a further response, I flip back to the magazines and pull out one written in what I assume is Arabic.

"I thought you took Spanish in high school." I hold up the magazine. "Can you read this?"

"Sure. You learn one language, you can learn another." He offers nothing more, and instead stares at me as he takes a drink.

"What's going on here?" asks Gigi.

She's referring to the silent dance we've been doing, me avoiding anything with substance and Hank refusing to engage in conversation until I ante up.

"Paisley owes me something," he tells her without breaking eye contact with me. His lips twitch and he gives me a bawdy wink. I try to suppress a laugh but holding it in makes me it come out in an unflattering way and Hank's smile gets larger.

"Come on, you can do it," he says.

An apology? Over Melinda Bane. Not going to happen. Never, never, never will I apologize to Hank Lancaster.

We continue to stare at each other, our version of a Mexican standoff. I don't even think he's blinked.

"All right. I'm sorry." I fling a magazine at him and we laugh.

"Was that so hard?" He catches the slippery volume with one hand and quickly drops it. He reaches across his sister and pulls me off the couch and into a one-armed half hug. He tucks me into the crook of his arm, trapping me in a headlock, and proceeds to briskly rub his knuckles across my scalp giving me the first noogie I've had in several years.

"Stop it." I push against him trying to break free. "Gigi, help."

"Oh, no. You're on your own." She's still lying on the couch.

Hank lets me go and walks away laughing, leaving me half on the love seat.

"You're a jackass." I yell as he walks into the kitchen. I pat down my hair then reach for another magazine. This time I pick up *Am Bràighe*, a magazine for Scots with pages of Gaelic words. I look at Hank, puzzled. He's leaning against the wall drinking a beer.

"Can you read this?" I ask snottily. Even raised in a house where it was frequently spoken, I'd stumble over some of the passages.

He shrugs and looks smug.

"How many languages do you speak?" I narrow my gaze. In high school he took Spanish and Latin.

"Lots," Gigi says. "Hank minored in foreign language." Her smile is proud, his shrug casual.

I fling *Am Bràighe* at him when he starts to laugh. I hate them both.

"When did this happen? All you ever talked about was the Academy. Besides I thought you were an intelligence officer?" Not a linguist, and I'm pretty confident there is a difference between the two.

He takes a slow drink of his beer before he answers, "Once you learn one romantic language, it's easy to learn the others. At the Academy, I found I had a natural aptitude for languages so I studied others there. It's not a job requirement, but it's come in handy on the rare occasion. It makes me marketable after I'm done with the Navy."

I roll my eyes, Hank and his ten-year plans. He's always thinking ahead. There is no doubt, I'm impressed.

To learn more than one language is amazing. I grew up in a home where Gaelic was spoken frequently, yet I only speak broken phrases and read it slightly better. I could never take on a third language, much less several.

"Hmm," is my lame response and I excuse myself to the restroom. When I come out, Gigi's left for a walk along the water. Alone with Hank, I'm instantly nervous.

"Gigi knows," I tell him.

Hank is lying across the love seat, flipping through the TV channels. I thumb through the magazines again and bite my lower lip to keep it from trembling. This awkwardness is a new experience for me.

"And yet you are still alive." He pauses on a sports channel.

"OK, you're right. Gigi did not find it to be such a big deal," I say.

"I'm sorry. What did you say? I didn't quite hear you." He smirks.

I stick out my tongue and blow a raspberry.

"Admit it. You were jealous," he says.

"What are you talking about?"

"Me dancing with Melinda." He stretches and looks over at me.

"This again? Don't start with me, Hank."

"Yup, jealous." He's so smug.

"Oh, brother. Could I *please* get some more tea?" I hold up my empty glass and give it a slight shake for emphasis. I'm not going down this road. He frowns at me and points to the kitchen.

"Help yourself. It's in the pitcher."

I make my way to the kitchen and jerk open the fridge.

A giant bottle of hot sauce comes flying out and shatters on the kitchen floor.

Instantly, Hank is at the kitchen entryway, "Don't move, babe. There's glass everywhere." He points to my bare feet.

He leaves and comes back wearing flip-flops. He steps his way into the kitchen and scoops me up in his arms.

"Did you step on any glass?" He carries me away from the shards.

"Nope."

It's hard to think, being this snug against him. Up close, his facial stubble looks longer and his dark circles even darker. He doesn't smell like cologne, and I realize his natural scent, a combination of soap and deodorant, is very intoxicating and much more pleasing than some cologne. I gulp, overwhelmed by a wave of such strong sexual desire, it makes me dizzy.

"I can help clean up." My voice is hoarse. Hank stops at the sofa and leans in.

Please let him kiss me, I pray. All I need is to kiss him. I know it's the surefire answer to curing my hangover, bad mood, and sudden wave of need. We seem suspended in time as I wait for him to make up his mind.

Guess it isn't my lucky day because one moment I'm flying through the air and the next I'm bouncing on the sofa. Hank's back is facing me as he heads to the mess.

I lie there to catch my breath and gather my bearings. Why am I such a sucker for him? I push off his couch, retrieve my flip-flops, and head back to the kitchen to help clean up. Hank is scooping up the glass, and I reach under the sink to pull out a kitchen cleaner and sponge and begin cleaning up the splatter.

"Sorry about the mess," I say.

"It's all right. When I put it in there, I knew I was asking for trouble, but was too tired to care." He watches me bend down to wipe up the floor and waits for me to hand him the sponge to rinse out.

"Good. I don't feel so bad then." I smile at him.

It's up to Hank to break the tension between us. The proverbial ball is in his court.

"What are you doing next weekend?" He hands me the sponge.

"Josie's getting married up at Amelia Island. You remember her?"

"Yeah, she's real mouthy and chatty."

"That's our Josie. What do you mean by chatty?"

"Nothing. Just said some interesting things when we were dancing. She seems real nice."

I give the cabinets one last wipe and hand the sponge back to be rinsed. My mind races at the possibilities of what Josie could have said to him. We finish cleaning the mess and Hank steps around me, heading toward his bedroom.

"Like what?" I follow him.

He turns and is about to say something, struggling with either the words or his thoughts. His face reflects a mélange of emotions and settles on one that looks a lot like exasperation.

"Nothing important."

I search his face. "I was wondering if you wanted to go with me to her wedding."

"What about the guy at your apartment? You aren't taking him?"

"No." I shake my head and sit on the edge of the bed. I'm pretty sure trashing a guy's car wipes out any chance of reconciliation. Not that I'm interested.

"I think she would be disappointed if you didn't come." I tell him. "I'm not trying to pressure you, but you're welcome to come."

Taking Hank has its perks. He's a great dancer and fun to boot. I know I'll enjoy his company. I don't want to go alone, especially since Jayne is going with Stacy, but if Hank's going to be this moody, I'm not sure I want to spend the whole weekend with him either.

"Are you asking me because your friend wants me to come, because you want me to, or you don't want to go alone?"

"Oh for Pete's sake. Don't come, jeez." I throw up my hands in frustration. "I asked because I thought you might like to come. I know we'd have a good time and you look worn-out. I thought a weekend at the beach relaxing might be the thing you need."

"I'm not trying to be difficult. I'm trying to make sure I understand what page we're on. I'd love to go to the wedding, but I want to know what the expectations will be."

Should there be any expectations? Wasn't that part of the no-strings deal? "Why don't we agree to have no expectations so no one can misconstrue anything."

"And if we have sex?"

I sigh with exasperation. "Why is this so difficult? Isn't

this exactly what you had in mind when you came up with your grand idea?"

A beat passes before he responds, "You're right. Sounds fine with me. No expectations."

Gigi calls to us from the living room, "I'm back."

"We're in the bedroom," I say.

"Can I come in? Is everyone decent?" She stands outside the doorway with her hands over her eyes.

"Yes." I sigh.

"Gee, too bad." She joins me on the bed. "Who's hungry for lunch?"

"I might be." I hold up my hand as my stomach loops over, though I'm not sure if it's because I'm hungry or still nauseated from last night.

"If you're treating, I'm hungry," Hank tells Gigi.

We agree on a restaurant and head out. Hank takes his motorcycle. I want to ask if I can ride with him but I hesitate, something I normally wouldn't do. It feels strange, everyone knowing we've slept together. As if they'll be watching our every move, speculating.

The lunch together isn't too awkward, when I don't think about Hank's hands on my body, which happens about two seconds out of every minute. Or try to make small talk with Gigi while refraining from leaping across the table and throwing myself at Hank. Instead, I'm trying to chew my nails but each time I bring my hand up, one of them looks at me as if they can read my mind.

It's a huge relief to head back to Daytona. Of course, once I send Gigi on her way home, with a large cup of iced tea and trail mix to snack on during the ride, I flop onto my couch and stare at my cell phone, my finger hovering over the message icon. I don't feel like things are settled between us. Plus, I want to see him.

Oh, what the hell.

I text him and use an emoticon, because who can resist? *Hi:-)*

Hi

Apparently Hank can. Such a buzz kill. I hesitate, second-guessing my next move.

It was nice seeing u. What r u doing?

Nothing. U?

Ack. This is painful. What was I thinking? *Same. Gigi's gone*

I told you she'd be cool

She wasn't 100% cool

She didn't kick your ass either

I want to point out that I was right, sorta, about his sister's reaction. She wasn't as pleased as he said she would be. *She threatened to*

LOL That's all he can say. Laugh out loud? This requires an exclamation point, or two. *Seriously!!*

She's posturing

OK, deep breath. Now for the real reason. Here goes nothing. *What r u doing for dinner?*

Dunno. Have no food here. Guess takeout

I have tons here. Plus great take out places

Good for you

If I could reach through this phone and shove him I would. *Don't be obtuse*

Was that an invitation? BC if it was it sucked

Ahh! This man is making me crazy. OK, another deep breath. *Oh all right. Wanna come here for dinner?*

I have to close my eyes and wait for the phone to vibrate, finding it unbearable to watch the screen and wait for his reply. When the phone finally hums in my hand, I swallow the lump in my throat and open my eyes.

It sounds like fun—long drive tho—Meet halfway?

I type quickly so as to not chicken out. *Or you could just bring an overnight bag*

I'm leaving here in 10

25

THE MOMENT IS PERFECT. It's been years since I've felt this at ease or right with the world. When he arrives, dressed in jeans and a leather jacket, having come on his motorcycle, I jump into his arms. We start at the front door, leaving a trail of clothes to the bedroom. Whatever awkwardness was between us is gone. Hopefully forgotten.

"I'm famished. Want to order delivery? We should get something now before it gets too late." He rolls toward me smiling, picks up a curl, and brushes it against my shoulder.

"Why do you do that?" I ask. Unfortunately, the move reminds me of Jake and I'm not interested in any reminders.

"What? Play with your hair?" He continues when I nod. "Your hair's been long since I can remember. Though it's either whipping me in the face or stuck to your face. I guess I like to touch it."

I raise up and press a light kiss to his lips. History. We have history. It warms me from within.

"Delivery sounds great. How about Thai food?" I roll toward the night table where I keep my iPad and reach to open the drawer. Hank grabs my arm before I realize what I've done.

"What's this on your arm?" His voice is quiet.

I look at the back of my arm and the fingerprint bruises are clear. Hank moves my pillow to look at my other arm, finding the other set of bruises. I roll back toward him, iPad forgotten.

"It's nothing."

"It doesn't look like nothing. Who grabbed you and why?"

He sets his jaw, his lips thin creases, his brow narrow. This is not a conversation he can be distracted from. I consider making something up, but Hank knows me too well and can sniff out a lie in an instant.

I go with honesty. "Remember the guy who was here the day you showed up, said he was my boyfriend?" I pull the sheet up, covering my chest, and tuck it under my arms before I continue. "It turns out he was interested in me so he could get to Josie's fiancé, Brinn. When I told him I wasn't going to see him anymore and he wasn't coming to the wedding with me, he got upset."

Hank takes one arm and lifts it up to look at the bruises and places his hand over the imprints. His hand assumes Jake's position.

"He grabbed your arms and what else?" He gently puts my arm down and moves to sit on the edge of the bed.

"Nothing else. Said some hateful things and that's it." I reach for him but he gets up and pulls on his jeans.

"Holy shit, Paisley." He jerks on his shirt and stands, clenching and unclenching his fist. "What is wrong with you?"

"Me?"

He gestures to my arms.

"I don't understand? I'm not still going out with him."

"Oh yeah? After how many dates did you decide not to see him again? Because I can pretty much guaran-damn-tee he gave you warning signs on date number one and you still went out with him again. Probably two or three more times. To think he was inside your place while I stood outside and I left you alone with him. And you knew he was capable of this—"

"I didn't know."

It's a halfhearted argument. He's right. I ignored my instinct throughout the whole ordeal. I follow him out of bed, throwing on a pair of shorts and a T-shirt.

"Bullshit. You knew. Deep down, you knew." He stops to pinch the bridge of his nose, as if it helps with regaining composure. "I never imagined your self-esteem was this low, Paisley."

"There is nothing wrong with my self-esteem," I shout, more embarrassed, less indignant.

"Is that so?" He stares at me and it's the first time he's looked at me with pity.

"I can't do this anymore," he says matter-of-factly, shaking his head.

I step back and sink onto my bed. "I knew doing this

would ruin everything. I knew it." It takes everything I have not to say I told you so, not to cry.

He shakes his head, grabs his backpack, and starts throwing his stuff into it.

"That's not what I'm talking about."

"I don't understand...."

He rubs his hand across his brow and shakes his head. "I've known you my entire life, and I'm pretty sure I've loved you just as long. Remember when you punched Michael Walters in the nose for calling Sarah Grace a bitch, you were ten years old maybe? I watched you ball up your fist and slug him. Watching you do that, I knew for sure. Do you remember?"

I nod. "Sure, but what—"

"Hear me out. You've always been sassy and courageous. So sure of yourself and determined. You're not that person anymore. This person now, I'm not sure I like. Yeah, when we're together I see glimpses of the girl I fell for as a boy and it gives me hope she's still in there. But this wishy-washy person, who can't make a decision, can't...won't...know her own mind, infuriates me."

"Apparently I don't infuriate you enough because you still slept with me every chance you got," I say.

He stops and looks at me and shakes his head, "I've waited a lifetime for you, and yeah, I slept with you whenever I could. Because I want to be with you. Because I thought if we slept together, you would see me as someone other than Gigi's brother or your friend. I thought you'd see how great things are when we're together and want it too." He looks away.

"Hank, I'm still trying to find my way since my divorce."

"Bullshit." He points at me. "You can use your divorce as an excuse for only so long. You know, it amazes me. You can marry the wrong person, go through what he put you through, and come out the other side weaker than when you went in."

It's a slap on the face. "You know nothing about being divorced. Nothing," I scream. "You know nothing about me." Tears run down my face.

He stops and looks at me; his pack falls to the ground. "You're right. I don't know you, or should I say this version of you, at all. The girl I know is lost. I guess you have been for some time. Maybe it started when your dad died. Maybe not. I guess it doesn't matter because the point is you've lost a part of you. The best part of you. The girl I know would've never let some jackass grab her. She would've never let it go too far. Not after everything she'd been through, but then the girl I know would have never let her sister punch her cheating ex-husband in the face either. She'd have done it herself."

The disappointment that crosses his face guts me. I know he doesn't see the person I think I am.

"I've always been there for you, Paisley. Ready to bail you out, ready to be your hero, but I won't be there anymore. I can't do *this* anymore."

"I never asked you to be my hero." My temper boils.

"No, you didn't. But you sure came running every time you needed one."

"Not true." I point my finger at him.

"'Hank, I have a flat. Hank, I don't want to go to this

party alone,'" he mimics. "'Hank, Austin dumped me before prom and I don't have a date. Hank, my friend's husband is an asshole, so aren't all men? Hank, come to my friend's wedding so I won't be alone.'"

"You asshole." I grab some of his stuff and throw it at him, tears blurring my vision. "I thought you were my friend and I asked you to come to this wedding because I wanted your company not because I don't want to be alone."

"Right. Good old Hank the friend. Remember my senior year when we were both single at the same time?" He doesn't wait for a response. "We hung out and walked the lake, ate ice cream, and had a good time. You asked me why I broke up with what's her face and I told you some stupid line. The truth is I broke up with her because you were suddenly single and I was leaving for the Academy in the fall. I thought maybe we could start something, maybe you'd finally see me as something other than a friend. But you've got it all wrong. I'm not an asshole, I'm a chump."

My knees are shaking as my mind races. I'm trying to process what he's saying but can't seem to focus. I only see the anger and disappointment etched on his face. His words flash through my mind, bring snapshots of our past, my past. He's walking around my apartment, making sure he has everything. When he does a complete lap, he turns to me.

"I don't want to be your friend anymore. Everything I did for you I did because I love you. Correction. I love the girl you used to be. I want to be with her more than anything in the world. When I found out you were getting divorced, I couldn't get back to the states fast enough. Hell, I even had orders to Norfolk, Virginia and changed them to be closer to you. I just wanted a shot to see if we could make something of it. Something good, true, and lasting. But this girl"—he points to me—"she's a coward, and I don't have the stomach for cowards, nor the time. I'm all done." He swings his bag over his shoulder, grabs his helmet, and walks out.

How I manage to walk on such wobbly legs I'll never know. I make my way to the window, watch him get on his motorcycle, and ride away, never once looking back.

It's not until the night gives way to morning that I turn away and go back inside.

26

"COME ON, Paisley. Help me impress Jayne with my Fred Astaire moves." Stacy holds his arms out and does a dance move with an imaginary partner. He nods toward the dance floor where a large portion of the guests at Brinn and Josie's wedding are twirling around to the ten-piece orchestra's big-band music.

I smile up at him. "It's OK, Stacy, I know the guys are taking turns dancing with me because I have no date. But there are plenty of single men here, and I can't meet even one with you all hovering." Not that I'm trying. I put my glass under the champagne fountain and watch the bubbles collide.

"Come on, help a guy out. I've got to show her I've got something going for me other than mad counting skills. She keeps giving me the old let's-just-be-friends line." He gives me such a look of earnest. It's too bad Jayne is overly cautious about getting involved with someone who has a kid because it's obvious they like each other,

"Oh, all right, but if I know Jayne, and I do, it's not going to help. She's nothing if not stubborn." I put my glass to the side and let him guide me to the dance floor, where we make it through a fast dance without anyone getting hurt.

"It's only six steps. I can count that high." He smiles and guides me back to our table.

By ours, I mean the same table where Gigi and John, Jayne and Stacy, Kenley and Doug, Samantha and her husband Mike, and Heather and I are sitting. I'm trying really hard not to be a wet blanket. It's hard enough being at a wedding surrounded by so much love and happiness, so foreign from my own experience. I plop into my seat next to Gigi.

"Can I drink this champagne?" I reach for the glass.

"Please do."

Her hand is on John's leg and he's entwined his fingers with hers. He's been smiling and laughing all night and he and Stacy have struck up a friendship.

"Can I ask you something?" I put down the glass and lean in to make it a more private conversation.

"Sure." She leans toward me.

"I may have the wrong impression of John. I mean, I haven't spent any time with the two of you together in years and I was wondering, um... Are you happy?" I whisper it.

She nods and smiles at me. "We've had our rough periods, in fact, we are coming out of one now. But even our rough periods are still pretty good. Our issues are more about external stresses like Pete's teacher and her concern about his attention or John's job."

The moment hangs there as I gain a new perspective on those memories, finally seeing the other side.

She continues, "Remember Poppy's party? When you showed up and Pete said John and I were inside wrestling?"

I nod and remember how disheveled and scattered she looked.

"A couple weeks prior, Pete walked in on us...you know...and asked what we were doing. We told him we were wrestling. The day of my dad's party, John and I were trying to get in a quick 'wrestle,' if you know what I mean, and John told Pete to go outside and play so we could wrestle." Her face turns red.

"He's always been so...grouchy." It's the mildest of words I can come up with.

Gigi laughs. "I know, mainly because of his job."

I know John works for the FBI, but I'm not sure what he does. I was told a long time ago, but couldn't remember, so I ask.

"Until a few days ago he was assigned to investigate pedophiles. He just got transferred to financial crimes. It's going to be a huge change, for the positive."

I look from Gigi to John and I see it, a couple, struggling with a difficult child, a stressful job, and still working together. Two people in it for the long haul. Two people who love each other, for better or worse.

I look over at Kenley and Doug who are holding hands and he keeps kissing her knuckles. They're no longer the laid-back, easygoing couple I believed them to be. They struggle trying to cross the divide caused by their fertility issues.

Heather looks better than I've seen her in years. Demanding Justin split custody has forced him to man up and be a father, yet allowed him to do it on his terms. Something Hank pointed out to me. Sure, her marriage is still up in the air but she's moving forward one day at a time.

It would seem Hank was correct on a lot of points. Maybe I did lose my way after my dad died. Dealing with his death was painful, is still painful. I reflect back on the various ways I've let loss rule my life. Certainly, it's expected to change your life, losing a parent. I completely shut down. In my family, my father was the person I was the most connected to. When he died, I became adrift, not attached to anyone. My mother's depression was all the more reason to shut down and protect my already wounded self.

At my own wedding, when my family asked me not to go through with it, I pushed forward without any regard to consequences. Marriage was the obvious next step for that phase of my life. And Trevor was just as good as anyone else. Maybe I knew, deep down, losing Trevor would be terrible, but not so terrible I wouldn't survive it.

I look at Josie, who is standing a few tables away, staring at me. I look back at Gigi.

"Did I tell you I'm pregnant again?" She squeezes my hand.

Tears spring forward and I hug her. I know she's not making a big announcement out of respect for Kenley. Everyone is moving forward and, as much as I pretend to be doing the same, I'm not. I'm still stuck. Afraid of forward because with forward comes risk.

Gigi sighs. "I owe you an apology." She's not meeting my eyes.

"For what?" I owe her a million.

"I've known how Hank has felt about you for a long time."

I search her face, waiting for the punch line. I take shallow breaths, afraid I might miss what she says next.

"What? What do you mean?" I stare at her.

"I think I always knew. I was certain the day your dad died. I could see it in his face."

"Why didn't you say anything?" I try to wrap my mind around it.

"I wanted to but Hank made me promise not to. My mom told me—"

"Your mom knows?" How did I miss this?

She nods. "Mom told me it was for Hank to tell you."

"Why didn't he? Why did he wait so long?" It's something I've been asking myself every day since our fight. How different would things be if he had?

"I dunno. Maybe he needed to make sure you wanted him for him and not because you were used to him. He wanted to make sure he could be a good provider as well. You know how he is." She does a slight eye roll.

I cover my mouth with my hands and think about what we've been through. I shake my head. "He never said anything."

"Remember spring break our junior year of college, when Hank came home on leave?" She's playing with the hem of her dress. I nod and wait for her to continue.

"I think he was planning on saying something then. You were dating Trevor, but you were pretty indecisive where he was concerned. Hank asked me if I thought you were done with Trevor."

I sit back in horror. "I was going to break up with Trevor when we got back to school. He surprised me when he showed up and proposed."

"Everyone was blown away when you accepted. Hank was devastated. I tried to get him to say something, but he said if Trevor was the kind of guy you wanted to spend your life with, you weren't the girl he thought you were."

My heart is breaking all over again.

"Why didn't you break up with Trevor? Why did you accept his proposal?"

She's never asked me this before, and I now know I mistook her silence as approval.

Conversations replay in my head. "He said... Oh my God. Fear. I've lost so much because of my fear."

I stand, bumping the table and causing the glasses to wobble. I look around at my friends and open my mouth to say something. Nothing comes out. I walk over to Josie.

She pulls me into a hug. "We're leaving in five minutes. When we drive off, I expect you to run your ass to your car and drive as fast as you can to his house. You understand?"

"I hope it's not too late." My voice trembles.

"Me too. Good luck." We hug again, and I make my way back to the table to get my purse.

Gigi stands and hands me my clutch. She's crying too. "John's gone to bring your car around. Please don't be mad at me."

We give each other a quick hug, and she brushes the tears from my face.

"Never," I tell her. "Please don't be mad at me."

"Don't let him turn you away. Don't give up," Kenley tells me and hands me my bag of birdseed.

"Come on, they're moving. Let's get you in a good spot," Heather says as they push me toward the exit, where people are waiting to send off Josie and Brinn.

I'm panicky, like time is crawling and every moment is a moment lost. I want to scream at the photographer, who apparently wants to get a picture of every single step Josie and Brinn take.

My hands shake as I toss the seed. As soon as they're in the car, I sprint as fast as my heels allow to my waiting car. My friends cheer me from behind.

27

———

SPEEDING DOWN THE INTERSTATE, I sit on the edge of my seat, clenching the steering wheel. When I left the wedding, my GPS told me it was going to be fifty-three minutes until I got to Hank's house. They're a long fifty-three minutes as memories from our childhood, high school, and even more recent times keep flooding my mind. Tears zigzag down my face at record speed.

I'm close to his house and pass each Jacksonville exit as fast as this car will move, pressing my luck with the state speeding laws. His exit is next, and my stomach clenches in a spasm, as if I might get sick. What will I find when I arrive? What will he say? I'm crying too hard, barely able to see past the tears, to keep driving, my legs are shaking, and I know I look a mess. I pull over onto the median, put on my hazards, and give in to my self-loathing. If I show up like this, nothing will be achieved other than making a fool of myself.

I've been so stupid. Incredibly shortsighted.

He's right about who I am now and who I used to be. He's right. I was delusional to think once Trevor and I divorced I would go back to being myself. But this change happened long before Trevor. This was more than letting myself be manipulated. This was a deeper fear.

Fear of loving and losing it, of being lost without them. Fear of having a lifetime with someone and it not measuring up to everything I thought, hoped, or wanted. Fear of not finding someone, or even worse, settling. Fear of loving with my entire being and not being loved in return.

For years after my dad died, my mom cried herself to sleep and wandered aimlessly through life. What would my life be like without Hank in it? My mind races with the things he said, with what I want out of life, with what I thought to be true and isn't. Like with Gigi and John.

He's right about everything. I always look to him for help. The only time I didn't count on Hank was when I was married to Trevor and those were honestly the worst four years of my life. I was lonely the entire time. Trevor was always at a study group, dissecting something, or hanging with the other med students. Being with Trevor was a constant dance of learning my profession, supporting our small family, and accommodating his needs.

I never complained. I liked having the mantle of marriage to prop me up. It showed I was normal, doing what I was supposed to. It was an achievement even when I knew Trevor wasn't reliable, dependable, or trustworthy. Toward the end was the hardest because I knew we weren't a couple trying to find our stride like my parents or Sarah Grace and Dan. We were two people who didn't work together. Had either of us recognized earlier that we were meant to do nothing more than date, we could have saved each other a whole lot of heartache.

My divorce was painful, but I'll never forget the overwhelming sense of relief I experienced when I moved out. I no longer held my breath or felt I was always compromising or sacrificing. The burden of carrying such a heavy load was gone, leaving me to face the open wounds left from marriage. But, even then, I didn't look deep enough, never fixing what was broken.

I bang my hand on the steering wheel before I start digging in my center console for tissues. In my search, I pull out the heart place mat Hank gave me during his drunken weekend a few months back. I'd put it there with the intention of bringing it back to him. I press it to my face.

Like a bitch slap from a higher power, I have the mother of all epiphanies. In this moment, this breath, it's clear how life would be without Hank. It's a sucker punch to the gut, sucking the breath straight from my chest. Losing him would be another epic failure on my part.

I tuck the heart into my bra, wipe my palms across my eyes, and gasp in air. I draw in my courage, bundling it up to hold in my reserves. Checking my mirrors and scanning for cops, I turn off my hazards, throw my car in drive, pull into traffic, and cut across the lanes to the exit. I make it to Hank's house in record time.

I slam my car in park behind his truck, jump out, stumble on my heels, but manage to run to his door. I don't give myself a second to chicken out and start banging on the door right away.

He pulls it open, takes one look at me, and walks away, leaving the door open.

I follow him, stopping at the living room. He keeps walking toward his bedroom.

"I'm sorry." It's easy to say when he isn't looking at me. He comes back and stands in the doorway. Looking me square in the eye.

"You were right about everything." I don't break eye contact. Tears start to flow again and the lump in my throat makes my breathing shallow. "You aren't the first person to call me a coward. Sarah Grace has, Gigi, my friends. All in roundabout ways, of course. You're right. I am a coward and I have changed." I wring my hands.

He stands there, hand on his hip and looks away, toward the floor. "OK, well...is that it?"

I shake my head, unable to talk. His expression is ragged, as if my words fatigue him. I've done this to Hank, and it rips at my core. I no longer have any doubts.

"I love you, Hank." I wipe tears away.

He brings his hand up from his hip to cross his arms over his chest and leans against the door frame. "That's great. I'm glad you figured it all out. I bet being alone at a wedding really helped you see the light."

"I wasn't the only one alone and that's not why I'm here." I step toward him, wanting to cup my hands around his face. I need to ease the furrow in his brow.

The air hangs thick between us. He sighs and walks to his room. I stand there, uncertain. That's it? I turn to leave, even walk to the front door. I stop, turn back, and march to his room.

"That's it?" I cross the threshold.

He stands inside the room, facing the door.

"You walk away? At the very least you can gloat because I admitted you're right." I take a step closer to him and push my finger in his chest, repeatedly. "You can rest assured I won't be saying those words again. And for the record, I've loved you for just as long, too. It only took me a while to figure it out."

"And of course it has nothing to do with your fear of being alone and your need to be 'married.' Thanks for sharing. Now if you'll excuse me." He tosses a towel into a sea bag he's propped up on his bed.

Using my palm to wipe away my tears I look past Hank's face and see he's dressed in khaki uniform pants and a white T-shirt. How I didn't notice until now is beyond me.

There's a sudden pounding on his front door, followed by a booming voice, "Get your purse, Nancy. We're wheels up in two hours." Surge comes around the corner, where he stops short, gaze darting between us.

"Paisley. Smoking-hot dress," he says. "I'll wait outside, brother." With a nod to Hank, he leaves.

"I'm right behind you, Surge," Hank says and puts on a matching khaki shirt, his last name across his left breast pocket, a series of small ribbons below that. He puts on a small hat, straightens it, and runs his hand along the crease down the center.

"Are you going somewhere? I mean, when will you be back?"

He no longer wears a haggard look. Instead his face is without emotion. He's all business. "We're all done here, Paisley. I hope you feel better, said what you needed to." Cinching the bag closed, he slings it over his shoulder. Outside, a horn blares three short honks.

"Make sure you lock the door when you leave." He walks out and doesn't look back.

I knew loving someone so fully, completely would break me, especially if they never returned that love. Knowing I had his love and lost it leaves me raw, exposed. As if the sun has burned my skin, making me hot and three shades past pink. Only the pain is on the inside and it's deep and writhes, scraping against my bared soul. I can't live with this. Like this.

I could ball up, hide within myself and build protective walls. A part of me screams to do just that, the part that's broken, but I've come too far to stop now.

Hank Lancaster hasn't seen the last of me.

28

I WAKE up to the sun streaming in, and I know it's going to be another beautiful day. Beautiful and silent. It's been one week and six days since Hank left me standing in his house. Thirteen days without any form of communication from him.

Not that I haven't tried, because I like to punish myself. Though I still ache from our encounter, it's more a chafing of the heart. I refuse to accept this finale.

I roll over and check my phone. Nothing. I check my spam mail just in case, nothing there either. To punish myself even more, I flop onto my back and scroll through the e-mails I sent him. It can't be the silent treatment if one of us is still talking. On day one, I wrote:

This isn't over. I'm home alone (that means by myself) and I'm perfectly happy with the exception of you. I miss you, your face, your laugh—everything about you.

. . .

On day two, I wrote:

Still feel the same way in case you were wondering.

Day three I try something new:

Today I have doubts. Maybe all I really want is to have you take me around on your Harley. BTW: I drank all your beer before I left.

And because I didn't know when to shut up, by the fifth day of no return communication, I wrote:

It's weird having a one-sided conversation. If I didn't know better I would think something has happened to you. I've mulled over the possibilities. This is my list:

1. *You are a real life James Bond and incognito.*
2. *You are a zombie hunter and as I type this you have saved the world, again.*
3. *You've been kidnapped by aliens (hopefully a cool one like in the movie* Paul *with Simon Pegg).*

4. *You've been hit on the head and forgotten how to read or write this language (and wonder why in the hell you even know Gaelic).*

5. *You've been hit on the head and forgotten who you are (word would have gotten out by now if this was the case).*

Funny enough, I still miss you. Not the things you do for me. But talking to you. Laughing with you. I even miss your stupid face.

In case you're wondering, yes, I'm frustrated that you haven't e-mailed back and I'm secure in admitting that. So there.

No response scares me out of my wits. Maybe he realizes now he has me, and he no longer wants me. What he wants is the chase, not the prize. Not that I think I'm a prize or anything. Maybe I've pushed too hard or have hurt him too deeply. If he felt anything like I did the day he left me standing in his room, no wonder it's radio silence. I wouldn't give me the time of day either. Thing is, I'm not so sure I deserve a second chance with Hank.

I groan in frustration as I journey down this path again. This is the same fear and self-doubt that may cost me Hank, cost me this chance at love. I will not let it get me again.

It's weird to think of Hank in these terms. A few months ago, I would've never imagined I could scare him off with anything. Solid is how I would've defined us.

Uncertain is the word I use now. Uncertain makes my stomach ache.

I toss my phone to the other side of the bed and jump up. There are a few short weeks of summer left. Getting back to work is right around the corner, and I'm going to enjoy what's left if it kills me.

I shower, eat a light breakfast, and dress in a vintage periwinkle-blue dress, circa the 1950s. The boat neck and flared skirt make me feel pretty and happy and a dose of those right now is what I need.

My destination of choice is St. Augustine, Florida's oldest town. Its Spanish roots and quaintness is what I seek. I want to stroll the brick streets and shop the eclectic stores. What I get isn't something I expected. The streets are packed, full of supporters for the Wounded Warrior Project. The finish line of the Wounded Warrior Project 8K is at Castillo de San Marco National Monument, a three-hundred-year-old fort resting at the heart of Old Town St. Augustine.

Amazing people surround me. Men and women with permanent injuries, some visible and some not. People run on a prosthetic leg or even two, others sit in bikes using their upper body and arms to peddle. Next to them are their friends, spouses, and kids.

It's beautiful, wonderful, and crushing in the same breath.

I grab a coffee and a few pastries from my favorite French bakery and head toward the finish line to watch and cheer. As a therapist, I know of the struggles these individuals encounter on their journey of healing. As a girl in love with a Navy guy, I see a whole new possibility. This could be my life.

Could I go through this with Hank? My mind cannot even wrap around how difficult rebuilding a life would be, together. For better or worse you proclaim on your wedding day and this certainly adds perspective to "worse."

As the last of the stragglers come through the finish line, I continue to cheer.

When it's over, I make my way to the event table and make a donation. It seems the very least I can do. The mood, the euphoria, and the camaraderie makes me hesitate to move away. But, the crowd is dispersing and I'm just a bystander.

I browse through a few stores, art shops, typical tourist shops with shells, sand dollars, and shot glasses, before I find myself standing in a collectibles store.

In the center of the store, a framed chalkboard hangs from the ceiling. Painted in bold orange letters are the words "Fears Erased Here Daily" and the numbers one through five are listed below that. Underneath the sign are more chalkboards with the same inspiration only in a variety of colors and next to those is a large five-tier stand of journals.

I like the sentiment. It calls to me, my new proverb. The idea of putting my fears down on paper, giving them a voice but not allowing their energy to sit and swell and consume, appeals to me on all levels.

I stand next to a lady who looks to be the same age as me, and she's looking at the journals. She's dressed in running clothes and her number is still pinned to her shirt.

I reach for a pretty, hardback book, decorated with minty-green chevrons, and flip it open.

"Oh, chevrons are pretty," she says. "Too bad the pages aren't lined."

I didn't even realize. "Is that bad?"

"For me it is. Especially if you plan on using it as a journal. I need the lines or else it will start to slant off the page."

"Good point." I put the book back and pick up a second hardback book, this time in floral.

She picks up one I hadn't noticed. It's decorated with a pretty paisley pattern and scrawled across the front is a different version of my new motto, "Fears Released Here Daily."

"Hey, babe," a guy behind us says.

We both turn, another runner stands a few feet behind us, holding a squirming toddler on his right hip. He's got two prosthetics; one is an amputation below his left knee and the other is below his left elbow.

"Yeah?" my journal-seeking friend says as she holds the book.

"I'm gonna take baby girl outside to run around. She's going to break something in here any minute now."

"OK, I'm going to get this book and be right out."

I watch them smile at each other. He turns and carries their daughter out of the store, making her laugh by blowing raspberries on her arms.

"That's sweet." I put the floral book back and pull out the last one with paisleys.

"Yeah." She watches them leave. She looks lost in thought for a moment, then looks at me and whispers, "I'm thankful every day he's alive."

I don't know what to say that won't minimize such a statement. I'll take Hank any way I can get him.

"I'm sure you are," I say. "I watched the race, and it's inspiring."

"You know what he told me? Said he wouldn't change a thing. Even knowing what it would be like going through it again." She shakes her head as if reliving it and looks at me with watery eyes.

"I use these journals to let it go." She pats the book. "Without these, I think sometimes I might lose my mind." She laughs and holds the book close.

"Oh, listen to me getting sappy." She grabs my arm in a light squeeze, I can tell she's embarrassed. "Is your guy in the military?"

I don't know what to call Hank. He's not my boyfriend, yet. I go with the truth,

"The guy I'm in love with is in the Navy. The military is a new world for me."

I don't know why two people who don't even know each other are sharing such personal details. Maybe because it's sometimes easier to talk to strangers.

"Don't let this scare you." She gestures to the crowd. "It's not only this. It's more. Most days are very much like your life right now."

"How do you handle the worry?" I've noticed my worry level has increased enormously. Maybe it's because we have so much unresolved. I hope so.

"You just do. The beautiful thing about living a military life is you treat each day as if it's the last one before a deployment. You know, we, my husband and I, did a good job of enjoying each other before he was injured. Our lives take more work now but we are tackling this new adventure with the same premise. Don't get me wrong, there are days when I need these little books more, but most days are like before. Don't spend your time worrying about when he's going or while he's gone. It's a waste of energy. He could be killed in a car accident tomorrow. Grab on to today." She gives me a warm smile. I nod in agreement. There are no truer words.

"Thanks." I want to hug her.

"This paisley print is pretty, isn't it?" she asks.

I look at the book I hold. The colors are shades of blue and green and it's very calming.

"I'm a bit partial to the paisley," I tell her. "It's my name."

"Wow, that's cool. Now when I write in my journal I'll think of you and smile."

"I'll do the same," I tell her before we hug. "Thank you."

She moves toward the register. "Oh, poo. Don't thank me. If you come to the next 8K, look for me and say hi. I'm Andrea by the way."

"It's a deal. I plan on running in the next 8K," I tell her. I happen to know it's in Ft. Lauderdale in a few weeks and I already have the brochure in my purse. Josie plans on running it too, she just doesn't know it yet.

"Fantastic. I'll see you there." She pays and wishes me well before she leaves.

I pick up a nice pen to go with my journal. After I pay,

I find one of the small bistros for lunch and get an outside table.

I wonder what's become of Hank's friend who was wounded some time back. For all I know I may be running with him at the next 8K. I pull out my phone and send Hank an e-mail.

Hi, spending the day in St. Augustine. BOB says hi.

I include a selfie just for the heck of it.

While waiting for my food, I rub my finger over the embossed letters, "Fears Released Here Daily." Yes, I'm afraid it might be too late for Hank and I, that he's too hurt to overcome it. So that's what I write. But I won't accept that to be true, not yet anyway.

Maybe it's the wine or the conversation with Andrea, the journal lady, but I know what needs to be done. The plan comes to me with such clarity it could be mistaken for a vision. I whip out my phone and with three simple taps of my finger, it rings in my ear.

"Hello."

"Hey, Gigi," I say. "I have an idea but I'm going to need your help."

"Finally," she exclaims. "It took you long enough."

29

THE SUN PEAKS up over a clear blue sky as I navigate the Jacksonville morning traffic. The radio is off but I tap my hand against the side of my leg in anticipation. Three days ago, I met Gigi in Orlando and she gave me Hank's house key. Today, I put it to use.

My phone rings through the car's Bluetooth system and I fumble it, my fingers moist with apprehension. Gigi's smiling face, with Hank's same dimples, brightens the screen.

"Hey, you're up early," I say.

"Yeah, I couldn't sleep. I'm excited for you."

"Really? Because I'm scared as hell." I don't doubt my feelings, just my powers of persuasion.

"You'll do great. It'll work out. Trust me."

"You can't be so sure. You didn't see his face. I bared my soul and he walked out. He didn't even look back. What if this doesn't work?"

This isn't the first time we've had this conversation.

My confidence comes and goes in small bursts. Gigi's convinced me that he couldn't have turned off his feelings for me already, and I believe her. But then I experience a tremor of uncertainty. Have I hurt him too much? Is it too late? What if it doesn't work out like I have planned?

"Yeah, what if it doesn't? But what if it does? Are you so afraid it might not work out you're not willing to try? I might have a kid with ADHD. I might have a difficult delivery with this next one. I might—"

"All right, I get it." I laugh.

"Anyway, I called to tell you nothing has changed. Mom e-mailed Hank yesterday and he's still scheduled on getting in later this afternoon."

"I guess it's all systems go." I rub my palms across the skirt of my navy-and-white sundress before reaching for a piece of gum in hopes of steadying my nerves.

"Yippee," she says and I picture her clapping in happiness and excitement.

"Wish me luck."

"You don't need luck. If in doubt, get naked."

"Gigi," I exclaim.

We laugh, though mine's more from nervousness. Thinking about getting naked in front of Hank and being rebuffed, well, I'll take that risk if it comes down to it. But I really hope it doesn't.

"Did you get his favorite beer? How about the chocolate-covered strawberries?" Gigi asks.

"Yes, to both."

"You know, I was thinking, you should take off your underwear. Maybe even your bra. Guys can tell right away

if a girl doesn't have on those things and it might work to
your benefit."

"I'm going to hang up on you now," I say and park my
car a few houses down from Hank's, hoping to hide it
among the cars lining the street.

"OK, but you call me if you decide to chicken out or
something because that isn't an option. Remember, you
got this."

"Yeah." I try to sound convincing but it comes out
weak.

"You got this," she screams in my ear.

We laugh and say a quick good-bye. I put my plan into
motion.

Waiting for Hank is less about prepping his house and
more about prepping my nerves. I put the beer on ice in a
fancy table cooler and set out cheese, crackers, and strawberries, licking the chocolate off my fingers. I move the
cooler and food to the living room coffee table, then, move
it back to the kitchen. While I wait—Hank's window of
arrival spans four hours—I change the ice out twice.

Gigi made me promise I would practice my speech in
every room so I'd be as prepared as possible. I practice in
the kitchen and in the living room. When I start it in his
room it sounds stupid and I decide to scrap the idea.
Maybe I should get naked and wait for him on his bed. I
slip off my sandals and reach back to unfasten my dress.
Nothing says I love you to a guy like sex, or so I'm told. But
the thought of waiting, naked, for who knows how long is
creepy, wrong. Only thing missing from this crazy picture
is a bunny in a pot, on the stove, straight out of *Fatal
Attraction.*

I decide to wait in the living room and quickly refasten my dress. I forgo the shoes and walk to the kitchen to grab a beer. I'm passing between rooms when a key in the door makes the bolt turn with an audible *click.* I freeze. He's early. Do I dash for the couch? Move to stand before the door? Where are my shoes? I turn in circles and freeze again when the door swings open and Hank tosses in his sea bag, shuffling in behind it.

We stare at each other. It's only a guess as to what he's thinking but I'm experiencing a rush of thoughts. He looks exhausted. Where are my shoes? This isn't how I planned on starting this.

Man, I love him.

"I guess you found my hide-a-key." He steps back out the door and kicks over a rock. Damn Gigi. I bet she knew a key was there the entire time.

I shake my head when he looks at me and we say in unison, "Gigi."

"Hear me out," I say as I rush to him. I want to grab his hands, cup his face, or wrap my arms around his neck. I want to touch him but the wary look in his eyes and the heavy sigh falling from his lips stops me from going any further.

"I heard you last time."

"Yes, but you didn't listen. You didn't see. I love you. I want to be with you. I want—"

"I can't do this right now." He shoulders past me.

"I'm not leaving until you listen to what I have to say." I dog his footsteps, walking so close that when he stops at the kitchen, drops his sea bag, and turns, I bump into his side.

I mumble an apology and take a step back.

He pulls a beer out of my table cooler and twists off the top. He takes several long gulps and I survey his rumpled uniform, the stubble on his face, and the slight pink tint to his sun-kissed skin. Where did he go? Was he in danger? I suddenly understood the message Andrea had pressed upon me. Live everyday as if it's the one before a deployment. Yes, the specifics matter but only so much as they provide knowledge.

Specifics such as where he was or what he did aren't as important as how we live the day, together.

He brings the beer down and meets my gaze, cocking a brow, "I don't think there is anything you can say at this point." He shakes his head and walks away.

"Hank," I cry out.

He disappears into his bedroom. The shower turns on. I refuse to be dismissed so easily and chase after him.

"Hank," I say again when I enter his bedroom. "Please."

"Please what? I heard you." He strips off his khaki shirt and white undershirt.

He's going about his business as if this is no big deal whatsoever.

"Tell me what you want from me." I take a deep breath to steady my voice. I don't want to cry but it's inevitable. The tears are pushing against me, waiting to break free.

"I wanted it all. I wanted you to want me too. I wanted —" he says.

"I do want you. I've always wanted you but I've been too afraid. My mom lost the love of her life and it almost broke her. Losing you would be the same for me. Devastating."

He looks me up and down. "You don't look devastated." He sits on the edge of his bed, kicks off his shoes, and tugs off his socks. I'll convince him before he gets in that shower or by God I'll follow him in there, clothes and all.

"Just hear me out. I'm willing to leave once you've listened."

"It's too late." He doesn't look at me.

"I know I've let you down. I know I've hurt you. But if you could see past that, find it in your heart to give me another try, I'll spend every day showing you how much I love you. I'll show you, even during the times I'm the most afraid, how I no longer live my life behind my cloak of fear. I'll show you how I've embraced it and am using it to make me stronger. I'll show you that I'm the girl you remember. Your love wasn't wasted on me."

"Paisley—" He stands and puts his hands on his hips.

"Just tell me you don't still love me. Look at me and tell me that it's really over." I rush to where he is and place my hand on his chest, over his heart.

"Just say it," His heart races beneath my hand and it encourages me. He's breathing heavy through his nose, but his lips are no longer pressed in a thin line.

They've softened.

"I just got home. I need a shower and—"

A burst of courage and hope explodes in me. This is it, the moment that can change everything for us. I bend down on one knee, open my arms wide, and look at him.

"Hank Lancaster, you're the love of my life. I want to share every day with you. I want to fight with you, laugh with you, and touch you every chance I get. I want to be with you for the rest of my life and I don't care what that looks like, whether one of us is injured, angry, happy, sad, moody, or our families interfere. I don't care, I want you. Will you—"

He swoops down and lifts me, bringing me to my feet.

"Oh no, you don't," he says.

As soon as he lets go I drop down on one knee again. He picks me up, and I drop down again, arms extended.

"Dammit, Paisley. Do *not* say it." He picks me up, pausing.

Waiting for me to give some sign, a twitch, that I plan on going back on my knee or that I'm going to comply with his demand. I hold still. He lets go slowly, and I quickly drop down once more.

"I love you," I declare. "I want to make love with you in parks, in your truck, and on your motorcycle. Especially your motorcycle. That's really hot. I want to be waiting here when you get back from a long trip, a deployment, at the end of a day. *You* are what I have always wanted. You—"

"Would you stop already? You don't get to finish this. That's my job, so shut up." A small rumble of a laugh escapes from between his lips as his arms go around me, pressing me against his chest. I dangle briefly before I wrap my arms around his neck, my legs around his waist.

"I was only going to ask you to be my boyfriend," I say. "I don't know what *you* thought I was going to say."

"Shut up."

"I love you." I look into his eyes. "I'm sorry."

"I love you," he says.

Of this I have no doubt. I see it in his eyes, feel it in his touch. He's proven it over and over again with his actions. Now it's my turn to prove it to him. When our lips touch, it brings the giddiness of a first kiss and the tenderness of true love. I cup his face and deepen the kiss, branding him with the promise of my forever love.

"Thanks for waiting for me," I whisper when we come apart. He walks us to his bathroom, heavy with steam from the shower, and unzips my dress.

"I never had a choice. I've always been yours," he says.

"Not the bee upon the blossom,
  In the pride o' sunny noon
  Not the little sporting fairy,
  All beneath the simmer moon;
  Not the poet, in the moment
  Fancy lightens in his e'e,
  Kens the pleasure, feels the rapture,
  That thy presence gi'es to me."
-Robert Burns

———

Are you feeling like these gals could be your friends? Jayne's story is next! She's determined to not risk her heart. But there's something distracting about single dad Stacy Cunningham. Only she's not wife or mommy material, and it's just a matter of time before he realizes she's not **the girl he wants.**

Grab a copy today!

BOOKS BY KRISTI ROSE

<u>The No Strings Attached Series-</u>

(Romance) The No Strings Series has a chick lit vibe and some are available in audio.

The Girl He Knows

The Girl He Needs

The Girl He Wants

The Girl He Loves

———

<u>Like cowboys?</u>

<u>The Wyoming Matchmaker Series</u>

(Romance) Sweet and sexy romances on the ranch. There's action, adventure, and heartbreaking angst paired with feel good rewards.

The Cowboy Takes A Bride

The Cowboy's Make Believe Bride

The Cowboy's Runaway Bride

———

<u>Samantha True Mysteries</u>

<u>Also in audio</u>

(Mystery) These laugh out loud, action pack books take place in the Pacific Northwest. Join Samantha, an adult with dyslexia who's hid behind photography, on her adventures in her new life as a Private Investigator. A job she inherited when her new husband died unexpectedly and left behind a mess and another wife.

<u>*One Hit Wonder*</u>

<u>*All Bets Are Off*</u>

<u>*Best Laid Plans*</u>

<u>*Caught Off Guard*</u>

<u>*Two Time Loser*</u>

<u>*Dodged A Bullet*</u>

<u>*The Meryton Brides*</u>

(Sweet romance) The Meryton Brides is a complete series (for now) that is a light, pleasant modernization of Jane Austen's Pride and Prejudice with a twist on the characters. These sweet contemporary romance books are full of love, friendship, trust, and family. Darcy and Elizabeth's story spans the series and ends in book 5, but each book provides the happily ever after we seek.

To Have and To Hold (Book 1)

With This Ring (Book 2)

I Do (Book 3)

Promise Me This (Book 4)

Marry Me, Matchmaker (Book 5)

Honeymoon Postponed (Book 6)

Matchmaker's Guidebook - FREE

The Coming Home Series

(Sweet Romance) A collection of small-town short stories that take place in Lakeland, Florida where Kristi grew up. These sweet romances are bite sized stories of happiness, wit, and laughter and invite you into the lives of 5 women and leave you happy because of the feel, good endings.

Second Chances

Once Again

Reason to Stay

He's the One

Kiss Me Again

or purchased in a bundle for a better discount.

The Coming Home Series: A Collection of 5 Second Chance Short Stories (Can be purchased individually).

Love Comes Home

Standalone Mysteries:

Campus Murder Club

Perfect Place (Using pen name Robbie Peale)

MEET KRISTI ROSE

Hey! I'm Kristi. I write romances that will tug your heartstrings and laugh out loud mysteries. In all my stories you'll fall in love with the cast of characters, they'll become old, fun friends. **My one hope** is that I create stories that *satisfy any of your book cravings* and offer a getaway from everyday life. When I'm not writing I'm repurposing Happy Planners or drinking a London Fog (hot tea with frothy milk).

I'm the mom of 2 and a milspouse (retired). We live in the Pacific Northwest.

Here are 3 things about me:

- I lived on the outskirts of an active volcano (Mt.Etna)
- A spider bit me and it laid eggs in my arm (my kids don't know that story yet)
- I grew up in Central Florida and have skied in lakes with gators.

I'd love to get to know you better. Join my Read & Relax community and then fire off an email and tell me 3 things about you!

Not ready to join? Email me below or follow me at one of the links below. Thanks for popping by!

You can connect with Kristi at any of the following:
www.kristirose.net
kristi@kristirose.net

ACKNOWLEDGMENTS

I am indebted to the following people to whom I offer my
deepest gratitude:
My family—My mom, sister, and in particular my
husband and children. Thank you for sacrificing so much
mom-time so I could get that next line typed, jotted,
written,
scribbled, or saved before it drifted away. You gave up
Sundays so I could participate in my weekly writer's
group, helped me juggle every day and didn't mind
(much) that I always had a smartphone in one hand and a
laptop in the other.
My Lyrical Press family—Paige Christian, I couldn't have
asked for a better editor. Your insight and guidance were
the final puzzle pieces to this story. You navigated me
through the editing process and fielded a thousand
questions with grace, patience, and a teacher's heart. You
turned my story into a book I'm tremendously proud of.
You are simply awesome. Thank you. <insert serious
fangirling here>. Renee Rocco, thank you for
always being accessible, acquiring my book, and for my
incredible cover. Working with you and the Lyrical staff
has exceeded my expectations and I'm so happy to be a
part of

this great House.

To the most amazing, wonderful and encouraging critique group. Ever. Eryn Scott, Anya Mora, John Pelkey, and G.L. Snodgrass. #bestgroupever. #writemybook. #hashtagfingers. #fingerlakes. Thank you for the weekly goals, catching the missed opportunities, the candid and honest feedback, the brainstorming, the laughter, the bees and mobsters on the mountain, the encouragement and the list goes on. Without you, where would Paisley be? Thank you. Thank you! #Thankyou

My Beta Readers and additional advisors: Rachel Cross, Jessica McKay, Letitia Archer, and Kim Smith. You all gave such invaluable feedback. You tolerated my many email questions even though you have busy lives. Thank you. Dianna- You gave me the line that became the impetus for this story. Thanks for the friendship that's spanned decades.

Thanks to my dad for always talking books with me, my friends who cheered me on, and to the teachers that encouraged me to write. Thank You. As with any opportunity to thank people who have, whether big or small, had a hand in helping me achieve this dream, someone will be left out. My apologies. This "Thank You" is for you. You know who you are.

JOIN KRISTI'S READER NEWSLETTER

I hope you enjoy this book. I'd love to connect and share more with you. Be a part of my reader newsletter and let's get to know each other. There, I'll share all sorts of book information. You're guaranteed to find an escape. You'll also be the first to know about my sales and new releases. You'll have access to giveaways, freebies, and bonus content. Think you might be interested? Give me a try. You can always leave at any time.

If you enjoyed this book I would appreciate if you'd share that with others. I love when my friends pass along a good read. Here's some ways you can help.

Lend it , Recommend it , Review it

XO, Kristi

www.ingramcontent.com/pod-product-compliance
Lightning Source LLC
Chambersburg PA
CBHW032113180726

48284CB00002B/550